Julie Cohen studied at Brown University, earning a summa cum laude degree with honours in English. She moved to the UK in 1992 to pursue a postgraduate degree in English Literature at the University of Reading and currently teaches English at secondary level. She lives with her husband in Berkshire.

SPIRIT WILLING, FLESH WEAK

Rosie Fox is a really good liar. But when you're a stage psychic who's not actually psychic, you have to be. One night, while pretending to commune with the dead relatives of her audience, Rosie makes a startling prediction — which tragically comes true. Suddenly she's trapped in a media frenzy, spearheaded by the handsome journalist Harry Blake, a man intent on kick-starting his stalled career by exposing Rosie as a fraud. Yet when his interest in her goes from professional to personal, she thinks she can trust him not to blow her cover — but maybe she's making a huge mistake.

JULIE COHEN

SPIRIT WILLING, FLESH WEAK

Complete and Unabridged

ULVERSCROFT
Leicester

First published in Great Britain in 2006 by
Little Black Dress, an imprint of
Headline Publishing Group
London

First Large Print Edition
published 2007
by arrangement with
Headline Publishing Group
London

British Library CIP Data

Cohen, Julie, 1970 –
   Spirit willing, flesh weak.—Large print ed.—
Ulverscroft large print series: romance
1. Psychics—Fiction 2. Love stories
3. Large type books
I. Title
823.9′2 [F]

ISBN 978–1–84617–934–1

Published by
F. A. Thorpe (Publishing)
Anstey, Leicestershire

Set by Words & Graphics Ltd.
Anstey, Leicestershire
Printed and bound in Great Britain by
T. J. International Ltd., Padstow, Cornwall

This book is printed on acid-free paper

To Lillian Bronstein Cohen, my Grammy.

With thanks to some masters of deception for their inspiration: magicians Ian Rowland, James Randi, Derren Brown, and Harry Houdini.

And to Kathy Love, Anna Scamans, Jaquelin Bduard, Lee Weatherly, Jenny Harris, Brigid Coady, and Cathy Wade for always telling the truth.

1

'Here goes nothing.'

As always, I raised my antique Russian tea glass towards the ceiling in a gesture like a toast to heaven. I could see the whisky glinting golden where the backstage light caught it.

As always, I took a deep breath. Then I brought the glass down to my lips and downed its contents in one.

And as always, I almost puked.

The teenage boy sitting in a plastic chair beside me must not have noticed my grimace, nor the gagging I managed to subdue, because he looked at me admiringly and said, 'Wicked. You can really do shots.'

The nausea passed; the whisky was a warm fire in my belly and a familiar relaxation in my knees. I smiled at the teenager. He was wearing the same nu-metal T-shirt, baggy black jeans and pocket chains that a teenager in New Jersey would be wearing, but this teenager had a public television English accent. I'd been in the country a few weeks, and I still hadn't gotten used to hearing everybody talk that way.

'It helps me get more receptive to the spirits,' I said.

He nodded sagely, as if he talked about whisky-fuelled spirit reception every day. Maybe he did; kids these days did some pretty weird stuff, whatever country they were in.

'Well, break a leg,' he said. 'Do you want me to get you another one?'

I handed him the glass. 'No, one is good,' I said, and stood close to the gap in the curtain to hear whether this local guy who was introducing me could manage to follow the script.

' . . . converted hundreds of nonbelievers from New York to Los Angeles with her extraordinary ability to communicate with the other world. From the age of thirteen, Rosie has helped countless people get in touch with their loved ones and shown us all that, despite loss, life does go on.'

I'm going to have to rewrite that script, I thought. Way, way too corny.

'So without further ado, let me introduce you to Rosie Fox, all the way from America, and I can tell you, I had a drink with her earlier, and though she might be a medium, there's nothing medium about her. She's the sexiest psychic I ever met.'

I definitely did not write that part.

'Rosie Fox, ladies and gentlemen!'

Applause. It was nearly a full house, but the clapping wasn't so loud. I was used to that. People don't usually clap too energetically for a psychic before she's proven herself. There were a few people in the crowd who totally believed I was going to contact their dead relatives for them; there were a few people who were absolutely convinced I was a liar; most of them weren't really sure one way or the other.

They'd applaud when I was done, though.

I tossed back my hair, put my best welcoming 'you love me' smile on my face and walked out through the gap in the curtain. I could hear my heels thumping against the wooden floor of the stage, and my bracelets jangling with every movement I made.

'Thanks, Dan,' I said to the MC. He hadn't hidden his attempt to look down my cleavage when I'd met him earlier, and he barely hid it now, walking past me to the wings. I stood in the centre of the stage, and as soon as he was gone I gave my full attention to the audience.

They watched me. The lighting guy had done a good job. The seats and the stage were lit up enough to be clearly visible, but it was still dim enough to be atmospheric. I knew my red, sparkly, silky top stood out like a beacon against the black curtains; my faded jeans made me look down-to-earth, while my silver hoop earrings, silver bangles and rings and necklaces, and jumble of curly dark hair gave me an air of a gypsy fortune-teller. I let my eyes wander over the people sitting facing me and I knew what they saw: a slender, smiling woman. Normal-looking enough to be trustworthy, exotic-looking enough to be mysterious. Sexy enough to be interesting, but not so sexy as to be threatening.

I gave eye contact to the women first. They were my audience; there was no point alienating them by eyeing up their men. I started somewhere in the middle of the crowd, a young woman's clear hazel eyes, and moved from left to right, up and down, looking frankly into every female face I could, as I began my spiel.

'Hi, everybody. It's great to be here in Reading, England. Before I begin, I want to thank you for coming to see me, and I want to ask you all a favour.

'As you know, I'll be trying to contact the spirits of your loved ones tonight, and I want to apologise in advance if you came here hoping to hear from someone and you don't get the chance to talk to them. I try my best, but sometimes spirits can't get through, even when they really want to. Anybody ever try to

4

get a drink at a bar, and no matter what you do, nobody seems to see you?'

A few nods. A good audience tonight.

'The boundary between this world and their world is shifting constantly; sometimes it's clear, and sometimes it's fuzzy. It's like sometimes I've got a hundred channels of digital television, and sometimes I only have a really bad snowy picture of a rerun. You know what I mean?'

Vague laughter. *Trust me*, I beamed, and continued.

'It helps, though, if you help me. You know, good vibrations, stuff like that. I might not get everything right. Your good wishes can help make it easier for me to get a better reception. And one funny thing I've noticed about talking with spirits, though it's not that weird when you think about it — they're not so definite, sometimes, about whether they're talking about the past or the present or the future. Remember they've passed on to the next world and time doesn't mean much to them any more. Also, pretty often they know what they're talking about, and you'll know what they're talking about, but I won't have a clue. So your help counts.'

Setting-up done, I stood for a moment in the expectant silence. I let my wide smile melt away, and tilted my head slightly in a

5

listening posture. Then, slowly, I began to smile again.

'I've got a lady standing next to me right now,' I said. 'She's very lively and wanted to get to me first, she says! She's pointing at you, ma'am.' I walked closer to the audience, and gestured with open palm to a woman in the fourth row.

I'd seen her in my opening sweep of the audience: in her late forties, with long hair held up by a clip, sitting next to a man who was obviously her husband. She raised her hand to her throat, blushing and surprised to be picked out, her mouth half open, uncertain whether to reply.

'This lady is a mother figure to you, and she's full of energy, bursting with life. Does that make sense to you?' I asked the woman, who nodded.

I tilted my head still more and laughed. 'She really is lively, this lady. I'm sorry, I'm American so I'm no good at accents, but hers sounds very strong to me, and she's telling me something about family recipes? Or some sort of food tradition, and she's laughing?'

The woman's husband smiled and nudged her, and she gasped. 'It's my grandmother, she was Welsh. I tried to make her Christmas cake last year and I forgot to add the eggs. None of us could eat it.'

The audience laughed along with her, and I congratulated myself on a good first choice, while filing away the information. The woman tried very hard at domestic things but didn't always succeed; her family was important; she probably had more than one child.

'The eggs!' I agreed. 'And that's what she's saying to me. The kids all teased you about it, didn't they? Do you mind me asking your name?'

'Janet,' said the woman. Her surprise had melted into openness, trust, and a kind of hope.

'Janet, your grandmother knows she was special in your life, and she's telling me that she loves you. She has a message for you, but it's sort of personal. Do you mind if I repeat it?'

'No, please do.' Her husband took her hand.

I waited for a moment more, and when I spoke, my voice was soft. 'Janet, she says you are a truly giving person. I don't mean giving things or presents, though of course I mean that too, but she's saying you give time. You give love, you give yourself to others. It's important for you to feel needed. Do you understand this?'

Janet nodded. Oh, I was good tonight.

'But she says that sometimes, and one big

time — and I get the feeling that this is within this year, though it could still be in the future — you've had to say no. You've had to put yourself first. And when that happened, you felt so selfish, so bad about it, but you didn't have any choice.'

Janet gasped again. She was still nodding while I carried on.

'Your grandmother wants to tell you that that's okay. You shouldn't feel bad, because she wants you to love yourself as much as she loves you. She trusts you to do the right thing. And you should trust yourself. If you're honest about your needs, people can accept you for who you are, even if you disappoint them sometimes.'

She wiped away a tear. I glanced at the audience around her: rapt, fascinated, believers.

Oh yes, it was great to be in Reading, England.

I took a few minutes to deliberate while I walked around the stage, letting them see me concentrate. When you start out this well it's a balancing act whether you relax a little, or whether you press on and really get the audience on your side. On the one hand, if they've seen firm reason to believe in you, they're hooked and they'll happily ignore almost any number of misses. On the other hand, if you play your aces too soon you haven't got them up your sleeve in case disaster strikes.

It felt good tonight, though. I felt strong, almost invulnerable, in a way that had nothing to do with the whisky that still pooled warmly in my stomach.

Janet was smiling through her tears. And that was why I was invulnerable: Janet believed me.

I stopped wandering the stage and held both my hands to the sides of my head, in a position of fierce attention. 'There's someone else here,' I started slowly, and felt the faces that were still turned to Janet focus back on me. 'It's a man, and I'm getting a name . . . sorry, it's so hard to hear him . . . it starts with a J — no, I'm sorry it's a G, and it sounds like J. George. It's George with us.'

I looked over the audience slowly, drawing out the tension. There she was in the second row — short brown hair, bright pink shirt, trendy. I took another minute, and then nodded to myself and walked down the stage steps and straight to the second row. I met her eyes, and unlike Janet, she didn't seem surprised or embarrassed; her eyes were glowing and her cheeks were flushed.

'He's your father, isn't he?' My voice was a

murmur but the audience drank in every word.

'Yes.'

She was in her early twenties, young to have a dead father. *Ha! Try to explain how I guessed that one,* I mentally exulted over the nonbelievers in the audience. If there were any.

'He knows you miss him. He's saying that you're wearing something of his right now, around your neck — a ring. Do you understand that?'

She was grinning as she reached inside the neck of her shirt and pulled out the chain she wore, a gold ring looped on to it. 'It's his wedding ring. I wear it every day so he'll be close to me.'

I stepped forward; the man who was sitting beside her shifted his legs to the side so I could get nearer. 'He's close to you every day, he says he's with you all the time. I want to use your name but he's not saying it, he's saying a pet name of some kind, does that — '

'Is it Stinky?' she interrupted. 'He always called me Stinky.'

Fortunately, everyone else laughed, so I didn't have to cover up my own giggles. Stinky laughed herself, twirling the wedding ring on her finger and looking so, so happy.

How long had it been since her father died? Years, or months, or weeks? How often did she smile and laugh when she thought of him?

I couldn't ask that, of course. The rules wouldn't permit it.

I couldn't ask any of the other things I wanted to either: what George had been like, in what way had he been special, why he called her Stinky.

How it felt to know her father's love had been real.

'He's loving how you're laughing now,' I said fervently. 'You should see him, he's grinning. Please be happy, he wants to say to you. He's with you always. Don't mourn, be yourself and take what he's taught you into the world to share.'

I stretched out my hand to her and she took it. She nodded, and her smile brought tears to my own eyes. The room was in a hush as she clasped my hand in hers and shared her grief and happiness with me.

It was soon, it was near, he hadn't been dead long. I knew that, not through any psychic powers, but because of how her hands shook and held me tight.

No. This was going wrong, suddenly. Where was my invulnerability now that I needed it? I tried and tried to blink back my tears.

And I did. Of course. I was a professional. 'Thank you,' she said finally, and let me go.

The audience applauded, and that brought me wholly back to myself. They loved Stinky and her father. They loved the fact that I'd nearly cried. They believed me.

They were in the palm of my hand.

The next forty minutes were normal, or as normal as it gets when you're translating for spirits. We had an anniversary in June, a stack of letters in a closet, a childhood accident. An uncle called John and a sister called Ruth. Family heirlooms and a hamster that tunnelled into the wall of a house (I didn't tell them that one; a guy filled it in for me when I mentioned a lost pet). I had a few misses, but so few that even I hardly noticed them. There was a lot of laughter; Janet and Stinky had set the tone for how the rest of the messages would be interpreted, and there was something funny about nearly all of the information that the audience revealed to me.

Except for my dangerous moment holding Stinky's hand — which was an odd aberration, but nothing to worry about, nothing I couldn't control — it was the best show I'd done in England. It all was flowing easily, but I signalled the teenager in the wings for a glass of water anyway. I stood for a minute, hands on hips, looking at the audience, my new friends.

Who next?

I think it was adrenalin as much as anything else that led me to the lady in the back row. As always with a great show, I felt excited, light on my feet, as if I was about to float up into the spotlit air any minute.

So I flew past the rows of seats to the back of the audience, faces swivelling to follow me. My bracelets jingled. I stopped next to the woman on the end of the row.

She was thin, dressed in beige, with straight mousy shoulder-length hair and brown eyes. Even though the walls around her were black, she seemed to blend into the background.

So, where to start with this woman? 'Hi, I'm Rosie,' I said.

'I'm Moira,' she replied. A small voice, shy.

'Do you have anyone that you're trying to get in touch with, Moira?'

'Well, um, not really,' she said. 'Maybe my brother.'

I screwed my eyes shut, showing I was concentrating hard. 'I feel a male presence trying to get through,' I said, 'but it's not very clear yet. Would you mind giving me your hand, Moira, maybe to make the connection stronger?'

Her hand in mine was bony but warm, except for her rings which felt cold and hard.

13

I held it and tried to figure out whether her brother had died as a boy or a man.

'I'm getting a picture of brown eyes, and a few freckles, and I think he wants to tell you about something that happened in January?' I began, and opened my eyes to look at her brown-eyed, lightly freckled face.

And then, holding her hand and looking into this stranger's face, it happened.

I'm not sure even now *how* it happened. It didn't feel any different from anything else that evening — there wasn't a flash of lightning or any sort of major insight in my head. I felt totally like me, totally normal, like I was opening my mouth to say the sort of thing I was so used to saying.

But I didn't.

I opened my mouth and I said, 'Don't get on the nine twenty-seven train to Swansea.'

Just like that.

I dropped Moira's hand. I didn't feel normal then. I felt practically blind, nearly deaf, and not at all like the usual Rosie Fox I knew and often loved.

'Oh my God,' I said. 'Really. Don't take the nine twenty-seven train to Swansea.'

And then I turned and ran out of the theatre.

14

2

I had no idea where I was going.

I ran downhill, in the direction I thought the station was probably in. It was a guess. I didn't know Reading or how close I was to the station, and I certainly didn't hear any spirit messengers telling me which way to go. All I felt was urgency gripping my heart and lungs, making me pant as I ran across a double-lane road. The centre had a low brick wall planted with scrubby bushes; they snagged my jeans as I climbed through them and my heels sank into the damp earth, and then I was over the wall and across the other side of the road and running over a narrow bridge.

The sidewalk was uneven. It was full of people. At nine o'clock on a Saturday night, groups of very young drinkers lined the street, the boy-men all dressed the same, the girl-women wearing nearly nothing, talking loudly and weaving slightly. I burst through a group of them who were blocking my path and I heard one girl squeal.

'Oi!' a male voice called after me. 'What you playin' at?'

I kept running. Nine twenty-seven train. I had nearly half an hour. It would be okay. It would be okay.

It wouldn't be okay.

My heel caught in a crack in the paving stones and I stumbled, twisting my ankle and crying out at the bolt of pain that shot up my leg. My momentum carried me forward and I pitched on to the sidewalk. The skin of my palms scraped off as I tried to catch myself. I heard the people behind me laughing.

Then I was back up on my feet, limping in these shoes that were no good for running. I saw another group of people in front of me.

'Where's the station?' I gasped, and as soon as one of the boy-men pointed vaguely behind him I took off again, sprinting as fast as my heels and my twisted ankle would let me.

It wasn't far. It felt like a lifetime. But then I was stumbling up the steps and through the glass doors and I was in the bright, echoey station concourse.

Where do you go? How to stop a train? I saw the sign saying *Information* and I ran there. I had information. Even if I wasn't sure where it had come from.

'You've got to stop the nine twenty-seven train to Swansea,' I told the man behind the counter.

'Platform four,' he said, and turned his attention to the person behind me.

'No,' I said, and when he didn't look at me, I yelled, 'Sir! You don't understand. You have to stop that train. The nine twenty-seven. It can't leave this station.'

The guy looked at me. 'I don't stop trains,' he said. Then he went back to the person behind me.

'Idiot,' I muttered, though I wasn't sure whether I was talking about him or me. Of course he didn't stop trains. He was the info guy. Where was the guy who stopped trains?

Superman stops trains, I thought, not stage psychics in stupid high heels. Seeing a sign for *First Great Western*, I clicked at a rapid pace to that glass door. Locked.

'Damn British opening hours.' I kicked the door. Then I looked at the big clock above the information desk.

Nearly ten past nine. Seventeen minutes to go.

At the thought, the urgent, ill-formed dread that had had hold of me since I had held Moira's hand tightened its grip. My insides were an acid mass of fear. And I had absolutely no idea why, just a burning knowledge that I had to stop that train, in any way possible.

Platform four, the info guy had said. I'd

have to go on to the platform and try to convince the driver to stop. I'd have to talk to people who were going to get on the train and try to stop them. If necessary I could stand in front of the train and trust that it wouldn't run me down.

People believed me. I'd just made a whole audience do it.

The way to the platforms was blocked by a line of turnstile things that you had to put your ticket in. I glanced back at the clock. Nine eleven. Sixteen minutes left.

I went straight to the man guarding the turnstiles, my mind processing strategies. Tell the truth: no. He'd treat me like I was crazy, like the info guy. Buy a ticket: no. My purse was back in my dressing room.

The lie came easily to my lips. 'Excuse me, sir. I'm meeting a friend's train, and he doesn't speak any English. Do you mind if I go through and make sure he gets off okay?' Despite the now full-scale panic churning my stomach, I smiled at the man.

'That's fine, love,' he said, and pushed a plastic card into the turnstile so I could go through. I sprinted to platform four.

Next train: 21.27 Swansea.

The red digital sign flashed in front of me. When I blinked, I could see it still imprinted on my vision.

I grabbed the person beside me.

'Are you going on that train?'

It was an Asian teenage boy, heavy gold chain around his neck, gold hoop in his ear, hair shaved into a spiky pattern on his scalp. He assessed me and my shaking hand that gripped his arm. 'Yeah, so what?'

'You can't get on it. Please, please don't get on the train.'

He narrowed his eyes. 'You on drugs?'

'Just don't. Okay?' The platform was clotted with people, dozens, all planning to catch that train. I couldn't wait for the boy to promise me. I let him go — he stepped away from me with an exaggerated shrug — and reached for somebody, anybody else.

She was a middle-aged woman holding the hand of a boy who was about six years old. She recoiled in shock when I grabbed her. Then she wrenched her sleeve from my hand. The blood still seeping from my scraped palm soaked into her tan coat, bright red darkening to maroon.

Everything was too loud, all the colours were too bright; the platform was hot with the bodies of so many people about to get on that train and the little boy's eyes were blue, bright blue, and starting to be scared.

'Don't take him on the train,' I told the woman, who was glaring at me. 'Please.

19

Don't take the little boy.'

She turned away from me and marched down the platform, pulling the boy after her. He stumbled with the quickness of her steps and looked back at me.

I felt sick.

'Excuse me!' I yelled. Usually, onstage, I hushed to a shaky whisper when I wanted to be noticed. Hollering wasn't my style. But despite that, my voice was strong. It was a tool of my trade.

On the platform, though, it didn't carry. Bad acoustics, I thought, and sucked air into my lungs and tried again, striding down towards the centre of the platform and hitting every word with my diaphragm to give it emphasis.

'Excuse me, ladies and gentlemen! I'm sorry to disturb your evening, but it's absolutely vital that you listen to me. Do not get on the nine-twenty-seven train to Swansea. I repeat: do *not* get on the next train.'

About half of the people on the platform stared at me; the other half pretended not to. I remembered how I was dressed. My outfit was perfect for making me credible to the audience of a psychic stage show, but it wasn't the best choice for making a platform full of people think I was an authority on trains. Glittery top, jeans, high heels, lots of silver jewellery: I probably looked like one of the twenty-something drinkers from the street.

'You probably think I'm crazy, but I'm not. I wouldn't be embarrassing myself here if it weren't really, really important that none of you get on this train. In fact we need to stop this train from leaving the station at all.'

People were nudging each other and exchanging looks and comments. I tried to catch the eye of a man who was standing near me, but he looked away quickly. The same thing happened with the woman I tried next.

'Ma'am? Sir? Please, I mean what I'm saying. Sir?'

British people. I hadn't been in the country long but I'd seen this happen before, on the underground in London. A man had gotten into the carriage and started singing a haunting song, walking down the carriage holding out his hat for any spare change. Nobody had looked at him. They'd let their eyes skip over him as if he were a blank space in the air. Nobody had smiled at his song, not even the few people who gave him a bit of change. Nobody met his eyes.

In America, people look at you, they talk to you, they don't let their eyes skitter past. My thoughts were frantic. Person after person

21 00619384

treated me like a blank space in the air. Americans try to pick a fight with you, they tell you to shut up and try to get you arrested, but they don't ignore you, they don't —

'Please!' I cried. 'I'm telling the truth!'

'The next train to approach platform four is the twenty-one-twenty-seven service to Swansea. Calling at Swindon, Bristol Parkway, Newport, Cardiff Central, and Swansea. Platform four for the twenty-one-twenty-seven service to Swansea.'

The announcement was made by an automated voice, male and hollow, inevitable as death. It echoed as my own voice had not done.

Swindon. There were going to be more people getting on at Swindon. Panic tasted like blood in my throat.

'OH FOR GOD'S SAKE, PEOPLE, WILL YOU LISTEN TO ME!' My voice broke on the last word and I felt a hand clasp my shoulder.

Finally. Someone was paying attention. I turned and saw a large man in a British Transport Police uniform.

'Now, miss, if you'll calm down, we can try to sort thi — '

I grabbed the lapels of his jacket. 'Oh thank God!' I cried, and I have no idea what I

22

looked like at that point, but I felt as if I were about to explode, or collapse, or both, and I only had one thought because now I could hear the train coming towards us.

'Thank you, you've got to stop that train, you can't let it leave the platform, you might think I'm crazy but I'm not, I know, it's something bad — '

The transport policeman murmured, 'Yes, yes,' and we were moving fast up the platform. In the middle of that chaos I had a moment of lucidity and I saw that the people we passed were staring at me now. I was being dealt with by authority. I was neutralised, no longer blank air.

I noticed for the first time that the policeman had a partner, who was talking rapidly into a radio or a cell phone. Through the blood pounding in my ears, above the assaulting roar of the train coming up to platform four, I heard what the second guy was saying.

'Yeah, mate, we'll get her off the platform and try to calm her down . . . . We'll get her out of the station once the train's left.'

He wasn't going to stop the train.

And now I could see the bright yellow front of the train, with windshields like blind goggles. A big worm curving towards the platform. It was coming, then it was here, and its doors opened and people lined up to get on it.

Desperation must have lent me strength, because the policeman was pretty much twice my size. I broke free of him and ran for the train.

How do you stop a train? If you're nobody special with no special powers? How do you stop a train if you're just an ordinary person?

I didn't know. I'd only been on a train once or twice. In America, we drive. I ran through all the people who were getting on and reached the front. I pounded on the blue door where the driver was, but my fists didn't make any sound over the hissing of the train and the rumble of its engine. As I pounded, I heard a whistle and doors shut all the way down the line and I still couldn't hear my fists, and the two transport police had nearly reached me.

I don't remember grabbing hold of somebody's suitcase and trying to fling it on to the track, but that was what I was holding on to when the policemen reached me, because I remember them holding me and me holding it and the train pulling away.

With all the desperate sharpness of a nightmare you've just woken up from, I remember that.

And the faces that looked out at me from

the windows as the train went past. I wasn't a blank space in the air. They saw me.

I still see them now.

★ ★ ★

At the police station they took away my watch and my jewellery and left me to sit in a room. A woman police officer stood by the door. I presume she was there to stop me from hurting myself, though as I've never been arrested before, I don't know. In any case, I wasn't interested in hurting myself or anyone else by then. I felt drained, empty and cold.

I sat in a plastic chair and looked down at my feet and realised that they really hurt. I eased off my shoes to reveal the burst blisters, the angry red lines where the shoes had rubbed against my feet as I ran.

'What's the good of psychic powers that don't tell you to wear sneakers?' I muttered.

'Pardon?' The policewoman sounded bored.

'Nothing.' At the sight of my sore feet, I began to feel the other aches and pains in my body. My ankle throbbed, and when I looked at my palms they were scraped and ragged, though they had stopped bleeding.

I sighed and leaned my head against the wall behind my chair.

'How much did you have to drink?' the

policewoman asked conversationally.

'I haven't been drinking.'

'Huh. Rashid said you stank of whisky.'

I remembered my one shot before my show. The memory of its warmth in my stomach seemed ancient, and so did the memory of the whole audience believing me. What I felt now was an echo, what was left when desperation was taken away.

I dug in the front pocket of my jeans. They'd patted me down, but they hadn't turned out my pockets. I fished out a folded slip of paper. Slowly, feeling the cuts on my hands open and pull, I unfolded it and read it in the fluorescent light.

It was in Gina's neat, looped blue ballpoint handwriting. *Pink blouse, short dark hair, twenties. Father, George. Wears his wedding ring around neck.*

I counted the words: fourteen. It wasn't much truth to build a lie around, but it had worked.

The more I stared at the slip of paper, the more I started to feel like myself. Okay, this had been freaky. I had freaked out. That thing with Stinky had shaken me earlier. Maybe I'd started to believe in all this crap I put in my publicity handouts.

This slip of paper was from the real world. It was how things really worked. The real world made sense, it followed patterns and probabilities. In the real world you got inside information from your manager who was listening to people drinking in the bar before your show. I could shape the real world with words. Not like —

I shuddered.

The door to the room opened and another police officer came in. I vaguely remembered him as the one who'd booked me. He'd looked grim then, but he looked grimmer now.

'Rosie Fox isn't your real name.'

'No.'

In fact, he looked worse than grim. He looked ghastly. Nearly green. 'What is your real name?'

'Rosalyn Markovitz Jones.'

'You're an American citizen?'

I stood up. The linoleum floor was cold against my bare feet. Everything was cold.

'What's happened?'

I don't know why I bothered to ask, though. I knew it already, from the sick, helpless panic that had begun to crawl back inside my belly.

'The train you were making the fuss over. The nine twenty-seven from Reading to Swansea.' He swallowed. 'It crashed between Swindon and Bristol. You're under arrest.'

3

'Good news. You're famous.'

Gina unceremoniously dumped a pile of newspapers on the foot of my hotel bed.

'Gina, I've only just gotten to sleep.'

'Well, time to get up. We need some better shots of you than this.'

I blinked at her. My head pounded, my body hurt all over, my throat felt as if it was lined with sandpaper. I knew, from the way Gina was regarding me, that I looked at least as awful as I felt.

Gina, on the other hand, looked great. Gina always looked great. She was in head-to-toe Donna Karan in chocolate brown and orange, her auburn hair perfectly styled. She couldn't have gotten much more sleep than I had, so it was totally unfair that she looked five thousand times better.

Then again, she hadn't been manhandled by the British Transport Police and then questioned for four hours on suspicion of terrorism.

Nor had she seen the entire fabric of the world she thought she'd known unravel before her eyes.

'Let me sleep, please,' I said.

'Sleep is for people who aren't on the verge of a career breakthrough. Look.' She held up a newspaper in one manicured hand and raised her shaped eyebrows.

I squinted, trying to see the article without moving my head from the pillow.

MEDIUM PREDICTS TRAIN DISASTER! the headline read. Underneath was a blurry CCTV still: me, on the platform, my hands raised in supplication, my mouth open and my eyes wide.

Gina was right. It wasn't a flattering picture. But what woke me up completely, with a wave of nausea, were the people standing around me in the picture. They were facing away from me, trying not to listen. I sat up and grabbed the newspaper from Gina's hand.

'Apparently one of the people at your show yesterday was a reporter for the *Reading Post*. She followed you to the station. She's got the first story on you, but it won't be the last. My phone's been ringing all morning.'

I ignored Gina and stared wildly at the front page of the newspaper.

RAIL CRASH KILLS SIX.

The picture was of a crushed carriage. Off to one side I could see the yellow-fronted, goggle-windscreened engine.

I wondered if any of the people I'd talked to, who'd treated me like blank air, were in that carriage. I scanned the article, though it didn't tell me anything new. The crash had been caused by a luggage trolley falling into the path of the train as it sped through a station. The train had derailed and ploughed into a bridge support.

The whole thing had been caught on CCTV cameras in the station. The police had held me until early in the morning, until they were sure I wasn't a terrorist and the crash was an accident caused by the wind and the trolley and bad luck. Eventually they had reluctantly realised there was nothing they could charge me with, advised me not to leave the country, and let Gina take me back to the hotel, where we'd been glued to the news channel.

So I knew already that five passengers and the driver had been killed. Fifty-two people had been injured. Railway officials were praising the driver, a man called Robert Branwell, saying his quick application of the brakes had probably saved several lives.

'Don't you cry,' warned Gina.

I shook my head. I'd cried all I was going to.

I must have looked like I was threatening tears, though, because Gina sat down beside me on the bed. 'It wasn't your fault,' she said for what felt like the thousandth time.

'I know.'

'And you did all you could have done to stop it.'

Now there Gina was wrong. In the hours since the crash, I'd thought of about a dozen ways that I could have stopped that train. The most obvious one being getting on the train and pulling the emergency cord. And several more inventive ways, too.

True, most of them were illegal, but laws seemed pretty trivial compared with the lives of six people.

'I should've pulled the cord,' I said.

'Rosie, you didn't know there was an emergency cord until that policeman told you so. You've hardly ever been on a train. It's not your fault.'

'I should've called in a bomb threat,' I said. 'Or left a suspicious-looking package on the platform.'

'You did the best you could. Trust me, it is not going to help you to think about the past on this thing. It's over. You need to think about the future now.'

I shuddered. 'If you want me to try to do some more predictions, forget it. I didn't mean to make this one, and I have no desire to repeat the experience.'

'That's not what I mean.' Gina picked up the newspaper I'd discarded and turned back to the photograph of me. She smoothed the page. 'I mean the future of your career. Today you're the best-known psychic in Reading. Tomorrow you'll be the best-known psychic in the country. You've got a press conference in half an hour.'

I shouldn't have been surprised at how quickly Gina switched from sympathetic mode to full-steam-ahead manager mode; I knew she was good at her job as a manager, even though she was only starting out, doing it part time, and she'd only signed a handful of small-time acts like me.

Though it didn't look like I was small-time any more.

'A press conference?' I felt nauseated.

'Uh huh. The hotel has got us a seminar room for it. The train crash is the most important news story in the UK right now, which means you're the second most important. We've got most of the tabloids, Channel Five news, and believe it or not, somebody from *The Guardian*. I'm figuring once they see how gorgeous you are, we're going to get offers for exclusive interviews. So you need to get up and get yourself looking human.'

'Gina. I don't want to give a press conference.'

'Yes you do. This is going to make a huge difference to your career, Rosie. You have to do it.'

This is going to make a huge difference to *whose* career, exactly? I wondered, and then squashed the thought. Gina had a lot riding on this. She had a lot riding on me.

I sighed. 'Can't you postpone it till this afternoon? I've only had two hours of sleep.'

'This afternoon we're driving to Birmingham. You've got a show there, remember? It's sold out.'

That sick feeling came back a hundred times worse. 'No.'

'You mean no, you didn't remember the show?'

'I mean no, I'm not doing it.'

Gina crossed her arms. 'Rosie, this is probably the most important show in your life. You have to do it.'

I tried to run my fingers through my hair, but they got stuck in the tangles. 'Gina, I do not feel like talking to dead people today. Not after last night.'

'Don't be silly. You're not responsible for those people's deaths.'

'But those people really did die.' My voice

was high and quavery to my ears. I hated that sound.

'And you had nothing to do with it.'

I didn't want to hear my voice again, so I shook my head vehemently.

'Be sensible. You said that you have no idea how or why you made that prediction. It wasn't anything like what you normally feel when you're performing. So why are you afraid to go on stage?'

'I'm not afraid. I don't get afraid. I just — I've had enough death for a while.'

Gina stood up and reached into her briefcase, which I hadn't noticed before, and pulled out a sheet of paper. ''From the age of thirteen,'' she read, ''Rosie has helped countless people get in touch with their loved ones and shown us all that, despite loss, life does go on.''

My stupid, corny intro speech. Three paragraphs of bullshit on a page, that I'd typed myself. Moreover, Gina knew it was bullshit. She had to; she'd written me cheat notes every night since we'd started the tour. It was a script, it wasn't real, not like the deaths of these six people were.

I looked at Gina. Her hands were on her hips.

'Come on,' she said. 'You've got reporters waiting for you downstairs. Pull yourself together.'

Suddenly I knew with total clarity that she hadn't wanted me to cry because she didn't want my eyes to be puffy and red for the cameras.

I lay back on the bed and pulled the blanket up over my head. The space underneath was like a womb: warm and soft and safe.

She patted my head through the blanket. 'Have a shower and put on some good clothes. I recommend some concealer underneath your eyes. I'll be back in twenty minutes to take you downstairs.'

Once she was gone, I got up and prepared to face the consequences of what I'd — somehow — done.

4

As media frenzies go, this was a pretty moderate one. About two dozen people sitting in chairs lined up in a room. I'd dressed to impress, in my 'I'm-a-sensitive-sexy-medium' style: flowing beaded skirt, clingy silk top ('Good, you've got some cleavage for the cameras' was Gina's observation). I'd pulled knee-high suede boots over my protesting feet, and threaded my silver hoops back through my ears.

I guess, in the back of my mind, I pictured walking into the press conference and being immediately swamped by flashing cameras and hordes of reporters calling out my name. Sort of like what happened to Hugh Grant in *Notting Hill*. But this was Reading, not Notting Hill, and it was a heck of a lot less glamorous.

Still, one camera flashed in my face when I entered the room, and that was enough to fill my vision with orange spots.

'Hi, guys,' I said, and heard the media frenzy mutter back at me as I went to the front of the room, to the table and chair Gina had prepared for me. She followed me in.

We both stood in front of the table. Standing people make better photographs than sitting people, and the Channel Five news camera was trained on me.

'Thanks for coming,' I said. 'First, before I say anything, I'd like to have a few moments of silence for the six people who lost their lives in last night's rail crash. Their spirits have passed to the other side, but they are with us now.' I bowed my head and heard the rest of the room subside into a rather embarrassed hush.

And it was that easy — I had control over them, and over myself. I'd reduced the awful sense of guilt back down to the words I was used to saying. A patter. A game.

I took a deep breath, pushed the last shred of my nightmares down, and raised my head.

'As you know, last night, while I was onstage here in Reading as part of my nationwide tour, I had a premonition that a disaster was going to hit the nine twenty-seven train from Reading to Swansea. I immediately left the theatre and ran to the station, where I was arrested while trying to warn the passengers. I tried to convince British Transport Police to stop the train, but they didn't believe me. I was in the custody of the Thames Valley Police when the news came in that the nine twenty-seven had derailed and crashed. All of this can be corroborated by members of the audience last night, the British Transport Police and the Thames Valley Police, and CCTV footage taken at the station.'

'Miss Fox, have you had premonitions like this before?' one of the reporters asked.

Gina had pointed the important ones out to me — the ones from the main tabloids and television stations, and the woman from *The Guardian*, the single broadsheet that had bothered to send anyone. I didn't recognise this man, so maybe he was local.

'Oh yes. Since I was a little girl, I've been able to tell the future. Spirits exist on a different plane; to them, time means very little. I've often had messages about things that were going to happen. They've saved my life twice. One time when I was a teenager I had a premonition that our family home wasn't safe, so I made my mother take us to a hotel for the night. That night, the house caught fire, though fortunately it was saved before it burnt to the ground. Another time the spirits told me not to drive my own car, and when I had it checked out, I found out the brakes were about to go.'

What a crock of shit. Still, they were taping it, and writing it down, and taking my picture. British journalism is supposed to be among the best in the world? I thought.

'Have you made predictions before that didn't involve you personally?'

'Yeah. All the time. I predicted the last American presidential election results within a hundred votes. And I usually get the Oscar winners correct, don't I, Gina?' Gina smiled and nodded; she didn't know anything about elections or Oscar winners, but she knew the camera was on her too. 'This is the first time it's happened in front of an audience, though, or been caught on CCTV cameras.'

The door at the back of the room opened, and a man walked in. The first thing I noticed was his hair. It was blond, wavy, longish, rumpled to the point of wildness.

Then I saw his face. He had high cheekbones, a strong chin, full lips. It was nearly the face of a movie star, except for the nose, which was crooked, slightly off-centre, where it must have been broken at some time.

Uh oh. I was in trouble.

I couldn't help smiling anyway. I'd thought about this moment for a long time.

'Hello, Harry Blake,' I said.

The man stopped. He considered me, his hands in the pockets of his leather jacket. 'Hello, Rosie Fox. Have we met?'

His voice — a low-pitched, casual tone that contrasted wonderfully with his perfect clear

British vowels and crisp consonants — was as familiar to me as his hair and face.

'No, we haven't,' I answered. 'But I'm a psychic, you know?'

'Oh. Yes. I see.' He walked across the room towards the closest available seat. It was beside the woman from *The Guardian*. Harry nodded at her and she looked at him as if he were an odd creature at a zoo.

'Sorry I'm late,' he said as he sat down. 'Had a breakdown on the M4.'

'No problem, Harry.' I didn't feel tired any more. Apparently seeing Harry Blake was as good as a cup of coffee and a couple of NoDoz.

And God, he was *cute*. Even better-looking in real life. He dug inside the pocket of his jacket and pulled out a notebook and a pen. He had nice, long-fingered, masculine hands; the pen looked small in them.

I felt a sharp dig in my side. 'Stop gawking at Harry Blake and start paying attention to the people who can actually help your career,' Gina hissed in my ear.

I smiled at the room in general. 'So where was I?' I asked.

'The Oscars,' said the *Guardian* woman, making no effort to conceal the boredom in her face or her voice. 'Is this the first time you've had one of your alleged precognitions objectively substantiated?'

'Oh no,' I replied, as charming as I could make it for her. The snob. 'As a matter of fact I've been approached by several police forces in the States and have helped them with their inquiries using my clairvoyant abilities.'

'Which police forces are these, Rosie?' the man from *The Sun* asked.

'I'm sorry, I can't share that information. I'm sure you'll understand: it could compromise an ongoing investigation.'

'Of course,' muttered *The Guardian*.

'However,' Gina cut in, 'if you look at Rosie's press release, you'll see the names of several happy clients in America who are willing to share the stories of how Rosie has used her amazing powers to help them. I have copies up here for those of you who haven't received one by fax or email.'

'Go on, Rosie,' called the *News of the Globe* guy, 'what are the spirits telling you about me now?'

I tilted my head and looked into the distance. This was the paper Gina was hoping would ask, and pay, for an exclusive.

'They're telling me you're a cheapo who's trying to get a reading without buying a ticket to my show.'

Most of the room laughed.

'Tell us about how you discovered you were

psychic,' said someone from another newspaper.

I sat on top of the table — tall enough to still look good on camera, but relaxed in my pose. 'It was when I was six years old. My parents thought I had an imaginary friend when I kept on talking to what they thought was thin air. I was an only child and they figured I was lonely. I was far from lonely, though. I had loads of friends. Only nobody could see them except me.

'I had this one friend who was a little boy even younger than me. One day he told me to tell my mother it was okay, he didn't blame her for not getting him out of the ice. When I told my mother, she went pale and asked me what my friend was called. 'Robbie,' I told her, and she fainted.

'Well, I was only six so of course I freaked out and thought my mommy was dead, but she came round right away and sat me down on her lap and told me, very gently, that she had had a younger brother who had died when he was very small. They'd been sliding on a frozen pond and he'd fallen through. My mother had tried to rescue him but she was only nine years old and she wasn't strong enough.

'She'd never talked to anybody about it, not even my father. She felt too guilty. So my

42

uncle Robbie had told me to tell her it wasn't her fault, so she wouldn't feel so bad.'

It could have been the TV camera, or maybe Harry Blake in the audience, but that was the best I'd ever told that story.

I liked the echo of my own situation: in the story my mother couldn't rescue her brother, and yesterday I hadn't been able to rescue those six people. Okay, maybe I was rationalising things, but the words 'it wasn't her fault' sounded really good to me.

I wasn't sure how far I believed them, though.

Harry Blake lifted his hand to signal he wanted to ask a question. When I nodded to him I noticed that his pen was still capped, and he hadn't written anything in his little notebook.

'How did you feel when you realised that something was going to happen to that train and you couldn't stop it?' he asked.

His posture in his chair was laid-back and casual, his voice was neutral and friendly, and his hair looked like it belonged on a Californian surfer. But his blue eyes were clear and keen and looking into mine.

'Horrible,' I said. 'It was absolutely horrible. One of the worst things I've ever felt. I felt helpless, and weak, and desperate, and very, very scared.'

And I didn't have to think about putting sincerity into my voice, because that was the only wholly true thing I'd said for the past twenty minutes.

Harry nodded, and uncapped his pen.

5

Gina threw her mobile phone down, frustrated. Though I noticed she wasn't frustrated enough to throw the expensive slim silver phone on to the floor — she made sure it landed squarely and safely on the hotel lobby armchair beside the one I sat in, my suitcases piled in front of me.

'The *News of the Globe* say they're considering making us an offer. 'Considering' it. It's the biggest objective proof since Nostradamus that the supernatural exists, and they're 'considering'?'

'What did you say to them?' I asked, kicking my suitcase with the pointed toe of my suede boot.

'I told them we had a very attractive offer from the *Sunday Sport*.' She sat in the armchair opposite me.

'An offer that's contingent on my posing topless,' I reminded her. 'Which I am not going to do.'

'Okay. You're right. You're too classy to go topless. It would give you a lot of exposure, though.'

I didn't even bother to make the obvious

joke. 'No money or publicity is worth showing my nipples to the nation.'

'Now that really is a shame.'

The familiar low tones, the precise yet lazy diction. I looked up and saw Harry Blake leaning a hip on the armchair beside me, his arms folded. My body did that NoDoz thing again.

'Hi Harry,' I said. 'I thought you'd left with the other media types.'

'No. I wanted to talk with you. But I had to discuss something with my editor first.' He bent down and picked up Gina's phone from the armchair and offered it to her. 'May I join you?'

'Please,' I said. Gina took her phone and he sat down beside me.

Harry Blake was taller in real life than on TV. He was less perfect; the camera erased smile lines around his eyes and a slight weariness in his features. The imperfections made him even sexier.

And of course TV could never show how wonderful he smelled. I caught it when he leaned forward in his chair — a breath of the leather of his soft, well-worn jacket, the clean cotton of his jeans and shirt, the spicy scent of his soap.

He smelled . . . well bred, I guess. I can't think of any other word for it, although that's a British phrase instead of an American one. Sophisticated, but like he wasn't even trying. Like he was born knowing how to move and how to talk and how he should smell.

'I'm a huge fan of yours,' I told him. 'Your show is practically a cult thing with psychics. We all watch it.'

'Really?' he said. 'Psychics watch *Amazing TV*? I'm rather surprised, given what I have to do occasionally.'

'Oh yeah. It's on late on Wednesday nights on cable TV in the States.'

'It's not exactly prime time here in the United Kingdom, either.'

'We all call each other the next day and talk about it. You're essential viewing to everybody on the medium circuit.'

'Well,' Harry said. 'That's a compliment indeed. Thank you. Although technically speaking, it's not my show, it's a show I work for.'

I shook my head. 'No, it's definitely your show. While I'm flattering you, I might as well mention that I've read your stuff in *Amazing News*, too, and I loved it.'

He chuckled, and stretched his long legs out in front of him. 'So you didn't need to use your psychic powers to tell who I was this morning.'

I held my hands up. 'I'll admit it.'

'I can flatter you in return. What you did last night is one of the best-substantiated pieces of precognition I've ever reported. Getting arrested was a particularly brilliant move.'

'I didn't plan that part.'

He inclined his head in a gesture that wasn't quite a nod. 'In any case, it ensured that your prediction was officially documented by impartial witnesses. And that's very rare.'

'Um. Thanks, I guess.'

He ran one hand through his wild hair and smiled at me. 'I'll tell you something else that's rare. I haven't been at a press conference with a reporter from *The Guardian* since I left *The Times*. The broadsheets don't tend to cover the same stories as *Amazing News*.'

I remembered the look the *Guardian* reporter had given Harry. I knew his story, of course. Everyone did. Now *that* had been a media frenzy.

I'd been in the States when I'd heard about it, three years ago. It was sort of surprising that a British press scandal should have reached America. But looking at Harry, I could tell why it had been big news.

He was a golden boy. He was handsome, and intelligent, and everything about him screamed *class*. He'd been educated at Cambridge and he'd been the young rising star of British journalism. In a short time he'd gone from some sort of assistant to one of *The Times's* best-known writers and editors.

When people fall from that height, they fall hard, and everybody feels the thud.

Though to my mind, the downward career trajectory from star journalist at *The Times* to staff journalist at a sensationalist rag like *Amazing News* was more interesting than how he'd risen to *The Times* in the first place.

One day, Harry had been interviewing the Home Secretary. Practically the next, he was interviewing people who'd had their bottoms probed by aliens. At *The Times*, his scoops had been on the Northern Ireland peace process or racism in the police force. At *Amazing News* — and on its companion late-night cable TV show, *Amazing TV* — he got to present worldwide exclusives on people who'd given birth to werewolves.

Now that was a story nobody could make up.

'No, I don't imagine you do cover the same sort of thing as *The Guardian* these days,' I said.

'Well, today we did, and I found it very

interesting. So thank you for that, Rosie.'

'You're welcome.' I wanted to offer a few choice words about how snobby that woman from *The Guardian* had been, but I thought maybe it would be a touchy subject for him. 'Next time I do something worthy of the broadsheets' attention, I'll make sure I call you.'

He folded his arms across his chest and looked comfortable enough to own the whole hotel. 'Well, that's more or less what I stayed to talk to you about. I have an offer for you.'

'We've already got an offer,' Gina cut in. I thought she'd been quiet lately. 'From the *Sport*. And the *News of the Globe* is calling me back in a minute.'

'Great. Well, you should feel free to take them up on their offers. They're bigger newspapers, and they're dailies, while *Amazing News* is a weekly. And *Amazing TV* is only on once a week too. Late at night, as you mentioned, Rosie. Not a huge audience.'

I sat up in my chair. 'You want me to be on *Amazing TV*?'

'Yes. We'd like to tape your next show in Birmingham and air it on Friday. And I'd like to come with you on your tour and base four or five weekly columns on your work. The next issue of *Amazing News* isn't for another five days, though. So if you've got bigger and better offers, you should take them.'

'You're some salesman,' said Gina drily.

'I'm being honest. We want this story very much, but we're not very big. We also don't mind if someone else beats us to the punch, as long as we get the story too. So taking our offer doesn't necessarily mean messing up the exclusive you're hoping to sell to the *News of the Globe*. When they call you back, of course.'

Gina frowned at his last comment. 'Rosie isn't the only one who's seen you on TV. I don't think we can trust you. I think you want this story so you can try to prove that she is a fraud.'

Harry snorted. 'Oh come on. If you know anything about *Amazing News* you'll know that the paper isn't exactly unsympathetic to psychics.'

'But you are,' I said.

Harry tensed a little bit. He still looked casual, but extremely alert at the same time.

'Okay. I've debunked a few people who claimed to have supernatural powers. But they were charlatans.'

'More than a few, Harry,' I said. 'You've exposed Ted Grayson, Eleanor Starr and Unicorn Riley within the past two months.'

'Well, they deserved to be exposed. They were clumsy fakes. Especially Unicorn Riley.'

He shifted his long legs. 'If you've followed my career, Rosie, you'll know there are plenty of paranormal stories that I can't conclusively disprove.'

'Yes. But even when you can't disprove them, everyone can tell you don't believe a word of the stuff you're reporting.'

'I have never said a single thing to indicate that, without evidence.'

'Never *said* it,' I persisted, 'but it's obvious. You look at your subjects that little bit too long. You focus in on their weaknesses, the ways that they're ridiculous. That's why we all call each other up the next day to gossip about you and the poor sucker who you've made look like a fool.'

A smile twitched at the corners of his lips. 'So you're not a fan of my show because of my dashing good looks after all. I'm disappointed. I thought I'd pulled.'

'You can stop flirting with my client, Mr Blake,' Gina cut in. 'We've got a lot of publicity already. We don't need someone nosing around trying to trip Rosie up, trying to prove she's a fake.'

'*Is* she a fake?'

'Of course not,' Gina bristled.

'Then I won't be tripping her up.' He turned to me. 'Did you know that Unicorn Riley had told twenty-three clients that they were the reincarnation of Cleopatra?'

I giggled. I shouldn't have. Because Gina's suspicions were right. Ninety per cent of the time, *Amazing News* and *Amazing TV* never questioned the paranormal stories they reported. It was credulous, sensationalist pap. But when Harry Blake took the stage, *Amazing TV* suddenly became energised. Anything could happen. Careers were suddenly on the line.

He was intelligent. He was observant. He was dangerous.

And good Lord, was he sexy.

'I'm not worried about you tripping Rosie up, Mr Blake,' Gina said, all business. 'Because that's not going to happen. You've told us what you want, but not what we'll get out of it. Right now Rosie is the biggest paranormal story in this country, and your publication is all about paranormal stories.'

'That's not strictly true,' Harry told her. 'We've always covered a wide variety of issues. For example, last month I interviewed the woman who's had the world's largest breast implants, and while they were impressive, they weren't exactly supernatural.'

I laughed, and Gina gave me a glare that clearly said *Whose side are you on anyway?* 'Breasts apart, Mr Blake, it's pretty clear that

Amazing News needs Rosie more than she needs you.'

'That could be true,' Harry agreed. 'Though it might not always be. This story could run and run. Then again, it might not. *Amazing News* will be guaranteed coverage in any case. Plus, ninety-two per cent of our readers unreservedly believe in paranormal phenomena, despite any sceptical stories I might do occasionally. They're your demographic. It's targeted publicity right at your most receptive potential audience.'

'That doesn't take away from the fact that you're a sceptic and your coverage is likely to be biased.'

Harry paused. 'So you'd rather have me write about Rosie without seeing her work?'

Gina stiffened. Harry regarded her levelly. If we didn't let him come along on the tour, we looked like we were hiding something from the man who sniffed out fakes.

Harry turned to me.

'Rosie. I want your story. Your prediction was stunning and I find you intriguing. And I think we've established that we need each other.'

Whoa, boy.

'It's fair enough that your manager is suspicious,' he continued. 'I do expose frauds

54

when I find them. I'm going to keep on doing it whenever I can.' He raised one eyebrow, like he always did at the end of his TV spots. 'But if you're as good as I think you are, you won't have to worry about a thing.'

If you're as good as I think you are. If those words weren't a challenge, I'd eat my tarot cards.

'And you don't have to take your top off,' he added. 'Unless you want to.'

I let my eyes travel the length of Harry's body, sprawled elegantly in his chair. Six feet of eye candy talking about taking my top off could be a welcome distraction from delivering spirit messages in second-rate theatres.

Plus, I could fool him. I'd been fooling everybody for so long. Harry Blake wouldn't be an exception.

'Sure.' I shrugged. 'Come along to Birmingham and we'll see how it goes.'

That would have been a great moment for any of the psychic ability that had shown itself so unexpectedly the night before to rear its spooky head.

But it didn't. I didn't feel any premonition at all. I felt delicate, as if I'd been shattered and put back together with spit and hope. All I could predict for the future was Gina berating me all the way to Birmingham.

If I had actually been able to see what the future held in store for me, my answer would have been very, very different.

6

The whisky in the antique glass had a definite shiver to it. The dim backstage light danced in it like amber sparks.

I brought my hand down to eye level and observed this phenomenon. The liquid seemed to have a life of its own.

That was when I realised how badly my hands were shaking.

'Shit,' I said under my breath.

I sat down heavily in the plastic chair and felt a lump form in my throat.

'Rosie, are you all right?' Harry turned from where he was standing near the curtain; I couldn't see his face clearly but I could see his figure silhouetted in the stage lights behind him. They caught his hair and made it into a wild halo.

My mouth seemed frozen shut and my hand held the whisky glass so hard it hurt.

'Hey. What's wrong?' He stepped towards me and reached out a hand as if he were going to touch my shoulder, and that got me unstuck. I jumped out of the chair and retreated behind it. There was no way I wanted him finding out how much I was trembling.

Though for a split second, I did. I wanted Harry Blake's arms around me and I wanted to relax and breathe in his smell, which was so effortlessly right.

Oh God. I was losing it big time.

'I'm fine,' I said quickly. 'I just need a minute to myself to get in tune with the vibrations.' And to stop myself from vibrating. I swallowed to try to get rid of the lump in my throat. 'And I guess I'm nervous about the TV cameras.'

'Right. Well, no need to be nervous about them. Pretend they're not there.'

Easier said than done. There were three of them, two on tripods pointed at the stage and one held by a cameraman stationed in the audience. Every time I saw them I thought about how I'd been caught on CCTV cameras at Reading station: panicked, alone, in black and white. Printed in the paper next to the news about the train crash.

I took a deep breath. In through my nose, out through my mouth. I was bound to be a little jittery. I'd tried to sleep this afternoon, before the show. I'd found a quiet spot in the corner of a dressing room, pulled my coat up over my head, and fallen asleep.

But my dreams were not kind.

The hot, oily smell of the train, the driver's door surprisingly warm under my fists. A half-glimpsed image of the driver. All mixed up with flat newspaper photographs of crushed carriages and empty goggle-windshield eyes.

I blinked and saw the same images again.

'Listen, I don't want to interfere with your vibrations, but you don't look well. Can I get you some water or something?'

Like I needed to have a gorgeous nosy reporter all concerned about me at the moment. I held up my glass of whisky. 'No thanks. This is fine.'

I could feel him looking at me, and in the moment of silence I could hear the audience beyond the curtain. They were waiting for me; they made small shuffling sounds in their seats, muffled coughs, a few whispers.

'I think it's probably time you went out there and introduced me,' I said.

Harry nodded slowly. 'All right.' He turned and went through the curtain to the stage.

I heard enthusiastic applause. Well, he was very handsome, and there were TV cameras there, after all. I edged back in front of the chair and sat down, trying to breathe slowly while I listened to Harry's patter.

'Good evening, ladies and gentlemen, and welcome to the Royal Theatre, Birmingham.

'I'm Harry Blake, of *Amazing News*, and tonight we're here to witness the psychic feats of Rosie Fox. As you can see, Rosie has allowed us to tape her show tonight for *Amazing TV*, and on behalf of the programme, I'd like to thank you for being our audience.'

It wasn't my scripted introduction. It was harmless and friendly, but it wasn't what I was used to, and the difference of it made my heart beat even faster.

I only had myself to blame for that. I'd suggested that Harry do the introduction and wrap up the show, for the cameras. 'If we can see what he's doing, it'll give us more control,' I'd said to a fretting Gina, who was of the opinion that it gave Harry that much more opportunity to call me a liar in front of a live audience.

I'd known he wouldn't do that; I'd seen his shows before, and he'd been unfailingly polite to his subjects. But now I wished I'd taken Gina's advice.

Harry introducing me made it feel too much like everything had changed since last night.

'Taping this show has been a last-minute thing and so I thank you even more for your patience with our cameras. Many of you already know the reason for my interest in

Rosie's career, but in case you don't, I'd like to fill you in on what happened at Rosie's show last night in Reading.'

My heart was doing all sorts of funny things: racing, leaping, and falling down to my stomach. Harry had mentioned, laconically, that he might talk about my prediction. And I'd said yes, of course. Like Gina said: it was going to make me the most famous medium in the UK. It was stupid not to make the most of it.

But I felt awful anyway.

'By all accounts, it was a normal show. Rosie had spoken with several people in the audience — an audience just like you, made up of normal people. And then, near the end of the show, while she was talking to a woman called Moira Castleman, Rosie suddenly stopped short.'

He knew how to work an audience. He never raised his voice from its habitual drawl, but he paused in all the right places, emphasised all the right words. I didn't look up, but I could picture him in his dark trousers and white shirt, fully self-possessed in the stage and TV lights, his golden hair a beacon.

'She said to Moira, 'Don't get on the nine twenty-seven train to Swansea.' And then Rosie Fox, without finishing her show, ran

61

out of the theatre. The time was two minutes past nine o'clock. With twenty-five minutes to go, Rosie tried to stop that train. At nine twenty-six, she was arrested by British Transport Police. And at twelve minutes past ten o'clock, as you all know, that train crashed on its way to Swansea.'

The audience had gone utterly quiet. I knew they were hanging on his every word.

I am exploiting the deaths of those six people, I thought.

And what did that make me?

I hadn't killed them. But I was sitting here and listening to a man telling an audience that I'd predicted their deaths. And I knew I could potentially make a lot of money out of this.

I'm going to choose a new career, I thought, and I stood up and put the glass of whisky on the seat of the chair. I'd have to go and apologise to the audience and to Gina, and then get the hell out of Birmingham as quickly as I could. I walked to the curtain and started to pull it aside, but was stopped by what I heard Harry saying.

'I spoke with Moira Castleman this afternoon. She credits Rosie Fox with saving her life. Because Moira was about to leave Rosie's show early, and walk to the station and get on the nine twenty-seven to Swansea to visit her sister for the weekend. She had a reserved seat in the front carriage, the one that was crushed in the impact. And because of Rosie's warning, she didn't get on that train.'

I dropped the curtain.

Moira. I'd forgotten about Moira. The beige woman. Harry hadn't told me he'd spoken with her.

Moira thought I'd saved her life.

I turned around and went back to the chair.

'That's the reason why I'm here tonight, ladies and gentlemen: I want to see the woman who's produced the most spectacular prediction I've witnessed in my career. And the woman who Moira Castleman says saved her life. Ladies and gentlemen, I give you Rosie Fox.'

I picked up the glass of whisky and raised it towards the ceiling in something like a toast.

'Here goes nothing,' I said, and downed it.

The minute I walked out in front of the audience, I knew things were different. The applause wasn't tentative, but it was hushed. I could feel the force of their belief as soon as I looked at them. Every face was serious, and every eye was on me. Including Harry's, and the three TV cameras.

My mic was live and the lights were dazzling.

'Thank you, Harry,' I said, and he nodded and went to sit in an empty seat in the front row. Next to Gina, I noted. She wasn't looking so annoyed that he was here any more.

'Hi,' I said to the audience.

I didn't smile. They all believed in me already. I could have been wearing a polyester Wicked Witch of the West outfit and they would've believed in me.

I started off with a moment of silence for the crash victims. I wondered how many of my appearances from now on were going to begin this same way, in remembering the public dead before going on to the private dead.

You know what I wanted to do? I wanted to tell the audience how I really felt.

I wanted to tell them that if I were offered the choice to see everything in the future on a platter, I'd run as fast as I could, no matter how much money it would bring me, because knowledge was responsibility.

I wanted to offer them the truth as raw as I could put it, and I wanted to feel their belief enfold me anyway like a pair of warm arms.

But that wouldn't work.

So instead I told them about how the

spirits were like TV reception and how sometimes they didn't know the difference between the past and the present and the future. Blah blah blah, all the normal stuff that told them, without saying it outright, that they should believe in what I said even if they thought I was wrong. Everything as usual.

Except it wasn't as usual. For one thing, I was being taped. For another, I had Harry Blake's intelligent blue eyes following every move I made. For a third, I didn't have any inside information gleaned from somebody listening to the audience before the show. I couldn't have risked something like that, with Harry pretty much watching Gina and me all day. I'd done plenty of shows without that sort of insurance, but the presence of the TV cameras and Harry Blake made me wish that this time I had it.

And for a fourth, I was half expecting another bolt from the blue. Another real prediction.

Just what the audience wanted, and what I really didn't.

I took a deep breath and smiled at the audience at last. 'You're going to have to forgive me. I'm drained from last night. I can feel plenty of spirits here, there are some strong personalities tonight, but I might be slow to pick them up. And that's my fault, not theirs. They want to be with you. But you might have to give me a little time.'

I surveyed the audience. Eye contact with the women. I gauged the expressions, some serious, some half smiling, all intent.

It was the most receptive audience I'd had in my entire life, and I had stage fright so badly I wanted to pee on the floor.

Okay. Start with an easy one. I took a deep breath and pretended to be listening to the empty air around me. 'I've got a man here who's saying the name Michael,' I began, 'and he's got some sort of tool in his hand; I think it's a saw. I'm sorry, ladies and gentlemen, I'm getting this man very clearly, but I can't quite see the direction he's indicating to me, though I think it might be on this side of the room.' I turned to the left half of the audience. 'Is there anyone who understands what I'm talking about?'

Slowly, a man sitting just to the right of the centre aisle raised his hand. Heads swivelled around him, and he cleared his throat before he spoke. 'My name's Michael, and so was my dad's. He was a kitchen fitter.'

The audience breathed together. An inhalation, an exhalation, a single collective expression of relief that their faith had been confirmed.

'Hi, Mike. I'm Rosie.' I climbed the steps

to him, the cameras and sound boom following, and held out my hand for him to shake. He was in his fifties, beside a woman who was obviously his wife. 'Your dad told some good jokes, didn't he?'

Mike nodded. 'He mostly told off-colour ones.'

'Oh, a man after my own heart,' I said, and couldn't help but glance down at where Harry sat. He had turned around to watch me, his arm draped over the back of his chair.

'Okay, Mike,' I continued, 'I'm not sure what this means, but your dad is referring to a job left undone. Do you know what I'm talking about here?'

'Yeah, I do,' Mike answered. 'He's talking about my brother.'

His brother is a job left undone? I thought. Oh God, have I got a botched gangster killing or something here?

I surveyed Mike: solid, thick around the middle, short greying hair, wearing a cheap watch and a gold wedding ring. With that watch, he wasn't a gangster.

'Your brother caused him some worry while he was alive,' I hazarded with an air of complete confidence.

'We both did,' Mike said. 'I haven't talked with Paul since 1997.'

I considered the probabilities. 'And your

dad tried to be a peacemaker that whole time? He's holding his hands like this' — I held my hands out in fists in front of me, and then brought them to clasp together — 'and then like this. Do you understand that?'

Mike didn't nod, though I felt anyway that I'd gotten it right, because he kept staring at me. Slowly, he reached out his hand and touched my clasped ones.

'Do you think we should try to make it up?' he said.

I nearly staggered backwards down the steps.

He'd asked my advice. It had happened before, of course. Plenty of times, especially back when I'd been doing one-to-one tarot readings.

But I'd never really felt the weight of it before now.

'What does my dad say?' he asked me.

'Mike,' I said, 'your dad says you know what he wants you to do. He wants you to get in touch with Paul. He wants you to put your differences aside. He wants you to love each other. It's all he's ever wanted, no matter what.'

The look on Mike's face told me that I'd said exactly what he wanted to hear. His eyes cleared, the lines in his face seemed to smooth out.

Then he smiled and squeezed my hands and turned to his wife. 'I'll call him,' he said, and his wife hugged him.

And I didn't feel the weight any more.

No guilt, no worry, no nervousness, nothing. It all lifted off my shoulders as suddenly as if someone had tied a helium balloon to all those bad feelings and let them float away.

The smile I gave the audience was one hundred per cent genuine. I caught Harry Blake with it for a split second as I scanned the theatre looking for who was next.

I'd try the spirit of a foreign woman, somebody French, or Italian, or Spanish. Somebody was bound to know a dead Continental, and it was different enough from Mike the kitchen fitter to keep everyone interested. I walked down the aisle back to the stage, touching my temples with my fingertips and adopting a slightly spaced-out meditative look.

When I got to the stage I took my time walking around it, feeling the cameras following my every move. A European woman, and a veiled hint about a family secret having to do with a child. If they denied it, I'd tell them to ask their relatives when they got home because it could be about the past. Or the future. Or about distant family. Or about somebody else's family. Hell, it could be so secret that nobody had discovered it yet.

I couldn't lose. I stopped walking and started to talk.

'I see a woman — '

I stopped.

Because I did see a woman. Not a dead one, but a live one. In the audience. Doing something I'd never seen anyone do at any of my shows before.

She was probably in her early seventies, with permed hair and a green skirt suit. She looked like a retired teacher. And she was standing up, looking at me and waving her hand rather tentatively.

'Yoo-hoo!' she called. 'Rosie, my mother and I fought before she died. Does she forgive me?'

I saw several people nod, not in answer to her question, but with fellow feeling. Another woman stood, four rows up. She was younger, probably mid-forties.

'I keep on feeling these cold draughts in the room. Do you think that's my uncle trying to contact me?'

Another person stood. And another. And my mouth fell open as I realised what was going on here.

These people didn't want me to impress

70

them. They didn't want names and facts pulled out of a hat and fitted to their lives. They believed in me already. What they wanted was reassurance.

They wanted help. My help. Help I could give.

I went to take the retired teacher's hand.

7

I first learned about the attraction of lies when I was thirteen, and my father's body gave out after nearly thirty years of abuse.

Three or four weeks after he'd died, I told my math teacher I didn't feel well, although I felt fine, and spent the last period of school in the girls' room. I'd never skipped class before. In fact I liked school; an A on a test was straightforward approval of the kind I rarely got at home. But I couldn't concentrate and the math teacher, knowing I was recently bereaved, didn't question my lie.

I sat on a sink kicking my heels, and when two seventh-grade girls came into the bathroom, I smiled at them. They weren't my friends; I'd never spoken with them. They were younger than me, but they were tougher. They wore makeup and hairspray and big dangly earrings. They didn't smile back, but one of them dug a green packet of Kools out of the pocket of her acid-washed jean jacket.

'You smoke?' she asked.

I didn't. I thought the things were nasty. 'Yes,' I said, took the cigarette she offered me, and lit up.

I sucked on the filter, kept the smoke in my mouth without inhaling, and let it flow out in a smooth stream. I watched myself in the mirror out of the corner of my eye. I looked like I was smoking. The seventh-graders thought I was smoking.

It tasted like a wintergreen Life Saver rolled in an ashtray. I sucked on it all until it was burned down to the filter. There was a menthol-flavoured air of camaraderie as we sat out the last period together. They complained about the teachers, and I listened. It was a whole new world for me.

When the bell rang for the end of the day, I walked out of the girls' room and I got a whiff of myself. I stank of smoke — girly minty menthol smoke, but smoke nonetheless. And I knew that my mother, who'd nagged my father for the thirteen years I'd been alive (and probably long before) to quit smoking or at least not to do it in the house for God's sake, would kill me.

So I didn't go right home. I took a walk and I chewed my way through two packs of Wrigley's to make sure my breath smelt good. I went into a McDonald's and washed my hands and my face. I didn't head for home until I could whip my head around really fast and not catch a whiff of smoke from my hair. And to be sure, I went into a drugstore on the way and sprayed myself with a perfume tester.

It was close to five o'clock when I got home, and although I expected to get told off, I knew being late wasn't as bad as being a smoker. I was already preparing my story, so I didn't notice anything different at first when I walked into our living room.

Then I saw my mother sitting in her armchair and staring at the wall, a tissue clutched in one hand. Her glance flickered to me when I came in. She smiled a little smile then went back to staring at the wall.

My first thought was that she'd moved the TV. Then I looked at the wall. There was an enlarged photograph of my father hanging on it, framed in an elaborate gold frame, the kind you use for oil paintings.

'You got a blow-up of Dad's picture,' I said.

Mom nodded. 'Isn't he wonderful?'

I looked at the picture. Even allowing for taste and sentimentality, it was far from wonderful.

I'd seen the picture plenty of times before, because the original had sat on a table in our living room for years in a normal silver-plated frame. It was my dad standing on the end of a dock on one of our infrequent holidays to the Massachusetts coast. He was wearing plaid shorts and a button-down short-sleeved shirt,

74

and his legs looked very skinny and his belly stuck out. His large dark eyes squinted against the sunlight. The breeze lifted his thin hair off his high, balding forehead. He had a beer in one hand and in the other he held a cigarette.

'It's the same old picture,' I said. 'It's not exactly the cover of *Time* magazine.'

'I mean your father.' My mother delicately touched her tissue to one of her eyes, and then the other. 'He was a wonderful man.'

I looked at my mother, and then at the photograph, and then back at my mother. She didn't appear to be deranged.

'Mom, what are you talking about? He wasn't a wonderful man. He was never home. And when he *was* home, he stank of booze. He cared more about what was inside a bottle than he cared about us.'

My mother sat up straighter. 'Roz, I'm sorry, honey, but you're wrong. Your father was a good man. If he spent a lot of time away from home that was because he was working hard at the store to support us. He had to put in so many hours, but he did it for his family. Everything he did he did because he loved us.'

'Yeah,' I said, 'and I bet he drank himself to death because he loved us, too.'

My mother glared at me.

'Mom, look at that picture. Look at it. You've framed it like it's a picture of God or something. And there he is, look, he didn't even stop drinking long enough for you to take the picture. And he's smoking, Mom, that drove you crazy.'

'Rosalyn.' My mother's voice held her warning tone, but I was feeling the anger rising in me.

I dug my fingernails into my palms and thought something like, *I just walked five miles to get rid of the smell of one Kool and my father dies and he's forgiven for decades of smoking a pack and a half a day?*

It was a thirteen-year-old's thought. I was upset about a lot more than a single Kool.

I stomped over to the picture and stabbed my finger against the glass. 'Look, Mom. Look here. He's got a beer in his hand. Right here. Can't you see it? And it wasn't just beer he drank, was it?'

My mother stood up. Her voice had more than a warning tone in it. 'Rosalyn Markovitz Jones, I never want to hear you talking about your father like that again. You may go to your room.'

I stared at her. I opened my mouth and nothing came out.

'Go to your room, Rosalyn. Now.'

I whirled on my heel and ran, making as

much noise as possible, to my room, where I slammed the door and burst into tears and tried to figure out how I had been banished for saying nothing but the truth.

I had a lot of time to think about it. When I came down for supper I was sent right back upstairs. But not before I saw that my mother was in that chair looking at that picture, apparently still not seeing the beer, the cigarette, the thousand faults and hurts and drunken mistakes.

That night, I thought she had gone temporarily insane. But the next day when I came home from school there she was, still in that chair, and though I was beginning to worry I would have to call the child protection people to save me, she fixed dinner as usual and asked me about school and nagged me about my homework.

So she was normal, somehow, underneath the weirdness. But she kept on making little visits to the photograph, and snapping at me when I made a less-than-appreciative comment. And the next day, and the next, and all of the days following, she started saying more and more stuff about how much she missed Dad, and how good he had been to us, and how we would never find another man who was better.

Needless to say, after a while I kept my

mouth shut. I wasn't stupid. I watched as what I began to think of as 'the cult of Saint Ed Jones' became a permanent part of our lives.

But my mind was busy. I came to formulate an explanation for what was going on in my mother's head.

People like believing in lies.

Lies make their lives easier. Lies give them something to believe in a world that is, as you get older, less and less likely to hold any role models or any perfection. Given the choice between a beautiful lie and an ugly truth, most people will go for the beauty wherever they find it.

My mother found beauty in my dead father. Somehow.

As the weeks passed and it became clear that my mother preferred spending time with her dead husband to spending time with her living daughter, I began to experiment with lying myself, spinning a fiction for the pure, risky beauty of it. Being believed was like all the A's I'd ever got in school rolled up into one.

And I had a talent. It ran in the family.

8

I slept like the dead in the bed and breakfast in Birmingham. My stomach woke me up at half past eight. My calorie intake for the previous day had been two teensy bags of what the British insisted on calling crisps and an antique Russian tea glass full of whisky. I launched out of bed and pulled on my jeans.

The breakfast room had pink nylon cloths on all the tables and matching pink carnations in little ceramic vases. Cheap, but well accessorised.

Harry Blake sat at one of the tables on his own, a rack of toast and a stack of newspapers in front of him. The chair he was sitting on was pretty spindly and so was the table, but even though the furniture was on the verge of collapse, Harry looked absolutely, utterly, totally at ease.

He folded the newspaper he'd been reading and smiled at me. 'Morning, Rosie. Did you sleep well?'

I felt a throb of excitement. I'd had a largish crush on Harry Blake for ages, and every hour he hung around, my crush was getting bigger. Even though he was poison to

79

psychics, Harry was the reason why I made sure I was at home and awake every Wednesday at one thirty a.m. His show was cheesy as hell, but he was pure class, and he was gorgeous with it.

Considering the groupie-esque thoughts that were whizzing through my mind at that moment, my answer was pretty relaxed. 'I slept great, thanks. Didn't know you were staying here too.'

Harry shrugged. 'It made sense to stay close to my subject.'

'In that case, it makes sense for me to join you for breakfast.' I pulled out the spindly chair across from him and sat down in it.

What a great sight to wake up to in the morning, I thought. His hair looked like he'd just gotten out of bed and run his hands through it; his face looked fresh and smooth and newly shaven. I wondered if Harry ever got personally involved with any of his subjects.

'Tea?' Harry offered, and poured me a cup from a metal pot when I nodded. I added milk and took a gulp. It was very dark brown and strong and hot enough to warm me all the way down. Perfect.

'Most Americans prefer coffee,' Harry said.

'I like tea. Plus' — I topped up my cup from the pot — 'I've got a certain professional affinity with it. Tea leaves can always come in handy for giving psychic readings.'

Harry nodded. 'So you practise tasseomancy too.'

I waved my hand breezily in the air. 'I prefer to call it tasseology. It's quite a precise science.'

Though his expression hardly changed, I could see exactly how scientific he believed tea leaf reading was.

I took a piece of toast and spread it with Marmite. 'Did the tape come out well?' I asked.

'Extremely. Your rapport with the audience was exceptional. Is that the way it always is, or do you think your prediction had something to do with it?'

I pretended to think about it. 'I always have a rapport, though I've never had quite so many people asking me for advice. Usually I pass on messages without being asked.'

Harry's keen blue eyes narrowed. 'Why do you think people asked you for advice?'

I was interrupted before I could answer by a woman setting down a laden plate in front of Harry. The smell of fried sausages and bacon made my empty stomach roll over.

'Just scrambled eggs, please, and more tea,' I said to the waitress. Harry made no move to pick up his knife and fork after she'd gone. 'Please go ahead and eat your breakfast,' I said. 'It'll be cold by the time mine gets here.'

'Thank you.' He began to cut into his fried egg.

'Are you always such a gentleman?'

His full lips tilted into a smile as he chewed. 'Not always,' he answered after he had swallowed.

Our eyes met for a moment. Oh, I had a crush all right. Pity it was on the person who wanted to expose me as a fake.

I dropped my eyes to his plate, and then quickly glanced away as nausea hit again. I'd never been able to look at a full English breakfast.

'That stuff is a heart attack on a plate.'

His eyebrow lifted in that way he had. 'I'm hoping that's not a prediction.'

'No,' I replied. Not unless you were my dad and you followed it with a fifth of Wild Turkey for lunch.

We spent several minutes in silence, him eating his breakfast, me drinking my tea and eating toast and Marmite and looking at the pink carnation.

'You going to stay at the same hotel as me tonight too?' I asked.

'Unless you mind.'

'Depends. Are you going to rifle through

my underwear drawer looking for evidence that I'm a fake?'

'That also depends. Do you usually keep your psychic secrets in your knickers?'

My surprised laugh nearly sent my toast flying out of my mouth. I grabbed the napkin and held it to my face.

Fortunately the waitress came in then with my breakfast. The next time I looked up, most of my eggs and several slices of toast were gone, and Harry had finished his own breakfast and was pouring us both another cup of tea.

'Your manager was very excited about your presence in the Sunday papers,' he said, passing over the stack. They were already folded to the pages with the stories about me. I looked at the top one.

DON'T TAKE THE NINE TWENTY-SEVEN! WARNS PSYCHIC, screamed the headline.

''Their spirits have passed to the other side,' American medium Rosie Fox said of the rail victims yesterday, less than fifteen hours after she predicted their fate,' I read. There was a picture of me during the press conference — cleavage subtle but visible, I noticed — and below it, the publicity photo that Gina had given out with the press pack.

The article itself wasn't surprising. It called

83

me 'beautiful' and my prediction 'stunning', and repeated the story I'd given them about my childhood spirit friend, poor ice-drowned Uncle Robbie. To balance it out, they had a quote from a paranormal researcher from some university who said that to prove conclusively that I was psychic I would have to repeat my precognition under controlled circumstances.

'How can you predict the future under controlled circumstances?' I wondered aloud.

Harry shrugged. 'Nobody's ever done it. It's a circular argument: psychics say that the presence of sceptics and scientific controls stops them from working properly. But sceptics and scientists will never believe psychic claims unless they are proven scientifically. It's no wonder sceptics and psychics don't really mix.'

'Predictions don't work like science. They — '

I remembered how my prediction — my only real, true prediction — had hit me. Out of nowhere, stronger than anything I'd ever felt. The practised response died on my lips.

No thinking about the prediction.

I could feel Harry watching me, and I turned my attention to leafing through the newspapers.

Four minutes of reading was enough to

gain me back my equilibrium. Each paper had slightly different photographs, slightly different information, and slightly different experts. *The Sun* said I was 'gorgeous', the *News of the Globe* called me 'Foxy Rosie Fox', and the *Sunday Sport* had a close-up of my chest.

I bit the inside of my cheek to keep myself from smiling and flipped to the front page of the tabloid I was holding.

And froze.

Six photographs. Six colour photographs. Four men, two women. One was a posed, formal photograph; one had been taken in a photo booth. The other four were casual snapshots of people smiling at the camera and living their normal lives.

Six real, live people to whom I'd been a blank space in the air. Who weren't alive any more.

I recognised the driver from my blurred glimpse of him through the train window. But not any of the other people. They were all adults, though; no little boy with scared blue eyes.

His mother moved him away from me towards the back of the train, I thought. And everyone who died was in the front. So maybe I saved his life.

That thought was what kept me from

85

puking up my scrambled eggs and toast.

The six photographs seemed to get bigger, brighter, to float up from the page and hang in the air in front of me, almost alive.

As I stood up, suddenly desperate to escape, my knees buckled underneath me.

Instantly I felt hands on my shoulders. I hauled in a breath and tasted the effortlessly right smell that was Harry Blake. He was holding me, stopping me from falling to the floor. I squeezed my eyes shut, trying to keep the tears back.

I was kneeling on the floor beside the table, and Harry was kneeling too, inches from me. I opened my eyes and saw his shirt.

Harry's hand found my chin and tilted my face up towards his. 'I thought you were going to faint,' he said. 'You look as white as a ghost.'

'Ghosts aren't white,' I replied, from habit.

'Are you okay?'

Was I? I breathed in another lungful of Harry, and focused myself by looking at his eyes. Blue eyes. *I saved that boy's life.*

Maybe.

'It was difficult for you to see their pictures,' he said.

'Are you going to write about this?' I asked.

'Probably.'

I pulled away from him and walked

backwards on my knees on the carpet until I wasn't close to him any more. 'I'm fine,' I said.

'Why are you two praying in the breakfast room?'

I looked up and saw Gina standing over us, beside the table. She was freshly made-up, her hair immaculately styled, and she was wearing a pristine designer suit.

I stood up quickly. 'Hi, Gina. We were just checking out the carpet.'

'Are you done?'

'We're done,' I heard Harry say behind me, and I could feel him standing up.

'Good. Because the *News of the Globe* called to ask for that exclusive. We're driving to Milton Keynes and you're meeting their reporter for lunch.'

'Milton Keynes,' Harry said. 'Nice.' He sounded less than impressed.

I turned to him. 'What's wrong with Milton Keynes?'

'You'll see when you get there.'

'Well, it's where Rosie's next show is,' Gina said briskly. 'And then tomorrow we're going to London for a photo shoot. So if you're done with breakfast and prayer, Rosie, you can go upstairs and get dressed before we check out.'

I looked down at my jeans and Ramones

T-shirt. 'I thought I was dressed.'

'Ha ha. Good one. Come on, get moving, it's nearly nine o'clock already.'

'Imagine that. Nine a.m. on a Sunday, the day's a-wastin'.' My eyes wandered to the table, where my tea had gone cold. 'I hope there's a decent restaurant in Milton Keynes.'

Harry snorted.

'What?' I asked him.

'Let's put it this way,' he said, gathering together his newspapers. 'I have no psychic ability whatsoever, but I can confidently predict that by lunchtime you're going to wish you'd had my heart attack on a plate.'

9

'Booze?' I said hopefully to Gina as we walked from her car to the hotel after the show that night.

'No,' she replied. 'Bed. We've got to go to London tomorrow for that photo shoot, remember. You should be fresh.'

'After the past few days I've had, I need to unwind a little bit before I go to bed. I'll have a drink or two and then go up.'

Gina gave me a look.

'Promise,' I said. She just shook her head, and parted from me in the lobby.

Growing up with my father cured me of any desire to get drunk on a regular basis. But I'd been through enough recently to make me want to let my hair down.

I'd spent most of the afternoon on my interview with Duncan Grice, the reporter for the *News of the Globe*. That is, I'd had my interview with him. He'd had his interview with my chest. It's amazing how easy it is to lie to somebody who's staring at your tits.

'So how about it?' I said to the balding bartender as he poured me a small glass of white wine. 'Is Milton Keynes a big party town, or what?'

'Three pound ninety-five,' he replied.

'I'll take that as a no,' I muttered, paying and taking my glass to a table.

The bar was non-atmospheric in the way that only a hotel or airport bar can be. There were fake plants, upholstered chairs and sofas around low tables, inoffensive music, and soft light that failed to provide any ambience whatsoever. If people hadn't been drinking out of pint glasses and smoking, I could have been in California or New York.

I sipped my wine and looked around to see if there was anybody I could talk to. My show had gone well that night, but I could do with talking to some people who weren't out to pump me for information or advice.

There was a couple who weren't talking to each other near the fake plants, and some Japanese businessmen in one corner. A group of people in black tie and evening gowns laughed uproariously near the piano. There had been some reporters at my show, but they'd apparently got what they were looking for, because I couldn't spot any in the bar.

I had just finished my glass of wine when Harry appeared at the bar's entrance. As always, I noticed his hair first, and then his smile as he spotted me and came up to my table.

'Drinking alone?' he asked.

'Not any more. You going to buy me one? I think I need something stronger than wine.'

He inclined his head. 'What would you like? A whisky?'

'No, I hate whisky. Rum and Coke would be good.'

His eyes sharpened, but otherwise, he didn't change expression. 'Rum and Coke it is.'

While Harry was at the bar, I observed the group of evening-gowned and black-tied people. 'The girl in the pink dress hates the girl in the black dress,' I announced to him when he returned with two rum and Cokes.

'Is this your psychic ability at work again?' he asked, sitting in the sofa across from my chair and settling his long legs beneath the table.

I sipped my drink. 'Mostly it's because the pink-dress woman has a wedding ring that matches the ring of the guy with red hair. And he's been flirting with the black-dress girl for the past fifteen minutes.'

I'd thought maybe I'd get used to Harry's smile, but it wasn't happening. The rum bypassed my stomach and went straight to my head.

'Ah,' he said. 'Observation. Sometimes I think our two professions are more similar than it appears on the surface.'

I narrowed my eyes at him. 'Harry, are you going to get all journalisty on me? Because I could really do with a night off.'

Harry took a long drink. 'Let's have a night off, Rosie, if that's what you need.'

'It is. I'll be right back.' I got up and went to the bar.

This drinking was supposed to unwind me, but I felt stretched tighter than a guitar string. 'Two more rum and Cokes,' I said to the bartender.

Harry Blake's eyes hadn't been off me since he turned up late to the press conference. I could feel them on me now, though I couldn't resist a quick glance to check that I was right.

I was. He was looking at me.

And Harry Blake wasn't just looking at me because it was his job. I adjusted my seat on the bar stool, letting my skirt ride a little way up my thighs, and his gaze dropped to my legs.

Warmth flushed through my body.

I knew exactly what would relax me after the crash, after my show, after all the worry and stress: Harry, a bed, and several hours of nakedness. I could think about the consequences tomorrow.

I paid the bartender some ridiculous amount of money and went back to the table.

'Are we expecting company?' Harry asked in his lazy voice, looking at our half-full drinks and the two new ones.

'They're for us. We're going to play a game.'

He raised his eyebrows. 'What sort of game?'

'A drinking game, obviously. We need to have some fun.' I sat back in my low chair and stretched out my legs in front of me. I was wearing my suede boots and a relatively short skirt, and I watched as Harry's eyes dropped to the bare skin of my legs again.

'I'm up for having fun,' he said.

'Cool. Then you can choose the game we play.'

'All right.' Harry looked straight into my eyes, and the corner of his mouth went up. 'Let's play Truth or Dare.'

I considered Harry. Gorgeous, charming, and more dangerous than a cobra. 'That's not a drinking game.'

His smile was full-fledged now. 'We can drink while we're playing it.'

No matter how much fun it might be, this was not going to be a night off. For a moment

I wondered if it was wise to get drunk with Harry Blake. What if the rum loosened my lips and let something slip out I didn't want him to know?

No. I could handle Harry. Maybe in more ways than one.

'Okay,' I said. 'I go first. I'll take a dare.'

'How did I know you were going to choose dare?' Harry wondered.

'You must be psychic too. What's the dare?'

He thought about it. 'All right. I dare you to get one of the men in this bar to give you his tie.'

'You're not wearing a tie.' The top two buttons of his shirt were open. Nice view.

'I think it would be more of a challenge for you to convince a stranger to remove his clothes for you.'

'Okay.' I stood up and took a slug of my rum. 'Give me five minutes.'

Being in the bar for half an hour had given me enough information about the people in it that I didn't have to think twice about who to approach. A man from the black-tie group was standing at the bar. He was in his twenties and had fashionably sticking-up hair. He was good-looking, quite drunk, and not, as far as I could tell, attached to any of the women in his group.

I leaned against the bar beside him, letting

my arm just touch his. 'Hi, I'm Rosie,' I said.

He turned to look at me, and I saw a smile grow on his face. 'Well, hi there, Rosie, I'm Neil.'

I leaned a little bit closer. The bar pressed against my chest and deepened my cleavage.

One thing I'd learned recently: the way to a British man's heart is through the chest.

'I saw you up here at the bar, Neil, and I knew you were perfect.'

'Perfect for what?' He leaned a little closer to me too. 'Can I buy you a drink?'

'Oh, no,' I said, smiling suggestively. 'I'd like you to give me something a lot more . . . ' I trailed my fingertips over the back of his hand and up his arm, 'intimate.'

His face showed that he was absolutely certain that he'd gotten lucky. 'What's that?'

I turned to face Neil, glancing over at Harry as I did. Harry was watching with an amused expression. Slowly I walked my fingers up Neil's chest, and gently took hold of his bow tie with both hands. I pulled him towards me.

Neil licked his lips. He smelled of beer and aftershave.

'Neil,' I whispered, 'I want you to give me your tie.'

Neil blinked. He rested his hands on my hips.

'All right,' he said. 'You have to take it off me, though.'

'It'll be a pleasure.' It was a pre-tied bow tie. I reached round to the back of his neck to unfasten it.

Neil took this opportunity to let his hands slide down and grab my backside.

And then all of a sudden there were two pairs of hands on me, and the second pair of hands at my waist pulled me backwards, out of Neil's grip. Then I was being lifted up and carried in Harry's arms back to the table. The bow tie dangled from my hand.

'Thanks, Neil!' I called.

Neil looked surprised, then smiled, shook his head, and turned back to the bar.

'You were supposed to take his tie, not give him a handful,' Harry said. The fingers of one of his hands were touching the bare skin of the back of my thigh.

'You've got a couple of handfuls yourself,' I said to him. 'I didn't need rescuing. I was in control there.'

'I know. You usually are.' He placed me on the couch, and sat down next to me.

'So what was that? Male chauvinist pigness in action?'

'No. I didn't enjoy seeing my drinking buddy getting mauled.' He picked up my drink and gave it to me. 'Well done on getting the tie. It only took three minutes.'

'Well, Neil was a nice guy. So I did the dare; now you have to drink.'

'Fair enough.' He drained one of his glasses.

'Your turn,' I said. 'Truth or dare?'

'Truth.' He leaned back on the couch.

I curled up my legs, facing him. 'Truth? Anything I ask? Are you sure?'

'Yes.'

'Okay. Tell me about how you got fired from *The Times*.'

He sucked in a breath through his teeth. 'What about something easier, like my favourite colour?'

'Nope. I want to know your story.'

'My story is a matter of public record. Look at any newspaper from three years ago. August the twenty-fifth, to be precise.'

'I want to hear your side of it.'

Harry nodded. 'I was an investigative journalist. I'd built a relationship with one source in particular. One day he said he had this piece of information that would knock my socks off.

'It was a leaked memo from a senior Member of Parliament named Warren Greene. I knew Greene quite well; I'd written several stories about him, starting when I was still at university.'

Harry paused to drink. 'I didn't like this man. I'd learned enough about him to convince me that while he might be a perfectly adequate politician, he was personally pretty abhorrent. There was a rumour, not provable, that he'd flirted with belonging to a far-right racist political party in his youth. And believe me, I tried to prove it. I'd heard him say things off the record that — well, I didn't like him.'

'I thought journalists were supposed to be impartial,' I said lightly. Playing the game. 'Not make up their mind before they know the truth.'

'I *was* impartial.' He hesitated. 'At least my writing was. But you're right. I let my personal feelings make me eager for a story that would show the world what I believed this man to really be. I thought the leaked memo was my chance.'

'It said something racist?' I asked.

'Exactly.'

'And you published it.'

'It got published.'

'And it wasn't true.'

He shook his head. 'It was a remarkable forgery. Greene denied writing it. There was an inquiry. I'd written hard-hitting articles about this man in the past, and he accused me of fabricating the story to ruin his career.'

'Where did the forgery come from?'

Harry downed the rest of his second drink. 'I'm not sure. My source disappeared. The inquiry found that I'd been at fault: I'd either made up the story, which made me a liar, or I hadn't checked out my information properly, which made me a fool. Either way, I didn't have a job any more. Or any credibility. Or any money, once the lawsuits were settled.'

'But you were set up,' I said.

'I have no proof that I was. And it was my own fault. I shouldn't have trusted the information. It was my job to find out the truth, and I failed.'

Harry ran his hands through his messy hair, and exhaled sharply. Then he stood.

'If you don't mind, I need another drink.'

I watched him go to the bar: so effortlessly well bred, so classically handsome, and so sharply intelligent.

He had two public flaws — his broken nose, and his one cataclysmic mistake. And somehow he wore them both with so much grace that they were almost virtues.

Harry came back with two more rum and Cokes.

'Thanks for telling me your story,' I said as he placed a glass in front of me.

'It was no less than duty required,' he replied, sitting down next to me again.

'Besides, most people avoid mentioning it to me; it's refreshing to talk about it.' He nodded at my glass. 'I told the truth; now you have to drink.'

I finished off the half of rum and Coke I still had left.

'Your turn,' Harry said. 'Truth or dare?'

'Dare.'

Harry didn't even have to think. 'All right. I dare you to tell me what really happened when you made your prediction the other night.'

10

I narrowed my eyes. 'You sound a little too ready with that dare.'

'I'm curious.'

'And it's not really a dare, is it? It's actually a truth.'

'The question you asked me was much more difficult than charming the tie off a bloke. You owe me. Are you going to do the dare, or are you chickening out?'

'I never chicken out.'

'Good. So tell me.'

My legs were curled up underneath me, but I curled them tighter. I picked up my drink and held it in both hands. He had told me something painful because I had asked it. I could risk the truth, for once.

'It's the weirdest feeling, Harry, because it feels so natural. You'd think it would be like having something reach you from outside. But it's not. The knowledge was suddenly there, as if it had been there all along.'

I thought about how to put it into words. 'Sort of like a memory I'd forgotten, and then all of a sudden something triggered it, and it came flooding back. I didn't really see it, or hear it, or even feel it. I just knew it. Like how you know your own name.' I shuddered. 'I hope it never happens again.'

Harry's casual posture hadn't changed; he still sat elegantly slumped back on the couch, his hands folded over his chest. But he'd been intent on my every word. I was getting to recognise that intensity as he listened. It was exactly the same casual, sharp scrutiny he'd given my shows.

'It wasn't a trick, Rosie?' he asked, sounding offhand. 'Or a guess?'

'No, Harry. It wasn't a trick, or a guess.'

I met his eyes and held them.

For a beat. For two beats. For enough time for me to take three slow, steady breaths.

'It's my turn to drink, then.' He took a swallow of rum. 'I'll take truth.'

He emphasised the first and last words. Infinitesimally. But enough for me to know that Harry Blake hadn't believed a single word I'd said.

I felt annoyance grab at me. What was the *point* in being honest? Why should I *bother*? I wasn't any good at it.

I took a big gulp of my rum and Coke and said, 'Okay, tell me how you feel about working at *Amazing News* with all the alien abductees and breast implants.'

Harry threw back his head and laughed. It

came from deep inside his body and was warm and smooth and somehow lazy, like his voice.

'I'm an investigative journalist,' he said. 'I've never been anything else. *Amazing News* came along, and they liked me because my name was famous, and with the stories they cover, they aren't too worried about credibility. The newspaper is a rag, and the programme lets weirdos tell their stories on national television. But it allows me to do what I'm good at. In my situation, I can't really ask for more.' He shrugged. 'Plus, there aren't many other jobs where I could meet vampires.'

'So you're resigned to it.'

'Rosie, I'm famous for lying, and I spend my days trying to tell the truth even though nobody will ever believe me. Since I got fired from *The Times*, my entire life has been a dictionary definition of the word 'irony'. I'm not resigned to it. But I've got to try and see the funny side. If I didn't, I'd go mad.'

I nodded. I drank. 'I'll take a dare.'

'Things are falling into a pattern here,' Harry observed.

'You think?'

'Perhaps. All right, I dare you to tell me — '

'No,' I interrupted. 'You got away with that

once already. I'm not telling you any more about myself. You don't believe me anyway, so why even ask? Give me a real dare.'

Harry leaned back on the sofa we shared and slowly let his gaze travel over me once again. I watched him look at the tips of my suede boots, the spiky heels, my bare legs, and my thigh-skimming skirt.

I wondered if this frankly appreciative survey of my body was honest, or if it was a ploy to throw me off guard. Or both.

His eyes lingered near the top button of my blouse and I felt myself flushing. By the time he looked up into my face I knew my cheeks were pink, and that if this was a ploy, it was working.

He smiled slightly and held my gaze.

'I dare you to do what you want to do right now,' he said.

I was a bluffer. I knew a bluff when I saw one. Sitting close to Harry on the sofa, looking into his keen blue eyes, I decided to call his.

It was what I wanted to do, anyway.

As soon as I stood, I felt the alcohol for real. My head felt a little swimmy and my knees a little wobbly. I walked the two steps to Harry's side of the couch, glancing at the rest of the room as I did. A few people were watching us with interest; one man averted his gaze as I looked around. I didn't care.

One leg at a time, I straddled him. I sat down on his knees. His hands grasped my waist and pulled me closer so I was fully on his lap, kneeling on the couch. The fabric of his jeans was warm against the bare skin of my thighs, and my face was level with his.

I buried my fingers in his wild hair. It was silky, golden, a caress in my hands. I could hear Harry's breath catch in his throat.

'Truth or dare?' I murmured.

For a second, I thought he would choose dare and pick me up and carry me to the elevators and up to his room.

'Truth,' he said.

'Are you really as attracted to me as you're acting you are?'

'Yes.' I felt the vibration of his voice in his body.

'Then dare me.'

I'm sure my face told him exactly what I wanted that dare to be, because he said it.

'I dare you to kiss me,' he said.

I moved my hands from his hair to his face. His jaw felt solid and rough. I leaned forward and touched my mouth to his.

It was slow and warm, that kiss. Harry tasted of rum. Like his smell, it was effortlessly right. We opened our lips at the same time, and with a sigh from me, a rumble deep in his throat, we let our tongues dip inside each other.

His skin was hot under my fingers. His hand on the small of my back pressed me to him. And our kiss was sometimes deep and melting and sometimes a whisper of a touch.

The parting felt like part of the kiss. His breath whispered against my moist lips. He stroked my hair back from my face with one hand. I could feel his heart beating hard and fast.

'It's your turn,' I murmured. 'Do you want truth?'

His 'yes' sounded like the answer to another question, the one my lips had asked him.

I tangled the fingers of both hands in his exuberant hair. I stroked his cheekbones with my thumbs. As soon as he said it, I was his for the night. And I hoped it would be a long, long night.

'Tell me what you're thinking, Harry Blake,' I said.

'You're very beautiful, Rosie Fox,' he said, his eyes dipping down to look at how I sat on his lap, and then coming back up to meet mine.

Languid anticipation spread through me. I licked my lips and tasted Harry.

'You're charming,' he murmured. 'You're a

consummate performer.' He ran a finger down my cheek and across my sensitive mouth. 'You are very, very good at faking it.'

Something began to stir in my stomach. Something a lot sharper and colder than desire.

Harry cupped my face in his hand and brought it closer to his. Almost another kiss. His voice was low and seductive.

'And your mother never had a brother called Robbie,' he said.

The cold flooded out of my stomach and through my whole body. I pulled away and stood up.

I didn't feel drunk any more. I felt stone-cold sober, tense and livid.

'Good night, Harry,' I said, and walked out of the bar. On the way, I scooped up the bow tie and deposited it on Neil's lap, as he sat laughing with his friends.

11

I clutched my cardboard cup of tea in one hand and twisted my hair into a tight rope with the other and looked at the train. It was red and shiny. It said 'Virgin' on it. There was a gap of about half a foot between the platform and the open door.

None of this was helping my hangover any.

'That's like a safety hazard,' I said. 'Somebody could get their foot stuck there and really hurt themselves.'

'That's why they invented the saying 'Mind the gap',' Gina explained, sounding as if she were talking to a child. 'Can we get on the train now?'

I sipped at my tea instead of answering her. After I'd swallowed, I said, 'Don't you think it's sort of ironic that they've named a long, snakelike, thrusting phallic symbol after a virgin?'

'Rosie, stop procrastinating. We need to go to London.' Gina put her hands on her hips.

'I'm not procrastinating. I feel sick.'

'I told you it wasn't a good idea to go drinking,' Gina said. With her foot she pushed my bag closer to the train. She looked as if she'd like to do the same to me. 'I hope they airbrush those photographs they take of you today to remove the green tinge from your face.'

'As my manager, it's your job to be sympathetic to me and to bring me Alka-Seltzer. Not to call me green and make me get on a frigging train called 'Virgin'.'

'And as a professional performer, it's your job not to embarrass yourself by getting drunk and snogging a reporter who'd love to ruin your career.'

I blinked. 'You know about that?'

Gina sighed heavily. 'Of course I know about it, Rosie. The hotel manager took great pleasure in telling me about it. I wouldn't be surprised if it made it into the tabloids tomorrow.'

I wouldn't be surprised if it made it into *Amazing News*, I thought, sicker than ever.

But that wasn't what was bothering me, not really. Not the kiss or my hangover.

I looked around the platform. It was different from platform four in Reading; it was modern and it looked like it had been built by someone with no conception whatsoever of style or comfort. Whereas Reading had been Victorian and, in comparison, almost quaint. It was amazing how well I remembered platform four, considering I'd been yelling my head off the entire time I'd been there. But the image was frozen permanently in my mind.

I took another gulp of tea. 'Explain to me again why we can't drive? Or take a taxi?'

'Because driving in London is hellish, and because a taxi would cost a bomb,' Gina explained none too patiently. 'So we're taking the train to London and back and then we'll pick up the car and drive to your next gig in Leicester.'

A guard in a uniform started walking down the platform slamming carriage doors shut.

'Rosie, we've got to get on the train now. Come on.' Gina grabbed my suitcase and my arm and pulled both of us towards the open door.

I was going to lose this battle. I'd known I was going to lose it even before I'd started it. I found I often lost my battles with Gina for some reason. Probably because she was so damn bossy.

I stepped over the gap.

This train isn't going to crash, I told myself as I followed Gina down the aisle. The reason why your stomach is attempting to commit suicide is because you are a lousy drinker and you have a hangover.

I sat in the seat across from Gina.

'Happy?' I asked.

'Ecstatic.'

'I'm glad one of us is.' I finished my tea and shoved the paper cup into the space between the seat and the wall of the train. Then I settled back and closed my eyes. Maybe I could fall asleep.

I heard a whistle from outside, and after a few seconds I felt the train lurch forward. Instead of trying to leap out of my throat, my stomach attempted to crawl down through my bowels.

I opened my eyes and looked at Gina. She was totally crease-free and perfect. You couldn't be that perfect without an ulterior motive. People who looked perfect were terrified of being out of control. They were hiding something, and so was Gina.

In the past, I'd done some quite spectacular psychic readings based on that insight, even more impressive because they seemed to go against everything the person's appearance indicated.

I knew I was right; Gina had a secret. But how did I know it?

I'd met other mediums on the circuit, over the years, and we talked shop. I'd always assumed that most people's air of total confidence in their psychic powers was, like mine, something studied. Sure, I met

111

mediums who believed completely in everything they said they could do. I'd figured they were fooling themselves.

What if they weren't?

I let my eyes drift to the window, and then wished I hadn't. The train was going fast now.

I closed my eyes again and tried to concentrate on something else, something safe and comfy. *The Muppet Show*. Kermit, Scooter, Miss Piggy, Statler and Waldorf, the Swedish Chef, and what was the name of that big Muppet with fangs who was about eight feet tall?

No good. Even big Muppets couldn't distract me.

What if I really was psychic?

And what if I really was psychic and the reason I felt so bad about being on this train wasn't because I was thinking about the other train that crashed, but because I knew, psychically, that this train was going to crash too?

'Gina,' I said, 'do you ever wonder about whether or not I really have psychic powers?'

Gina narrowed her eyes at me. It was a subject, among a lot of others, that we hadn't brought up. She seemed to accept whatever I told her about myself. And when I'd suggested, offhand, that she could help me out by collecting facts about the audience

112

before the show, she'd accepted that too. I didn't know if she thought I was a real psychic who wasn't averse to a little cheating, or an out-and-out fake.

'Of course you have psychic powers, Rosie,' she said, sounding, again, like she was talking to a child. 'Without them, you don't have a show.'

I listened to her carefully controlled voice and heard what she meant: Gina didn't care how I did my show, as long as I did it.

Of course. Unlike me, Gina didn't have to worry about questioning the foundations of everything she believed in; she believed in success, and she was getting it.

I stood up. 'I need another cup of tea. You want anything?'

'No thank you,' Gina said. 'You know, I've been doing some calculations, and I'm thinking it would be a good move for you to start up a psychic phone line.'

I ran my fingers through my hair in pure incredulity at how Gina's mind worked. The woman never, ever took even a minute off. 'I'm thinking it would be a good move for me to have some more tea.'

The train shook as I made my way down the aisle toward the buffet car; I had to grab the back of seats as I went to stop from pitching sideways. My hands were sweating.

113

Ironic. I'd been all pissed off with Harry Blake last night because he'd taken advantage of our Truth or Dare game to try to prove that I was a fake. And now I was a bundle of pathetic hungover nerves because I was desperately afraid that I wasn't a fake after all.

'Stupid,' I said to myself, reaching the buffet car and leaning against the counter.

'Pardon?' the woman behind it said.

'Nothing.' I looked at the rows of baby bottles of booze on display and considered the virtues of hair of the dog. Bad idea. 'A cup of tea, please.'

She gave me a plastic cup full of hot water, a tea bag that appeared to be on a wire, two tubs of milk, a plastic stirrer, and two packets of sugar.

'I don't need these, thanks,' I said, pushing the sugar back towards her along with the money for the tea, and then my mind made the connection.

Sugar.

'Sweetums!' I cried.

The woman's expression transformed from bored to alarmed. 'Pardon?' she said again.

'It's the name of that Muppet, you know the big one? I was trying to think of it before.'

She nodded carefully, obviously reviewing in her head the 'Procedures for Dealing With

114

Insane Rail Passengers' manual.

I, on the other hand, felt much, much more relaxed.

The name had come to me, like that. Certainty, recognition, all at once. Just like how I'd felt when I'd predicted the train crash.

It was nothing like how I felt about this train. This train I was only nervous about.

'Do you have a cover for this cup?' I asked the woman, and she pointed at the stack of them on the side of the counter. I grinned as I took one and fitted it on; I grinned at the woman, who twitched her lips back at me; and then I grinned all the way down the aisle to where Gina still sat with her Filofax.

Making a prediction could be something as simple as my brain working without my knowing it — like how it'd come up with the Muppet's name. Or it could be something supernatural. Who knew?

The future, and the past, were both out of my control. I couldn't predict another prediction any more than I could bring the dead back to life. It was something I was just going to have to accept.

And that was something I'd had plenty of practice at. Accepting situations, adapting to situations, and using situations to my advantage.

It was the Win/Win game. And I was very, very good at that game.

For the first time since Reading station, I felt more or less like my old self.

12

The trick to being a psychic is to set up a situation where whatever happens, you win.

Let me explain it with a simple analogy. Imagine there's one last piece of pie — no, let's make this analogy really mean something: there's one last piece of amaretto cheesecake on the plate. And to settle who gets it, you or your friend, you decide to flip a coin.

So you flip a coin. And you call heads. And it's heads, and you get the cheesecake.

Or, alternatively, you flip a coin. And you call heads. And it's tails, and you say, 'Best of three,' and two heads come up, and you get the cheesecake.

Or, alternatively, you flip a coin. And you call heads. And it's tails, and you say, 'Best of three,' and it comes up tails again.

And you look your friend in the eye, and you say, 'Sweetheart, I hate to say this, but do you remember when you said I should do whatever it takes to make you stick to your diet? I'm sorry, but I'm going to have to show some tough love here, for the sake of your thighs.'

And then you get the cheesecake.

Or even better — and this was the solution I liked to use in my stage act — you flip the coin, and you call heads, and then before you see what's come up, you look your friend meaningfully in the eye and say, 'Do we really want this piece of cheesecake to come between us? Isn't it better, as friends, if we live together and trust each other? How about you give me half of the cheesecake, and we both feel good together?'

In psychic terms, the Win/Win game consists of taking a guess. If you're right, you've won. And if you're wrong, you manipulate the situation so it seems as if you've been right all along, and you hit an emotional jackpot on the way. Therefore, you've won even better than you would've done if you'd got it right the first time.

Which was exactly what I was doing on stage that night in Leicester, talking with a woman called Lynn. After some careful questioning without appearing to do so, I'd found out that her grandfather was a butcher, and that her grandmother had had four cats, and therefore I had filled in some details about them — that Gran cleaned all the time (to keep the cat hairs off the sofa), that the family always had a big Sunday roast from Grampa's shop, that Grampa drove a van, that they both loved tradition. All weighing probabilities, and all, as it happened, hits.

'And now, Lynn,' I said, 'I want to get more into the present, here, because your grampa and gran are both with me, as you know, and they're saying enough about them. Let's talk about you. They know that your relationships are an important area in your life.'

Lynn, who was in her early forties with short curly hair, big glasses, and a wedding ring, nodded. Of course she did. Relationships are important to one hundred per cent of people who want to contact dead loved ones. Lynn didn't have any husband sitting next to her, so that was my next clue.

'Your grandparents are telling me about a problem with your relationship, and it's a major relationship; your grandmother is pointing to her wedding ring, so I'm thinking it's your marriage.'

Lynn nodded again.

'Okay, Lynn. This isn't something that's earth-shattering right now, but there's a conflict to do with money, I'm sensing a disagreement with your partner about money and how it gets spent?'

Again, something that applies to most of the Western world's adult population. I could remember my parents fighting about money almost every day of the week. When they

119

weren't fighting about my father's smoking, or my father's drinking, or my mother's cooking, or my grandparents' interfering. But Lynn's brow furrowed behind her big glasses, she glanced at her friend sitting next to her, and she began to shake her head.

'No,' she said, 'we haven't had any argument about money.'

The technique here is not to believe the client, to insist upon the infallibility of your sources from beyond the grave.

'Are you sure, Lynn? Because I'm definitely getting a very strong message about money conflicts. It doesn't have to be this week, or this month even; remember that spirits don't keep track of time like we do, once they've passed over.'

Lynn looked as if she were thinking, but she continued shaking her head. 'No, there's been nothing like that.' She blushed a little bit. 'I'm quite recently married, you see.'

She didn't look like a newlywed. Another miss; another tactic called for.

'Congratulations!' I said, beaming all over the place. 'Then of course if you're still honeymooning, you're not going to argue about money. But your grandparents — and don't let this embarrass you, Lynn, because they are only saying this because they love you and want the best for you — they're saying this is something you should watch out for in the future. Though with their warning, you may well be able to avoid this sort of conflict in your relationship. That's what your grandparents are hoping for you, that's why they're mentioning it.'

See? Win/Win. If it hasn't happened, then it, will happen in the future, and if it doesn't happen in the future, it's because the prediction has stopped it from happening.

Classic.

I took a moment to step back on the stage and look around, pretending to be listening. There was an empty chair in the front row: the chair that had been reserved for Harry Blake. I hadn't seen him since our Truth or Dare game the night before, and now he hadn't turned up for my show. I wasn't sure whether to be relieved or angry or disappointed.

I raised my fingers to my mouth for a second, remembering, despite myself, how he'd kissed me.

I turned back to Lynn. What was the point in thinking about Harry Blake when I had a winning situation here right in front of me? It was time to go for the emotional truth.

'Your grandparents have another message for you, Lynn. They say you shouldn't worry, even if these arguments do come up. You're not the type to put too much emphasis on material things. You know what's important in life, don't you?'

I saw the door at the back of the theatre open, and a silhouette stepped into the darkened room and stood at the back. It was tall, with wild hair.

'And Lynn,' I continued, 'you know that what's really important in life is trust.' I gave the last word a little bit of emphasis. 'Whatever life throws at you, they're saying, you know you're going to be able to handle it, because you and your husband can find the strength to work out any differences and trust each other.'

Though I didn't look at him, the sarcasm that dripped from my voice was aimed straight at Harry, but as soon as I spoke, I wondered if I'd overdone it. Lynn shifted in her seat, and she appeared flustered and embarrassed.

'W-well, actually, Rosie,' she stammered, her cheeks getting redder by the second, 'I don't have a husband. I recently got married to my girlfriend.'

The woman sitting beside her, who I'd assumed was her friend, took Lynn's hand. I saw that they had identical gold rings on their left hands.

Oh God, a lesbian wedding. What were the chances of that?

Quite heroically, I avoided flicking my gaze to the back of the room where I knew Harry Blake was gloating for all he was worth.

I stretched out my arms and thought, *Win/Win*.

'Lynn!' I cried. The smile I'd plastered all over my face grew even huger and brighter. 'This explains so much! I thought when your grandparents were talking about tradition that they were stressing that aspect a little, but I didn't pick it up because the relationship issues were coming to the forefront. But now of course it makes sense — you haven't got a traditional relationship and you want people to accept you as you are. And you're worried that your grandparents wouldn't accept the choices you've made. But they do, Lynn, they've come here to tell you they love you the way you are.'

Both Lynn and her — wife? — were nodding vehemently, and there it was: I'd turned a spectacular and unforeseeable gaffe into an emotional truth that they both believed I had heard from beyond the grave.

I was untouchable.

I turned the full wattage of my smile on Harry as he walked down the dark aisle and took his seat in the front row.

That last slice of amaretto cheesecake was mine.

★ ★ ★

'So now you know my show so well that you don't actually have to bother turning up for it?' I said, sitting down on the edge of the stage and setting my water bottle beside me.

The audience had gone home, Gina was discussing something with the theatre manager, and the place was empty except for Harry Blake, still sitting in the front row, looking (of course) as if he owned the place.

He stopped doodling in his notebook and smiled at me. 'I'm sorry I was late, Rosie. My car broke down on the M1 and I spent most of today at the Watford Gap service area waiting for the AA.'

'Alcoholics Anonymous?' I asked.

He laughed. 'I don't think one night of drinking Truth or Dare calls for anything that drastic. No, the Automobile Association.' He nodded at my litre of Evian. 'How about you? Feeling a bit the worse for wear?'

'I'm feeling absolutely great.' I swung my legs back and forth against the stage.

I wasn't feeling great. I was feeling irritated as hell, despite my fantastic success onstage that night. The man swanned in late to my show, and then had the audacity to be all cheerful and to completely ignore the fact that the night before we'd shared the most passionate kiss I'd had in — well, ages. And then he'd casually give me a look that made it clear that he thought I was a liar.

Okay, actually I *was* a liar. But still, that's rude.

'Sounds like your car isn't too good, though,' I said. 'It broke down on the way to my press conference the other day too, didn't it?'

Harry grimaced. 'Yes.'

'What do you drive?'

He looked wistful. 'I used to drive an Audi S4 Cabriolet. V8 engine, quattro all-wheel drive, black leather interior. That car could move. Then I got fired. Then I got sued. Now I drive a ten-year-old Rover Metro. Or rather, that's what I drove.'

'Is it dead?' I asked. 'Even Alcoholics Anonymous can't fix it?'

'No. It's gone. The only way I'm going to hear from that car again is if you could call up its spirit at one of your seances.'

'I don't usually speak with machinery.'

'If you do get a chance to talk to it, make sure you swear at it a lot.' Harry shook his head. 'It was a horrible car. In the end I took a taxi all the way up here. My editor is not

125

going to be pleased to get that expense claim.'

I took a swig of my water, in a way that I hoped expressed the sentiment *It's your choice and therefore your problem.*

'I'm glad I got here in time for the lesbian newlyweds, though,' he continued. 'You handled them extremely well. I was impressed.'

I snorted. 'After last night, Harry, you have to excuse me if I interpret your compliments as being pretty double-edged.'

'Ah.' Harry nodded in that slow, annoyingly all-knowing way he had. 'You're angry with me for what happened between us last night.'

'I'm not angry,' I said, though the way I screwed the cap of my water bottle back on probably proved my words wrong. 'I'm grateful, in fact. You reminded me that I should trust you about as much as I'd trust a kleptomaniac with my jewellery collection.'

I could tell, from the slight movements of his lips, that Harry didn't know whether to laugh or not. Probably wisely, he decided not to. He took a long moment to close his notebook and to push his pen into the spiral binding before he spoke.

'Rosie,' he said, 'I mentioned last night that you and I had something in common: we're both good at observing people. The more I get to know you, the more I see that we're alike in several other ways. One is that neither of us has a very big gap between what's professional and what's personal.'

'It's sort of hard to separate the professional from the personal when your drinking buddy for the evening is trying to do everything in his power to catch you out.'

This time Harry did laugh, but it was brief and humourless. 'Oh come on, Rosie. That went both ways, you know it did. You used the game to get me to tell you some very personal things. And I told you them. Even when they weren't particularly flattering to me.'

'Why did you tell me, then?'

'Because you asked for the truth, and the truth is the most important thing to me. I wanted you to understand why I'm doing the job I'm doing, because you're involved in it now. I thought that you, maybe more than many people, would be able to identify with what happened to me. After all, you've recently had a career-changing experience yourself.'

I looked at him sharply. 'Is this your way of telling me that I'm headed for a fall? Like you had?'

He held up his hands. 'No, Rosie. You're very good at what you do. You were born to perform. There's no reason, with your talent, why you should ever drop the ball like I did.'

He leaned back in his chair and crossed his arms. 'If you can handle all your challenges as well as you handled the lesbian newlyweds tonight, I predict that you will have a very long and lucrative career in the spiritualist trade.'

'But if I do drop the ball, you'll be there to document the moment,' I said.

He shrugged. 'It's my job. I could try to hide it from you, but you're too clever for that.'

'And you're not above manipulating circumstances so that it's more likely that I *will* drop the ball.'

Harry held my gaze with his. 'Rosie, you and I both know that last night was never about having time off. For either of us. Time off isn't something we do.'

I jumped down off the stage, crossed the aisle, and slipped into the seat next to Harry. I leaned my elbow on the armrest between our chairs and looked straight into his face. His warmth and his scent brought me back to the night before, when I'd sat on his lap and felt his body beneath me, his tongue in my mouth.

'And kissing me, Harry?' I asked softly. 'Was that a professional move too?'

'That was . . . unavoidable.' His voice had sunk, too, to a deep murmur. 'Maybe it was the rum. Maybe it was' — I saw him swallow, and heard his voice get huskier — 'because you're beautiful. I wanted to.'

Again, we were close enough to touch. I remembered the feel of his face under my palms and I curled both my hands into fists.

'It's another thing we have in common,' he said. 'We both seem to be turned on by danger.'

Danger? Could be. Whatever I was turned on by, it had *Harry Blake* written all over it.

'You set it up,' I said.

The lift of his eyebrow was an acknow-ledgement that I was right.

He raised his hand and caught the end of one of my locks of hair between his finger and thumb. I felt the slow thumbstroke all the way down to my toes.

'You enjoyed it, though. Didn't you, Rosie?' His voice was another caress.

I leaned forward still closer. I laid one finger on his denim-clad thigh. And slowly, feeling the worn softness of his jeans, the hardness of his muscles underneath, I ran my finger up the length of his leg.

I heard him suck in a breath.

When I reached the top of his thigh, I stopped. I could feel the warmth of his body through the fabric.

I raised my eyes to his again. From the expression on his face, I knew that if I moved my finger a couple of inches to the left, I would find out exactly how much Harry Blake was turned on by danger.

'Like you said, Harry,' I breathed, 'I'm a born performer.'

And I stood up and left the theatre, in search of Gina and my lift to the hotel.

Now you have to give me credit. That was an excellent parting line.

When I found Gina near the back entrance to the theatre, my cheeks felt flushed, my eyes felt bright, I felt full of energy and triumph, and yes, I must admit it: I felt turned on.

'Ready to go?' I asked her.

'All right,' she answered, picking up her briefcase and one of the boxes of publicity material. I picked up the other one and made for the door.

When I got to it, I realised Gina wasn't following me. I turned round. 'What are you waiting for?'

'I said I'd — ' she started, but at that very moment Harry appeared. He was carrying a suitcase, a garment bag, and his laptop.

'Oh, there you are,' Gina said to him. 'Are you ready to go?'

I put down the box. 'Is he coming back with us?'

'I said I'd give him a lift to the hotel, since he hasn't got his car,' Gina said.

'But — I thought you hated him.'

'It's a lift, Rosie,' said Gina. 'It's not a kiss.'

Harry's smile told me that the effect of my excellent parting line had been completely undermined by the expression on my face right at that moment. And that instead of making the dramatic exit I'd planned, I was going to spend another twenty-five minutes with him in the close confines of Gina's Peugeot.

'Oh, crap,' I muttered under my breath, picking up the box and stomping out to the car.

13

The next morning Gina was at my door at eight o'clock sharp, hurrying me into a pair of jeans and chasing me out of the hotel, saying we had to get to Newcastle right away, no time for breakfast or a shower. Five minutes later we'd checked out and were dragging our baggage out to the parking lot. My suitcase was heavy enough and awkward enough to take up most of my attention, so I didn't notice what was lurking in wait for me until I'd nearly reached Gina's car.

I looked up and saw Harry Blake, his bag slung from his shoulder, his laptop at his feet, his garment bag dangling from one hand, his body lounging casually against Gina's Peugeot.

'Oh no he is *not*,' I said.

'Morning, Rosie, Gina,' Harry said.

'I offered to give Harry a lift,' Gina told me, 'because his car has been scrapped, and he needs to get to Newcastle too.'

'*Amazing News* is being tricky about me hiring another car,' Harry explained. 'Seems the paper is a little strapped for cash . . . Who would've thought it?' he added under his breath.

'Harry also has lots of useful information and contacts for us on how to set up a psychic phone line,' Gina said. 'Since he's helping us, it seems only fair to help him.'

I turned to her. 'I said I'd think about the psychic phone line. Not go ahead with it. And in case you've forgotten, this is the guy who ruins mediums for a living.'

'In any case, we need to get going now.' Gina hit the central unlocking key.

'Fine,' I said. I slammed my suitcase into the car and climbed into the back seat. Harry and Gina could have the front and chatter away about psychic phone lines.

'I like your top,' Harry said to me, getting into the car. 'You're a baseball fan?'

I looked down at my Red Sox shirt, the same one I'd slept in. Great. Not only had I shown Harry that I liked baseball, but I'd shown him pretty much where I came from, too.

He probably knew already that I was from Massachusetts, if he knew that I'd never had an Uncle Robbie. But the comment was a reminder that since Harry was going to be near me practically around the clock, I'd have to watch out not to give away any information about myself, even through innocuous stuff like clothing.

Just what I needed. Something else to be careful about.

'It was a gift,' I muttered, and checked myself out in the rearview mirror, to make sure I didn't have any other facts about myself emblazoned on my forehead or something. I had smudges of mascara under my eyes that I hadn't noticed earlier.

'Sorry I ruined your morning,' Harry said.

'Oh believe me, it's not just the morning.'

I pulled a thick paperback out of my handbag, opened it, and held it up in front of my face in what I hoped would be a blatant enough signal that I didn't feel like talking to reporters or managers.

I heard Gina get in the car and start it up. I pretended to read for about ten minutes until something struck me.

'Gina,' I said, 'my show in Newcastle isn't until tomorrow night. Why are we in such a hurry?'

'We've got two shows in Newcastle, and neither of them is sold out yet. The *News of the Globe* article won't be printed until tomorrow, and *Amazing TV* airs on Friday. So I've lined up some publicity events for you in Newcastle today.'

'Oh. Okay.' I wondered why Gina hadn't seen fit to inform me about this yesterday.

'What am I doing?'

'You've got a local radio interview, followed by a half-hour's phone-in.'

'That sounds like fun.' It also sounded like she was preparing me for doing the psychic phone line, which I wasn't keen on, but it was better to let that ride for now.

'And then you're going to be the guest of honour at a grand opening.'

I sat forward as far as the seatbelt would let me. 'Grand opening of what?'

Gina pretended to be concentrating on a roundabout.

'Grand opening of what, Gina?'

'A local business,' she answered, staring far too intently at the road.

'What kind of local business, Gina?'

'It's a fish and chip shop.'

I heard Harry conspicuously not laughing.

'The owner contacted me and asked for you especially,' Gina continued. 'This shop is the culmination of his entire life's dream, and he named it after his dear departed mother. He wants to celebrate the opening with a brief seance, so his mother can be with them in spirit.'

I let that sink in.

'I'm giving a seance next to a deep-fat fryer,' I said.

'You're going to contact a man's mother on

the most important day of his life,' Gina corrected me.

My stomach growled, and I wondered if I'd get some chips, at least.

'He particularly wanted you there because his mother's name was Rosie too. Think of the publicity. After this, whenever anyone sees the sign in front of his chip shop, they'll automatically think of you. You can't get better marketing than that, on a local level, of course.'

'What's the chip shop called?'

'Rosie's Plaice. Spelled like the fish. You know? Plaice?'

I nodded slowly.

'I can see why you waited until I was in a moving car before you told me that my name will be forever associated with fish,' I said.

'Rosie.' Gina's voice was tight. 'It's my job to further your career. And if that involves opening a fish and chip shop to make sure that the rest of your tour is sold out, then so be it.'

I couldn't help it. 'Is this the sort of advice you give your clients when you're doing your real job as an independent financial adviser, Gina?'

I could practically see Harry's ears prick up underneath his blond hair.

Stupid, stupid, stupid, I told myself. You've handed Harry Blake another titbit of information.

Gina tightened her hands on the steering wheel, and didn't answer me.

Several miles passed in silence.

'Do you know what I really hate?' Harry asked conversationally. Neither one of us answered him, so he answered himself.

'Being in a car with two women who aren't talking to each other.'

For once, mind your own business, I thought.

Harry twisted around in his seat and looked at me. 'What's that in your hair?' he asked, staring at the side of my head.

Oh God, what other major grooming task had I left undone this morning? I put my hand up to feel. Several locks had fought free of their elastic band, but I didn't feel any rat's nest or anything. Maybe it had toothpaste stuck in it.

'What is it?' I asked, resigned.

'Do you mind?' He undid his seatbelt, and turned fully around in his seat. He reached his hand towards me, and for a heart-stopping, adrenalin-sparking moment, I thought he was going to bury his hand in my hair and pull me to him.

He didn't. 'It's . . . here,' he said.

I felt a slight tugging on my hair, and then Harry pulled his hand back. My antique Russian tea glass appeared in it. It caught the morning light as the car sped along the motorway.

'Where'd you get that?' I gasped.

'It was in your hair.'

'No it wasn't. Where'd you get it? Did you go through my stuff?'

Harry chuckled and handed the glass to me. 'You left it behind last night at the venue. I thought I'd try a little minor illusion to lighten the mood.'

'Nice try.' I checked the glass for damage and put it into my handbag. 'Thanks. You've cheered me up no end. I'm in a car with my Stepford manager, and we've got Harry Potter for light entertainment.'

I opened up my book in front of my face, and started reading in earnest.

* * *

As I rubbed my hands dry under the hot-air blower, I wondered if anybody had ever bothered to write a guide to the historic and interesting motorway service stations of Great Britain. It would be a very short book.

A whiff of designer perfume let me know

that Gina had joined me at the hand dryers. I looked over at her; she was staring at the blower nozzle.

'I'm sorry, Gina,' I said. 'I shouldn't have made the remark about your other career.'

She shook her hands briskly, and then faced me, her arms folded. 'Rosie, this *is* my career now. I take it very seriously.'

'I've noticed. I'm sorry. I shouldn't have said anything in front of Harry.'

'I don't want you to do or say anything that will hurt our credibility,' she said. 'I could do without any details of my other career being publicised, especially since I'm looking to expand my client base.'

'Are you? Who are you looking at?'

She checked her hair unnecessarily in the mirror. 'I've got a lead on Max DeMilo.'

'Max DeMilo? That rock star from the eighties?'

She nodded and reached into her handbag for her lipstick. 'He's looking for a manager to run his comeback tour.'

'That's great, Gina. Didn't he sing that song 'Infamous'? I loved that one.'

'He had seven number-one singles between 1986 and 1991. 'Infamous' was in the charts for seventeen weeks. He's recorded a new album called *Playing the Field*.'

'Whoa. You know your stuff.'

'Yes.' She smoothed lipstick over her top lip, and checked the line in the mirror. 'As I said, it's my job.'

Ladies' room girly talks were supposed to be intimate and fun. I gave it another attempt. 'Max DeMilo was really hot, too. I remember he always wore all that leather.'

'Mmm,' Gina replied, blotting her lips with a perfectly folded tissue.

I felt like a silly immature American, talking about hot men in leather in the face of her efficient Englishness. 'Well, good luck anyway.'

'Thank you.' She turned back to face me again. 'Rosie, my job is important to me. I don't mean to be a bitch, but this is my big chance, you know. I want to make it work, for both of us.'

She was telling me the truth, I could see. But I still felt like a teenager being told off, and I could feel my hackles rising.

'I know. Believe me, Gina, my job is important to me too. I can take being pushed. I'm glad you made me do the press conference, and I'll do my best for the fish and chip shop owner today, because as you said, it's a special time for him. But I don't like being dragged out of a hotel without my breakfast, and I don't like being presented with reporters in the

140

morning, and I don't want to do a psychic phone line. That stuff is for La Toya Jackson, not me.'

At least three women were earwigging on our conversation as they washed their hands and checked their faces. Gina turned her back on them with far more dignity than seemed possible in a service station restroom, and gestured for me to follow her. We went to the far corner of the room, between two empty toilet cubicles.

'I need to ask you something confidential, about Harry.' Her eyes flickered around the room.

'We're safe in here,' I said. 'Harry is sneaky, but I think we'd notice a six-foot man in drag eavesdropping on our conversation.'

'I know I gave you some information for a few of your shows,' Gina said, ignoring my joke, 'and I know we've stopped that now that Harry is around. I need to know if there's — if he's likely to find out anything about you.'

Your mother never had a brother called Robbie.

'There's nothing to find out,' I lied.

She nodded, but she still looked tense. 'And one other thing. Yesterday you asked me if I believed you really had psychic powers. I've been thinking about this, and please don't take this the wrong way, but I need to know for certain. Are you psychic?'

I looked straight into Gina's eyes.

'Yes. I am,' I said.

14

Ten minutes later, I was in the restaurant spreading Marmite on toast.

'Is it safe to approach you?'

I looked up. Harry stood about five feet away. He held a cup of tea in one hand and he had a stack of newspapers under his arm.

'Only if you don't produce anything else from my hair,' I said.

'Agreed,' he said. He sat down beside me and pushed one of the newspapers towards me. 'Your feature is in today's *Globe*. Gina's in the shop buying every copy she can find.'

He'd opened it to the relevant page for me. There was a big photo of me with a crystal ball.

'The crystal ball is a prop,' I told him. 'I don't use them. They're too heavy to carry and they hurt if you drop them on your foot.' I reached for the rest of the newspapers. 'Is there anything else?'

'Well, there's rather a lot about the Middle East, but I guess that's not what you mean,' said Harry, amused.

'I do actually care about what goes on in

the world,' I said, flipping through the pages.

'What do the people back in Worcester, Massachusetts, think about your choice of career? Does your mother ever come to any of your shows?'

I took a sip of my tea. 'You know,' I said, 'it's sort of unnerving to have someone mention personal details about your life out of the blue like that.'

Harry smiled. 'Now you know how your audiences feel.'

And there Harry was wrong. I knew how my audiences felt already. They wanted me to help them, and I couldn't help them if I was exposed as a fake.

'So, Harry Potter, where'd you learn the magic tricks?'

'It's more Harry Houdini than Harry Potter. I'm a big Houdini fan. Read all about him when I was younger. Like him, I'm interested in deception.'

I nodded, taking a bite of my toast. 'Houdini used to investigate mediums. He'd go to their seances in a false beard and when he saw a medium faking it, he'd jump up and reveal himself as the Great Houdini and denounce the medium. You've got more in common with him than the tricks.'

'You've done your research,' Harry commented.

'Of course I have. I'm a professional.'

'So you chose your stage name in homage to the Fox sisters.'

I tilted my head in a 'could be' expression. 'You know, Houdini found it difficult to debunk a lot of the mediums he investigated. He could do the same things they could do using deception, but just because two people can produce the same effect doesn't mean that they arrive at it in the same way. And if somebody lies once, that doesn't prove that they're lying all the time.'

'Rosie,' Harry said quietly, 'I know all about what it's like to be condemned for one mistake. And I know how actions can be misinterpreted when the observer doesn't have all the information.'

'So you take my point.'

And, possibly, my challenge.

'I ruined Unicorn Riley's career because she was silly,' Harry said. 'She was so clumsy it was embarrassing to watch her. If I'd reported the things she was saying, I would have looked like a fool. Telling twenty-three people they were the reincarnation of Cleopatra was only the tip of the iceberg. I personally watched her communicating with the spirit of a famous movie star who was alive and well and the head of the National

Rifle Association in California. Since I published my article, Unicorn's changed her name back to Sandra and she's got a job at an estate agent's.'

Harry leaned forward, elbows on the table. 'Unicorn doesn't bother me,' he continued. 'She was going to be found out sooner or later. I hope she sells some houses. But do you remember the *Amazing TV* show in September about Ted Grayson? The spiritual healer?'

I nodded. 'He was pretending to pull raw chicken livers out of people's stomachs and calling it psychic surgery.'

'Grayson claimed he could heal any sickness. He convinced people to come to him with their medical problems instead of to a doctor. I unearthed four definite cases where because of Grayson, people died because they didn't get real medical attention in time. One of these was a twelve-year-old boy named Richie Becker, who had appendicitis. He could have been saved with a course of antibiotics.'

My mouth dropped open. 'My God. That's monstrous. You didn't put that on TV.'

'I had enough evidence to discredit Grayson without publicising Richie's story. His family was gullible and acted irresponsibly, but they've suffered enough.'

I shook my head. 'That poor kid. That's horrific.'

'Yes,' Harry said. 'So while I take your point about how difficult it can be to disprove paranormal phenomena, there's a lot more than trickery at stake here.'

I thought about Ted Grayson pretending to pull a chicken liver out of that dying boy's stomach, knowing full well it wasn't doing any good. I shuddered.

And then I got hold of myself. 'Ted Grayson is the kind of person who gives all psychics a bad name. A fake and a charlatan. Most of us aren't like that. We're real, and we fulfil a major human need. You must've seen how my psychic powers can help my audiences come to terms with death and improve their lives.'

'It's a laudable goal.' His voice was noncommittal.

'Damn right it's a laudable goal. Take this fish and chip shop thing, for example. If I can manage to make contact with this man's mother this afternoon, it's probably going to make him feel great. Unless she's a total bitch,' I added. 'Sometimes the spirits aren't what you expect them to be.'

'Looks like you've changed your mind about the seance next to the deep fat fryer,' Harry commented.

'I'm in a better mood now. And Gina's right. If I can make this man's important day even better, then I should try to do it.'

Harry finished his tea. 'I'm sure you'll manage it so that you do, Rosie.'

15

'Are you sure the people around here speak English?' I asked Harry in a low voice as we walked down the street towards where the fish and chip shop was supposed to be. Gina strode beside us, carrying a bottle of champagne, tapping the sidewalk with her high heels.

'We're in Newcastle,' he answered me with a smile. 'They speak Geordie. Haven't you ever heard it before?'

'I've never heard anything like it. They all sound like they're talking backwards and too fast. Or maybe Norwegian.'

I toyed with my hoop earring. I was in full 'psychic Stevie Nicks' gear for this seance: flowing hair, flowing skirt, flowing peasant blouse, and lots of bangles.

I hoped all the fabric I was wearing wouldn't dip into the chip fat and catch fire.

'You did well with the radio phone-in,' Harry said.

Now, that had been tough. My job involves observing people, listening to them, and making inferences based on what I've learned. In the radio studio, I couldn't see the people who were calling in, and with these ridiculous accents I could barely understand them either. Fortunately, I have a stock of ready-made character profiles and predictions that can fit just about anyone at a pinch. Wrap them up in enough spiritualist jargon and I could convince any audience, no matter what language they were speaking.

'Oh well, you know, if the spirits want to communicate, they'll overcome any barrier,' I said. 'They've crossed over from life to death; a little dialect isn't going to bother them.'

'Too bad you're not interested in the psychic phone line,' Gina said. 'You'd be a natural.'

Time for a change of subject. 'Where is this fish and chip shop, anyway?'

Gina opened her Filofax and scrutinised a page. 'It should be down this next left.'

I paused. 'This left here? You mean this alleyway?'

'Yes.' She snapped her Filofax shut and turned down the alley.

I shrugged and followed her.

'So are there lots of Geordie muggers in Newcastle?' I asked conversationally.

'Geordies are fine, upstanding people,' Harry assured me. 'Unless you insult Newcastle United.'

'And that's the local mafia, is it?' The

alleyway was getting darker and damper by the second. I skirted a puddle, but still got the pointed toe of one of my shoes wet. A piece of ripped newspaper caught on my heel, and I shook it off.

'Newcastle United is the local football team. The Magpies. My God, is that the place?'

I looked up from the gloom to see where Harry was pointing.

It lit up the alleyway. Pink.

The front of the building was painted pink, and the window was filled with hundreds of tiny pink fairy lights. A neon sign glowed the hot pink words 'Rosie's Plaice'.

'That is incredibly cool.' I hurried forward, leaving the apparently stunned Harry and Gina behind me.

A banner hung above the pink door, proclaiming GRAND OPENING AND SEANCE TODAY! Grinning, I pushed open the door.

The shop was full of people and furniture and gleaming chrome counters. Three reporters and two photographers stood near the door; I was getting to recognise the media by the way they hovered with intent. I looked around for the owner. He was by the counter: slimly muscled in a black T-shirt and tight jeans, with gelled-up streaked hair, his hands on his hips in an elaborately feminine gesture. Very camp, just the type to own a pink fish and chip shop. I stepped towards him, holding out my hand, and then a mountain got in the way.

The mountain grabbed my hand and pumped it up and down and I gawked up at him. He was six foot six at least, and built like a truck. He had a shaved head and tattoos of sparrows across his neck.

'Aalreet, Rosie, me nyame is Neville Bruce but yee can caal me Spuggy. Welcome te me chippie. Ahm git chuffed te meet ye.'

Gentle reader, this is my last attempt to render 'Spuggy' Bruce's speech in a manner that even comes close to how he pronounced it. I'll spare you the torture, and myself the risk of mortally offending the Geordie nation. If you're familiar with the Newcastle accent, you can imagine it in his words. And if you're not familiar with the accent, there's no way you'll ever be able to imagine it.

'I'm really glad to meet you too, Spuggy,' I sputtered, overwhelmed by the dialect, the tattoos, the spectacular un-campness of the man who was mangling my hand.

'This is my family,' he said, still shaking my hand and pointing around the room at each person he named. 'My wife Natalie, my sister Joyce, my cousin Colin, my uncle Dave, my other uncle Steve, my auntie Mavis. We're all so excited to talk to our mam.'

They all greeted me in muted voices. It was a grand opening, but the atmosphere was more like a funeral.

'Her favourite colour was pink,' I said, hearing the door open again behind me and Gina and Harry enter.

Spuggy renewed his assault on my hand. 'Aye, see I knew you'd be able to talk to our mam as soon as I read about you in the paper, like. And with your name, I knew we had to have you.' His eyes dimmed. 'I miss her so much, and this is my chance to honour her, see?'

I nodded and squeezed his hand back, glad that Harry had come in during my success about the colour pink and not when I'd mistakenly tried to greet Camp Cousin Colin.

A camera flashed. 'Well,' I said, 'I've never done a seance in a fish and chip shop before, Spuggy, but I think it's beautiful that you're honouring your mother. She was obviously a very special woman.'

'Oh aye.' Spuggy seemed near tears. Tiny Auntie Mavis stood on her tiptoes and patted him on the shoulder. He sniffed, and pulled himself together. 'We're all ready for you, Rosie. I've set up the chairs and some candles. Would you like a drink first?'

He still hadn't let go of my hand, and I could see in his big face that he wanted desperately to begin.

Spuggy, this huge, strong, macho man with tattoos on his neck, loved his mother more than anything in the world. He didn't care whether it made him look weak to show it.

For a moment the pain in my hand was overshadowed by a big, hot stab of pain inside my chest.

Imagine how it must be to feel so certain of love.

'Let's start now, Spuggy,' I said quietly. 'I know she wants to talk to you as much as you want to talk with her.'

He nodded and finally let go of my hand to arrange the chairs. I went round the room shaking everyone else's hand. It's important to establish personal warmth in a reading. Plus, I wanted a chance to observe all I could. Spuggy's uncles Dave and Steve were only slightly smaller than Spuggy himself, near-identical men with grey hair and stubbly chins, whose muscle had softened into fat. Sister Joyce, thankfully, didn't follow the family resemblance; she was slender, brisk and competent, a nurse or a teacher.

As I shook Cousin Colin's hand, he rolled his eyes. Don't believe in ghosts, huh? I thought, adding a bit of a conspiratorial edge to my smile and giving him a subtle wink.

The shop was gleaming and clean and glowed with reflected pink from the strings of lights in the windows. It smelled of hot fat and cleaning liquid. On the wall beside the counter was a framed photograph of a woman in a white apron, beside a van that said *ROSIE'S TEAS*. She was holding a little boy by the hand.

Spuggy, arranging folding chairs into a circle, looked as eager as that little boy he'd once been. This seance meant everything to him. A flutter of nervousness played on top of the ache in my chest.

I'm not nervous onstage that often. I'm a professional playing a Win/Win game. But this one mattered. Not only because of the press and because Harry was watching me as always, waiting for me to trip up, but because Spuggy believed in me so much.

Spuggy ushered his relatives into chairs. He offered seats to the reporters, but they all shook their heads. I'd have to prove myself to them too. Gina and Harry joined the circle, though. Uncle Dave turned off the overhead lights, and wife Natalie and sister Joyce lit an implausible number of candles and perched them on the counter and the heated glass case that would hold the battered fish.

Spuggy settled himself in the chair next to

me and took my hand again. Fortunately it was the other, non-crushed hand; wife Natalie, a smaller and much gentler person than her husband, took the other one. We all joined hands, including Gina and Harry. Candles, dim lights, and holding hands — it looked like Spuggy had been studying his seance clichés. Considering most of my ghost-talking was in a spotlight in front of a bunch of strangers, it was sort of nice.

And very, very mournful.

'Should we say a prayer or something?' Spuggy's voice was hushed.

'If you want to, Spuggy,' I said.

He nodded and closed his eyes, and delivered an 'Our Father' in broad Geordie. His family joined in, and so did I.

The words felt unfamiliar in my mouth; I hadn't said them since the very infrequent Sunday mornings as a child when my father had decided his daughter had had enough of that Jewish crap his in-laws fed her and took me to the nearest Anglican church. He'd sit beside me, smelling of stale whisky and guilt, nursing his hangover in the hard polished pew and repeating the rituals of his youth.

Saying the words, I was back in the pew, holding his hand.

'Give us this day our daily bread, and

forgive us our trespasses, as we forgive those who trespass against us.'

Odd to think of my father and the word 'forgive' together.

I swallowed back a lump in my throat.

At the 'Amen' I opened my eyes; I hadn't realised I'd closed them. Spuggy, wife Natalie, sister Joyce, cousin Colin, uncle Dave, other uncle Steve, auntie Mavis, perfect Gina, tricky Harry, assorted press, dead Rosie Bruce on the wall — they were all looking at me in expectation.

'You know she's with us, don't you, Spuggy?' I murmured, nearly a whisper.

'Way aye.'

What could I say to these people, who loved this woman so much, when all I had was a photograph and the colour pink?

I dropped my chin down to my chest, pretending to concentrate. My throat burned and my eyes prickled. Then I raised my head and looked into the empty air in the centre of the circle.

'I can see her. She's not tall, and she has curly brown hair. Her hair used to drive her crazy on a wet day when the curls were hard to control, do you understand that? And of course she's smiling at all of you. She's dressed neatly, a dress and high heels and lipstick, and I get the impression that this is how she likes to look, she always made an effort.'

I saw the family nodding, and from the corner of my eye I saw Harry glance quickly at the photograph on the wall, from which I'd taken nearly all of these details. To be fair, he was being subtle and wasn't ruining my show. But I knew him, and I knew what he was thinking.

I needed something to clinch the deal right away. A good hit could lead to another and then I could spend some time talking about love that lasted beyond death and make it so there wasn't a dry eye in the chippie.

And maybe then by the time I got there I could let out my own tears that were threatening badly despite all my efforts to keep them back.

I started with something general, that could be refined. 'Rosie always liked a joke, didn't she? Nothing cruel, nothing to hurt anyone, but some fun to help the working day go easier. She's saying to you, Mavis, don't forget your exercises? Isn't there something special you do?'

'For my back,' she agreed.

One baby step forward, but still not much. 'Yes, she was worried about a bad spell you had a little while back, and she says

— oh.' I turned to Camp Cousin Colin, the disbeliever, as if I'd had a sudden revelation about him. 'She wants me to tell you to be careful, Colin. She's pointing to her stomach and looking like she's in pain. I think you have to be careful about injuries or an illness around your abdomen.'

He rolled his eyes again.

I could see Harry through the tears that still lingered in my eyes and he had that casual yet calculating look on his face.

What could I use? I needed something that would confirm the family's beliefs, something that would knock Harry for a loop and something that would raise the energy in this chip shop so I could breathe and talk and laugh without feeling as if the tears were going to overcome me. It was too early to use the tea van from the photograph, and besides, Harry would know where I'd got it.

Think, Rosie, I told myself as hard as I could, and to fill the silence while my brain was working (I hoped) I said the first thing that popped into my head. It was a tried-and-true approach, one I'd used again and again.

'She's talking now, and this will probably make more sense to you than to me, but she's holding her hand about a foot above the floor and she's saying some things. It's not totally clear but one of the words is 'pet'. Do you understand this?'

'Way aye!' cried Spuggy. 'That was what she always called me and Joyce. 'Pet.' When we were small, like.'

'Aye and she called me 'pet' and all,' Mavis said.

'I know you're an American so you probably don't know, but it's a Geordie word,' Spuggy explained to me. 'And my mam was a Geordie lass through and through. Born and bred in Newcastle, never went farther than Gateshead in her life.'

'Aye,' said the family. 'We did take her to Whitley Bay that once,' added Dave.

And then I had it. I knew how to get my spectacular hits and win at this particular game. I smiled.

'Oh wow, that's awesome,' I said, in my most exaggerated American accent. 'I knew she was saying something important, but it's the way you guys talk, it's hard for me to understand. So I can tell you what I hear, even if I don't understand it okay, and you can tell me what she means. Like right now she's saying a word I've never heard before and I have no idea what it means. It sounds like 'hin' — correct me if I'm wrong, because this sounds weird to me — something like 'hinny'?'

They all nearly jumped out of their seats with excitement.

'Hinny, way aye, that's what you call folks, she said it all the time,' Spuggy told me, and squeezed my hand so hard that I almost yelped. 'You can see her, you're really talking to our mam.'

I didn't have to glance at Harry to know he'd be looking interested now. My smile grew wider.

One afternoon in Newcastle had given me enough Geordie slang to keep this trick going for as long as I needed it to — especially if the Bruces kept on giving me information every time I got a hit. I turned to Spuggy and said, 'Now this might sound strange, but I can only say what she's telling me. I'm getting a strong association of you with birds somehow.'

'Oh aye, Spuggy means 'sparrow'.' He touched the tattoos on his neck. 'It was my mam's nickname for me.'

'Yes, it's that, but it's more than that too. I'm getting a strong image of something black and white, a bigger bird. This doesn't make any sense to me, but I'm going to say it because she's so insistent here: does a bird like a magpie have any meaning to you?'

This time I did yelp when he squeezed my hand, but it was drowned out by his enormous roar of 'TOON ARMY!' Dave and Steve and even Colin joined in the chant.

I took that as confirmation that I'd been right in surmising Spuggy was a football fan.

This time, I did glance at Harry. He caught my eye and shook his head and laughed.

And just like that, with that loud chant and Harry's laughter, what we were doing was transformed from funeral to party. And I was totally in control.

They erupted into anecdotes about Rosemary Bruce and the family. Everything I said prompted more memories, and they believed I had brought them up myself. They took me through Rosie Bruce's life without knowing it, and I felt their love for this woman, who had only been a simple, ordinary person after all. By the end they were in tears, as I'd planned, but they were joyful tears.

Somehow, even my tears were joyful, too.

Afterwards they all hugged me. Spuggy picked me right up off the floor. Then they fried up an enormous amount of fish and chips and we all sat around eating them and drinking Gina's champagne. When that was gone, Spuggy pulled out cans of beer. Some customers came in, attracted by the chatter and laughter.

One of the journalists sidled up to me, a chip poised in his chubby fist. 'So, Rosie,' he said confidentially, 'you can tell me. You're not really seeing ghosts, are you?'

I glanced at the other disbelievers in the room. Harry was talking with Auntie Mavis. Colin was sitting apart from his family, raising his hand to his mouth as if about to cough, pinkie delicately extended.

I smiled at the reporter, my *you love me* smile. 'Do you feel left out because there were no messages for you?'

I heard a clatter and saw a convulsive movement across the room. Colin stood and kicked his chair over. He clutched one hand to his throat.

I shoved the reporter aside. Colin's head was thrown backwards, his spine arched, in a caricature of Mick Jagger.

When I touched him he gaped at me, lips flapping, eyes wide. I hit him hard on the back. His chest hitched.

I hugged Colin and sank my fist into his stomach, so sharply that it felt as if the knuckle of my thumb would puncture the thin, lean membrane. I did it again.

Colin gagged, and a small, wet white lump went flying out of his mouth and hit the side of the counter.

We were surrounded by Bruces; they were there so quickly that they must've been there all along. I held on to Colin's shoulder, feeling it heave under my hand as he dragged in sobbing breath after sobbing breath.

He was okay. I'd saved this one.

Spuggy helped him into a chair, where he sat, one pale hand around his throat, the other cradling his stomach.

'And you said he'd have trouble with his stomach,' Steve, or was it Dave, whispered beside me.

Dave, or was it Steve, picked up the lump of food that Colin had choked up. 'Chip,' he told us, and put it reverently in a bin. And then the Bruces were hugging me, thanking me, all of them at once.

I felt, rather than saw or heard, the cameras taking photos. I blinked the burning out of my eyes and let the Bruces hug me until they had finished and started hugging each other. I went back to my chair, away from their unintelligible words, and picked up my paperful of chips.

Harry brought his fish and chips over to the seat beside me. 'Well done,' he said, holding up his beer for a toast.

I took a deep breath and clinked my can with his. 'Thanks, Houdini.'

'You even managed another prediction for the cameras. And you're right, you helped them.'

He leaned forward and spoke quietly in my

ear, so close I could feel his hair brush against my cheek.

'How are you going to help yourself, Rosie?' he murmured. He took my chin in his hand and turned my head so I was looking into his face.

'You've been crying,' he said.

I stood, up and away from him. 'Sometimes I feel the dear departed's emotions. Excuse me, I'm going to get some ketchup for these chips.'

From the counter, I looked at the Bruce family. God, they loved each other.

I didn't need help. I didn't need to envy them.

I was Rosie Fox, and I was heading for the top of my profession. I was on top of the world. The past was gone, and who cared about the future?

Right now, I didn't need anything except ketchup.

16

The knock on my hotel room door came as I was getting out of the bath. 'Just a second,' I called, wrapping my hair in one towel and my body in another.

I looked at the clock on my way to the door; it was a little past one in the morning. Normally I'd be asleep, but it was Friday night, I'd just finished the second of my Newcastle shows, and tonight I had a good reason to stay up very late.

It was probably Gina knocking. She'd said she'd come to my room right before the two a.m. broadcast of *Amazing TV*, but she was probably too excited to take the nap she'd said she was going to have until then. I knew I was. I'd never seen myself on television before.

I reached the door and flung it open, about to cry, 'Welcome to the room of Rosie Fox, star of stage and screen!'

Except I only got as far as 'room', because it wasn't Gina standing in the corridor outside my door, but Harry.

He was wearing low-slung jeans and a T-shirt, and he had bare feet, and he was holding a loosely corked bottle of red wine and two glasses. His eyes widened and I saw his gaze travel, slowly, down the length of my body. Over the skimpy damp towel that just about covered my breasts, over the naked tops of my thighs where the towel ended, and down to my feet. And then back up to my face. I felt my skin, which had been cold, heating up.

He opened his mouth as if he wanted to say something, but no noise came out.

'Are you all right, Houdini?' I asked.

I saw him swallow. 'I . . . ' he said, and swallowed again. He took a breath.

'I really do not want to be this attracted to you,' he said.

The feeling was altogether mutual.

'Well,' I replied, 'I can totally understand why you find me irresistible. But you'll have to wait your turn; I've got the bellboy and the guy from reception in my room already.'

He nodded. He was keeping his eyes glued to my face now. 'I thought we could watch ourselves on TV together.'

'Sure. Come in.' I stepped out of the way, and he walked past me into the room. He'd had a shower too; I could smell his shampoo.

'You thinking about getting me drunk and taking advantage of me again?' I pointed at the bottle of wine and the glasses.

'It had crossed my mind, to be honest. Drink can make people drop their guard and say what they're really thinking. I don't expect you'd be tricked by that, though.'

He sat on my double bed, leaning back against the headboard and stretching his legs out in front of him. His smile was lazy and sexy as hell.

It was all I could do to stop myself from flinging my towel in the corner, and then flinging myself at the beautiful man on my bed.

I looked down at myself. Nipples standing out under the towel like Harry-seeking missiles.

'I'll get dressed,' I said.

I grabbed my jeans and a shirt and took them into the bathroom with me.

I'd shucked the towel before I realised I'd forgotten to bring underwear. I considered going back out there and rummaging in a drawer and pulling out a pair of lacy silky panties in front of Harry.

What would he do? Sit and watch? Get up from the bed and touch me?

Or whisper, 'Come here'?

I had to grab the side of the sink to avoid being toppled over by a rush of pure lust.

Why don't I just go out there and get it over with? I thought in agony.

Why not go back into the room, climb on the bed, take his face in my hands, kiss him, and spend the rest of the night fucking like hot, sweaty, gyrating, orgasmic, totally fulfilled rabbits?

Why not get it out of my system? What harm would it do? In fact, it would probably help. I could stop spending so much energy trying to keep control of my rampant desire for him, and start spending more energy on making sure I wasn't discovered.

I let out a big whoosh of air, and plonked my bare behind down on the toilet seat.

That was the problem. Being discovered.

It was hard enough keeping Harry from seeing the real me when I was onstage, in full swing, putting everything I had into my performance. How on earth would I keep the truth from him when I was naked with him, all of my senses full of him? When he was deep inside me and my nails were digging into his back and I was riding on the crest of an orgasm?

How would I hide from him then, if he whispered into my ear and asked me . . . well, anything?

'You okay in there?' I heard Harry call.

Lord, even his voice through a bathroom door made my knees weak.

'Great,' I lied.

Don't get me wrong. I'm not the squishy, sentimental type who goes to bed with a guy and then immediately starts to get all carey-sharey. I'd had a few relationships since starting this job, and not once had I worried that I'd drop my cover with my clothes.

They'd been fun relationships, for company and friendship and sex, and they'd necessarily been pretty superficial. None of them had even come close to making me feel the way I felt when I was next to Harry, like every breath mattered.

In my head I heard Harry's voice, saying, *Time off isn't something that we do.*

Sex with him would be far more spectacular, and far more dangerous, than I wanted to risk.

After a few moments' deep, careful breathing, I stood up, splashed my face with cold water and pulled my jeans on over my bare bottom. Bending down to pick up my shirt, I noticed I'd forgotten to bring a bra, too.

'Behave,' I told my breasts as I buttoned myself up. I suspected they weren't listening.

I put on mascara, ran my fingers through my wet hair, and took a long drink of water from the faucet; then I was as ready as I'd ever be to face the sex god in my hotel room.

He was still lying on my bed. His hands

were folded on his chest and he looked like he hadn't taken his eyes off the bathroom door the entire time I'd been wrestling with my libido.

'I don't like that outfit as much as your last one,' he said.

'Get used to being disappointed.' I walked around to the other side of the bed and sat down next to him. I leaned against the headboard, like him, and stretched my jeans-clad legs out in front of me, like him.

I might not be able to risk having sex with him. But I was damned if I was going to look like I was rattled by him.

'Wine?' Harry asked, picking up the bottle.

'Why not?' I answered, though I knew full well why not.

He poured out two glasses and handed me one. The wine was rich and chocolatey.

'The show isn't for another hour,' I said. 'I'm not playing another drinking game with you while we wait.'

Harry had a glug of his own wine. 'Since you've got dressed, I guess we'll have to talk. Have you ever seen yourself on television before?'

You ever have that sensation where you take one sip of something alcoholic and you can feel it in the joints of your legs? Especially when your legs are lying next to a pair of long, strong male ones?

'Yup,' I answered. 'I've been on the news loads of times. Predictions and all that.'

'Have you ever been the subject of an entire TV show, though?' Harry asked. 'I've looked but I haven't found any footage of you yet, beyond the Channel Five bit last week.'

I sipped my wine again. 'And would you be looking because you're researching my career, or because you have some voyeuristic interest in seeing me on screen?'

'No comment,' he said.

'Then no comment on the television thing.'

He rolled over on to his side, facing me, leaned on his elbow, and gave me that half-grin. 'You're excited to see yourself on *Amazing TV*, though. I can tell.'

'I always loved that show.'

'And you always loved me on it.'

'No comment.' I smiled into my wine.

'Tell me how you became a professional psychic,' Harry said.

I put my glass down on the bedside table. I could smell Harry's just-right scent, and hear his breathing, and feel every little movement of his body on the bed beside me.

My press release said I'd been talking to people's dead loved ones since I was thirteen, but Harry was asking when I became a pro.

I'll tell him the truth, I thought. It's a lot less risky.

'I didn't mean to,' I said. 'I started when I was at college. I did some tarot readings for my friends, for fun. I got a reputation on campus. Strangers started approaching me. I did it because I liked it. Then I went to a psychic fair one time and saw people giving readings for money, and they weren't half as good as I was. So I thought — '

'Your grandparents paid your tuition at the University of Massachusetts, but you didn't have a lot of spending money. So you thought you'd do some paid readings for extra cash.'

I blinked. 'You're very disconcerting, you know.'

Harry shrugged. 'Sorry. Didn't mean to put you off your stride. I took a guess based on the information I had about your family. You don't mind, do you?'

Mind? It was downright spooky. This guy was spending a lot of time researching me behind my back.

'Have you been in touch with my family?' I asked. I wondered what my mother would tell Harry about me. I didn't talk with her much; she'd never been to one of my shows. She thought being a psychic was a waste of time. Funny, since she spent so much time communing with the dead herself.

173

'Not yet. Everything I've found so far has been a matter of public record. The internet, record offices, there's lots of information out there about everybody. You must do something similar when you can, before a private reading, right? To give you a head start?'

Of course I did. 'Of course I don't.'

Harry's expression told me he didn't believe a word.

I sat up cross-legged on the bed. 'So how are we going to kill this hour before the show?'

'Why don't you read my tarot?'

I laughed. 'You want me to read your tarot? Harry Blake, the world's greatest sceptic?'

'I promise I'll keep an open mind. If only for tonight.'

'Whatever you say, Houdini.' I got off the bed and went to my suitcase. My deck of tarot cards was in one of the side pockets, wrapped in a silk scarf inside a wooden box. The cards felt worn and comfortable in my hand.

'Here you go.' I gave the deck to Harry and climbed back on the bed to sit cross-legged again. 'Handle them a little bit to get them in tune with you.'

Harry sat up too. I watched him shuffle the cards, and wondered if this was a good idea.

On one hand, reading Harry's tarot would

give me something to concentrate on so I could stop myself thinking about his body and how much I wanted it. On the other hand, this was the man who was trying to catch me out in a lie, and it seemed pretty stupid to start lying to his face.

Harry fanned the cards out in front of him. 'Nice deck.'

'Classic Rider-Waite. This particular deck is from the nineteen forties. I like the history in them. Feel how they're soft around the edges?'

He nodded.

'That's where hundreds of people have handled them, looking for answers. It makes me feel like I'm in very good company.' I held out my hand. 'Done?'

Harry gave me back the cards. As soon as I had them in my hands again, I didn't feel doubtful any more. Hell, I'd done countless tarot readings. I could do tarot readings in my sleep. I could deal with a sceptical investigative journalist.

If it really looked like he was going to catch me out in a lie, I could always flash my tits at him to distract him.

'So what do you want to know?' I asked.

His answer was immediate. 'The future.'

17

I gave him a sideways smile. 'That's all?'

'I should think that's enough.'

'Besides, you think that I know too much about your past and present to give you a convincing reading that'll show my powers,' I said.

'Could be.'

'Only problem with that is, you'll have to wait for my predictions to come true before you find out whether I've been right or not.'

'I don't mind waiting, if the result is worth it.'

I knew that he was talking about more than the tarot reading, but I couldn't work out whether he was being suggestive, or if he was talking about his investigation of me.

Just like I couldn't tell whether that idea about flashing my tits was a stroke of genius or stupidity.

'Okay,' I said, 'we'll do a short simple reading. These two cards' — I laid them face down on the bedspread between us as I spoke — 'are about your future career, these two are about your future love life, and this last one is about your future in general. Will that be enough for you?'

'Sounds fairly thorough.'

I rapidly calculated my approach.

Harry, the rational sceptic, would not be impressed by a lot of mumbo-jumbo about what the tarot cards signified. So a big line of my patter was out the window. Nor would he be taken in by statements that would be true whatever occurred, or by my simultaneously predicting an event and its opposite. I wouldn't be able to make general statements that would fit any human being, or more specific statements designed purely for flattery.

I couldn't play the Win/Win game. I was never going to be able to play that game with Harry. I was going to have to wing it, and say what felt right.

'Okay, we'll start with your career.' I turned over the first card.

'The Wheel of Fortune,' Harry observed.

'Yeah. An interesting card. Have you had your tarot read before?'

'Yes. It said I was going to meet a tall, dark, handsome stranger and make an overseas journey.'

'I wouldn't mind that prediction myself. I'm seeing something different for you, though. The Wheel of Fortune signifies change. You're heading for a reversal of fortune, possibly something as huge as what happened to you before.'

Harry raised an eyebrow. 'I'm not sure whether that's good news or bad.'

'Let's look at the next card and see what it says.' I turned it over: the Ace of Swords.

'This card symbolises justice. You're going to deserve whatever happens to you. The sword could indicate violence, possibly vengeance.'

'I see. A change of fortune, and violence. I'm going to win the lottery and then go on a killing spree.'

'Somehow I don't think you're taking this seriously, Harry.'

'I'm merely pointing out that these cards can be interpreted in a variety of ways, none of which are objectively verifiable.'

'You promised to keep an open mind,' I said.

He laughed. 'I'm considering the possibility of becoming a millionaire and a mass murderer. What's closed-minded about that?'

I put my hand on the cards, and shut my eyes. 'You're not going to become a mass murderer. I think you might give in to aggression, but I don't think it'll go that far.' I opened my eyes and looked slyly at him. 'Possibly it'll be too much testosterone.'

'Or sexual frustration? That can lead a man

178

to violent and unpredictable behaviour.'

'Speaking of which, are you ready for your love life?' I indicated the next two cards.

'I'm more than ready,' he said.

I valiantly refrained from glancing down at his crotch to find out how ready he was. I turned over the next card.

And immediately cursed my luck.

The picture was a naked man and woman. Adam and Eve in the Garden of Eden, about to discover the pleasure and pain of sin.

So much for no sex.

'The Lovers,' I said. My voice sounded strangled.

I swallowed and started again. 'The Lovers signify sexual attraction, and struggling with the implications of being attracted to the wrong person.'

Harry's smile was wide enough to park a car in. 'You're truly stunning me with your supernatural insight, Rosie. Who do you think that wrong person might be?'

'The tarot shows general trends and themes, not specific names.' I deliberately matched his smile with my own. 'For all I know, you might make a habit of being attracted to people who are bad for you. Maybe it means you don't have to deal with the commitment of forming a real relationship.'

'Especially when the wrong person I'm attracted to isn't interested in forming a real relationship either.'

I acknowledged his comment by inclining my head to one side so my hair fell down over my shoulder. 'Are you ready for the next card?'

'I'm waiting with bated breath.'

I turned it over. The Queen of Swords. 'Well, here's your real love,' I said. 'The Queen of Swords is honest and forthright. She's a person who cuts through the bullshit. She's probably connected with your career change, since both cards are in the same suit. She'll share your passion for truth. And you're going to be happy for a very, very long time.'

On the last words, my voice broke.

Why was my voice breaking? This was stupid. I was making half of this stuff up, and the other half I had gotten from a *Tarot Reading for Dummies* book. Why should it bother me?

I ducked my head and let my hair fall over my face, so Harry couldn't see my momentary irrational weakness.

Unfortunately, this meant that I was looking at Harry's feet.

He sat cross-legged on the bed, like me. His bare feet poked out underneath his legs.

He had long toes, fine long bones, smooth-looking skin. I could see a glimmer of blond hair on his big toes.

He had sexy feet. Of course. My inner pervert kicked in again and showed me a mental picture of Harry sliding his foot up the inside of my naked thigh.

'Does it mean anything that the Queen of Swords is upside down?' Harry asked.

'She's unexpected,' I said without thinking, my attention still on his feet. 'You won't know it when you find her, until it hits you between the eyes. That's how you'll know she's the one.'

I realised how stupid I must look, staring downwards, my hair covering my face like a curtain. I curved a smile on to my face and looked up, tossing my hair back.

'So, you ready for the last card?' I asked.

'Hit me with it, baby.'

Before he'd finished speaking, I'd flipped it over.

The Tower: a building struck by lightning, blasting its top off, kindling flame from the windows. A man and a woman fell to their deaths on the sharp rocks below.

'Oh Harry, you're going to get hurt.'

All the playfulness went out of Harry's face in an instant. He looked at me, hard. 'Are you threatening me?'

I opened my mouth. I couldn't say anything. I closed my mouth again.

I didn't know why I'd said that. According to the books, the Tower could mean lots of things: seeing the truth, letting go of your beliefs, a sudden change. None of them necessarily meant getting hurt. And whether I'd meant physically hurt, or emotionally hurt, I wasn't sure. The words had just come out. I was winging it. I was making it up.

So why'd I make up that?

Harry gripped both my shoulders. I felt his fingers pressing through my shirt. 'Rosie? What's going on?'

'I . . . ' I took a breath and closed my eyes, then opened them again.

I chose humour as the best strategy. 'You think I'm threatening you? Because you've exposed a few mediums? What am I, the psychic mafia?'

Harry didn't stop scrutinising my face. 'You're not the psychic mafia. But there's something strange going on here.'

'Yeah. I'm telling your future. Like you asked me to. Isn't that what you wanted?'

Still holding my shoulders, he stared into my face for a few more moments. I met his blue eyes with mine. I breathed slowly, in through my nose, out through my mouth, willing my heart to stop beating quite so

hard, willing my face to look calm, willing myself to stop feeling as if weirdness was lying in wait every second of the day, ready to pounce.

I could tell precisely when Harry's scrutiny stopped being suspicious and started being sexual. His pupils dilated; his breathing got shallower. His grip on my shoulders became gentler and yet more intense, a caress rather than a restraint.

'Yes,' he said, and his voice had deepened too. 'I wanted to know the future. But I was thinking more about what's going to happen in the next few minutes.'

The throb of desire that pulsed through me was almost painful.

'I think you can tell that as well as I can.' It came out of me half a whisper.

Harry lifted one hand from my shoulder, and laid his finger, warm and heavy, on the top button of my shirt.

'You aren't wearing a bra,' he said.

'I'm not wearing any underwear at all.' And I could feel it, where the seam of my jeans pressed against the swollen, aroused flesh between my legs. The sensation was unbearable.

'You're driving me mad,' he murmured, and he leant forward over the tarot cards and closed the distance between us. His breath feathered across my lips, and my mouth opened of its own accord, loosening, yielding to his kiss even before he started it.

There was a knock on the door.

Harry's mouth was a fraction of an inch from mine.

I could taste him already.

We both drew back at the same instant.

Although it hurt as though I was going from a sauna into an ice-cold pool of water, I scrambled off the bed.

It was Gina. She was wearing jeans, but they only appeared worn because she'd bought them that way.

'Hi, Gina, join the party.' She followed me into the room, blinking at the sight of Harry on my bed.

'Hello, Harry. Are you here to watch *Amazing TV* too?'

'Of course.' He stood and offered the bottle to her. 'Glass of wine?'

'No thank you. It can't be a new thing for you to see yourself on television.'

'No. But this was an extraordinary show. I'm curious to see what Rosie thinks of it,' Harry said.

I was curious to see what I thought of it too.

Harry turned on the television as the opening credits for *Amazing TV* came on to

the screen. The sight of the orange and yellow lettering brought back memories of sitting on my couch at home watching this show, alone and clutching the throw pillows in lust for Harry.

I was pretty sure I couldn't get much more lustful, but I hugged a pillow from the bed, just in case.

Harry appeared on the TV: tall, impeccably dressed, and gorgeous. 'Good evening, ladies and gentlemen, and welcome to the Royal Theatre, Birmingham. I'm Harry Blake, of *Amazing News*,' he said, and man, I guess my inner pervert kicked in again with this whole voyeuristic thing, because I loved watching this man on television while the real live version sat less than a yard away.

I imagined watching him on TV while the real him sat even closer to me, touching me, running his hands over my body.

My naked body. Of course.

I hugged the pillow tighter.

And then I came on to the screen. I said 'Hi,' and I led the audience in a moment of silence.

I remembered how I'd felt at that moment. Scared. Shaken. Desperate to share my feelings and my fears, and unable to.

But I looked . . . well, I looked good. I looked powerful and certain of myself. I was wearing a sequinned skirt that clung to my hips and legs, and shimmered in the stage lights. My velvet top outlined every curve of my waist and chest. Silver bangles on my slim wrists, silver rings on my long fingers, silver hoops in my small ears.

The clothes had been styled for effect, of course. As had my glossy tumbling curls, my 'look-at-me' stance. But I hadn't known about my eyes. They flashed, they probed, they softened as I talked to the people who had lost loved ones.

They were plain brown eyes. I never knew they did so much. I never knew they looked so convincing that they could convince even me.

I looked around the hotel room. Gina was watching the TV intently.

Harry was looking at me. The real me, not the me on the television.

He smiled when he saw me notice him. 'Bravo,' he mouthed at me.

It wasn't sareastic. It was admiring, like an art connoisseur appreciating a truly exquisite forgery, and wishing he could possess it.

I hugged the pillow still tighter and dragged my attention back to the screen. I was holding the hand of the retired teacher. I was telling her exactly the lies she wanted to hear.

186

I was manipulating her, using her emotions to make myself look genuine, and powerful, and certain of my place in the universe.

I was really, really good at my job.

So why did I feel like it was wrong?

18

'So. *Cosmo* want me to be their resident psychic,' I mused, shuffling through the stack of papers Gina had put in front of me on my hotel-room desk. 'A psychic for *Cosmo*. Would that make me a psycho? Or a cosmic?'

Gina took her gold-plated pen out of her mouth and gave me her look. 'It's an extremely lucrative offer. And one that I'd think would be right up your street.'

'Oh yeah. Definitely. Supernatural advice on orgasms and shoes. I love it. Sign me up.'

She narrowed her eyes. 'Are you being serious when you say that, Rosie, or are you being sarcastic again? Because I never know these days whether you're sincere or not.'

'Oh?' I pretended to be surprised. But I wasn't.

It was twelve days after Newcastle and *Amazing TV* and I was feeling the strain. My conscience, reawakened by the sight of myself on television, kept on niggling in the annoying way consciences did. In this case it was particularly annoying, because I couldn't do anything about it. The people who came to my shows needed me to help them, which

I couldn't do if I didn't lie.

'I'm being serious,' I said. 'I always wanted to be cool enough to be in *Cosmo*. What else have you got for me?'

'I hope you *are* serious, because this is the big time. We can't be amateurs any more.' Gina took a deep breath, and looked me in the eye. 'I've resigned from my financial adviser job. I'm going to be a theatrical manager and agent, permanently.'

'Good! Oh, congratulations, Gina. It's what you've been hoping for.'

And yet my real response wasn't so straightforward.

This was serious now. Gina was giving up a very good job to manage my career. That meant . . . well, that meant she was counting on me for her choice to be the right one.

I might as well forget about this whole conscience thing.

'I've got some other news. I've added another London date to your tour. On Hallowe'en.'

'Ooh, that sounds good. Spooky. I like it.'

'And Channel Five wants to air it live. Prime time, on terrestrial national television, for an hour-long show.'

Gina's cheeks were flushed with triumph. I didn't need to feel responsible for her; she was doing fine by herself.

189

'I'm impressed,' I said.

'Thank you. Are you impressed enough to take my advice?'

'Maybe. Try me.'

'You need to get rid of Harry.'

I put my hand on my stomach, feeling, bizarrely, as if she'd punched me there. 'Get rid of him?'

'He can't do any more for you, Rosie. At first he was useful. The *Amazing TV* show was fabulous; it helped me get the Channel Five deal. And his columns are good so far. They're well written, I'll give him that. But his audience is limited. We're going for mainstream popularity now with *Cosmo* and your TV special. We don't need his trashy newspaper any more. To be blunt.'

Blunt was an understatement. 'Remember we decided it was better to have the enemy close, where we could see him?'

Gina shrugged again. 'We don't have to worry about that any more. Your reputation is established now. Besides, he's not going to expose you as a fraud. He can't. Right?'

'Of course not.' Man, I was glad I was a good actress. I still had very little idea about what Harry knew — other than it was more than I wanted him to.

He'd been gone for the past four days, taping episodes of *Amazing TV*. I hadn't had

190

a battle of wits in over ninety-six hours. Things had been pretty quiet.

And sort of boring.

'You don't need a pet journalist any more,' Gina said. 'Especially a failed pet journalist. Face it, Rosie — his career's on the way down, and yours is on the way up.'

Anger burst inside me. 'It wasn't his fault he got fired from *The Times*. He was set up.'

'Come on Rosie. Think about it. Harry Blake can only hurt your career now. Remember I'm talking about my career, too, so I mean what I say. Besides the fact that he works for a fourth-rate rag of a newspaper, he's an infamous liar. Do you really want to be associated with someone like that?'

I gritted my teeth. 'I'm not — ' I started, but there was a knock at the door. I stomped over and opened it.

Harry wore a dark suit, white shirt, and bright silk tie, all of which looked as if it had been made for him. It probably had. 'I just got back,' he said.

My God. Had I ever missed him.

I had to step back and grip the doorknob tighter at that revelation. 'Hey,' I said, doing my best impression of cool, 'how'd the taping go?'

'Bloody interesting. Or rather, bloody and interesting. We had some vampires, I nearly got my neck bitten off. Come have a drink and I'll tell you about it.'

'Okay. Let me get my purse.' I went back into my room and scooped up my handbag from the bed. 'Thanks for your advice, Gina. I'm going for a drink with my pet journalist now.'

She furrowed her brow. 'And you'll tell him we don't need him any more?'

'I'll think about it,' I said. 'Don't wait up.'

Walking down the hotel hallway with Harry was the most pleasurable thing I'd done all day. 'I've had enough of hotel bars,' he said. 'There's a pub across the road that looks all right. How have your shows been?'

'Great, as usual. *Cosmo* want me to write a regular psychic column. And Gina's arranged a live broadcast of my show on Hallowe'en.'

He whistled low. 'Those are great gigs. Well done.' He opened the hotel door for me and we crossed the lamplit street. It wasn't raining, but it had been, and the road was shiny jet beneath our feet.

I let Harry open the pub door for me too, and we walked into a fug of cigarette smoke and sepia-coloured walls. Harry ordered me a Diet Coke, himself a pint of Old Speckled Hen, and we sat at a highly polished table in a corner. He launched into his story about Gretchen and Scott, the self-styled teenage vampires from Glasgow.

About the time he got to the part about Gretchen pulling a Scooby Doo lunchbox out from under her long, flowing black velveteen cape and opening it to reveal two plastic bags full of blood and a can of Irn-Bru, I was holding on to the sides of my chair, laughing so hard that I'd nearly forgotten my manager wanted me to get the hell rid of this man as soon as possible.

'I don't even know what Irn-Bru is,' I sputtered.

'I'll get you one.' Harry came back from the bar with an orange can and a glassful of liquid that looked as if a radioactive tangerine had died in it. I took a sip and made a face.

'Gretchen said that she always has an Irn-Bru chaser after drinking blood. Apparently it gets rid of the aftertaste.'

'She's right. This stuff would remove paint.'

I smiled over at Harry and he smiled back at me, and my only thought was *Screw Gina. He's staying.* If only so I could look at that face every day.

But I couldn't discount completely what Gina had said. I had to admit, I didn't know exactly why Harry kept on coming back to me and my shows. He'd written plenty of columns about me. Surely there wasn't that much more to say, unless he thought he was going to expose me. If I asked him about that, though, it would appear I was worried.

Then there was the possibility that he kept on coming back because he was as addicted to our dangerous flirtation as I was.

Asking him about that seemed nearly as foolish as asking him if he had proof I was a fake.

'How did you break your nose?' I asked instead.

He ran a finger over its crooked contours. 'Haven't the spirits told you already?'

'The spirits don't talk to me about your nose. How *did* you break it? Falling off a polo pony?'

'Oh come on. I've never been on a polo pony.'

'You sound very posh to me,' I said, imitating his accent. 'All those round vowels.'

'Did your father have a strong south London accent? Or did he lose a lot of it, living in Massachusetts?'

And to think I'd spent two days without having unexpected facts about my past come up in conversation.

'My father could swear fluently in both English and American. I guess you found out he grew up in England, huh?'

He grinned. 'I've been watching you eat breakfast. I'd never met an American who

194

loved Marmite before. I thought you might have a British influence. It was easy enough to find out that your father was born in Lambeth and didn't go to the States until he was in his late twenties.'

'You're really bad at minding your own business.'

His grin got wider. 'You missed me, didn't you?'

'No.'

It was so easy to see when he didn't believe me.

'So fair's fair,' I said, feeling the need for a change of subject, but enjoying this whole conversation much, much more than I had any right to. 'My past is obviously an open book to you. Tell me how you broke your nose.'

'My sister Clarissa jumped out in front of me when I was riding my bicycle. I swerved and crashed head first into an oak tree. I was fourteen.' He held his hand to his heart and looked heavenward. 'It was only the first of many, many wounds inflicted upon me by women.'

'Somehow I doubt you've always been the innocent party. And you *are* posh. You had a sister called Clarissa. Did you have a happy childhood, Houdini?'

He nodded. 'Yes. Very.'

195

I wondered what it felt like to be able to say that.

'Private schools? Lots of toys?'

'No. My parents are diehard liberals. I went to local schools and then got into Cambridge. Every Christmas my mother and father had us choose toys to donate to charity. I spent a lot of my school holidays on peace marches.'

'Did you like the marches?'

'Well, when I was ten I would rather have gone to a theme park. But I didn't mind, not once I realised why they were doing it. I admire my parents' principles. That said, my mother was furious when I took the job at *The Times*. The paper's far too right-wing for her.'

'But she forgave you.'

'After she gave me a lecture on the dangers of conservatism, yes.'

I regarded Harry. He had loving parents, a secure income, a family who cared about other people and the world. No wonder he knew so effortlessly how to behave, how to move, how to dress. Life had been kind to him from the beginning.

He rubbed his chin contemplatively. 'I was very lucky growing up,' he said, nearly echoing my thoughts. 'You know, I don't think I ever failed at anything I tried, until I printed that memo.'

He sat looking at the wall behind me for a moment, his mind obviously busy. Then he sighed, picked up his pint, and looked surprised when he saw he'd drunk it all.

'Anyway,' he said, putting the glass down, 'I'm off again, I think. There have been some UFO sightings near Belfast.' He stood.

'You're going now?'

His slight smile told me he'd heard the dismay in my voice. 'Finish your drink, and I'll see you later. I'll stay for your show tonight and catch a plane in the morning. You've got plenty to think about without me around. *Cosmo* and — which network for your TV broadcast?'

'Channel Five.'

He whistled low again. 'Terrestrial. Well done. I'll be back for that.' Harry leaned down and dropped a soft kiss on the top of my head. 'Good luck,' he said, before I could react to it, and left the pub.

19

Dishonesty seems to have run in my family. What makes me different is that my mother and my father never fooled anybody but themselves with their lying.

I never actually saw my father drinking during the day. In fact I never saw him drinking heavily at all. He'd have a couple of beers when he got home at night, but by then he'd already be pretty far gone. But I was still very young when I realised that my father's distinctive smell, on his breath and on his clothes, seeping out of his pores, came straight from a bottle of whisky. He kept one, or several, at work, and then he'd always go to Malone's after he'd shut the store up for the night. The phone number of the bar was up on the corkboard near our phone, so my mother could call Malone and ask him to send Ed home if it got too late. She called a lot. He didn't always come.

She pretended it was normal to have the phone number of a bar next to her shopping lists in the kitchen. I thought it *was* normal, for a long time.

I can see now why my father drank at work.

He hated Markovitz's General Store and Deli, and he hated working there as the failure son-in-law who couldn't get a decent job on his own and had to be given a place in his wife's family business. Sitting behind a counter and getting slowly, steadily, secretly drunk while he sold toilet paper and kosher corned beef was like giving his in-laws the finger.

But I think the main reason he didn't drink the hard stuff at home was because he thought, on a deep, illogical level, that if he didn't show his family that he was an alcoholic, they would never know. And therefore there wasn't a problem. Drinking at work was an act of defiance, and justified. Drinking at Malone's was what every hardworking man had the right to do after spending the day earning a crust for his family. Drinking in front of his wife and his young daughter . . . well, that wasn't what a good man did.

I wasn't very old when I noticed that my father was a different person late at night than he was in the mornings, or on days he didn't work. Daddy in the mornings was forbidding, grouchy, and scary. He smoked and sat over cup after cup of strong milky tea and complained if my mother made it too weak. He didn't like to be touched and he didn't like little girls to make noise.

On Saturdays when the shop was closed he demanded breakfast and there was always an argument. My Jewish mother resented cooking pork, especially on the Sabbath, but of course she'd never outright refuse her husband. Instead she'd burn the sausages and bacon, fry the eggs too hard. As soon as I came down the stairs and smelled the fry-up, my stomach would start to curdle with dread of raised voices and slammed doors.

But Daddy in the evenings would sweep his precious Roz up in his arms and sit with her in his lap and tell her over and over again how pretty she was, how clever, and how much he loved her. I beamed and wriggled closer and buried my nose in his shirtfront and breathed in his sweet, smoky smell.

I got to appreciate my father's displays of affection a lot less once I'd figured out that they were born out of a bottle of Wild Turkey.

I think I was about seven when I was playing shop behind the counter one day at the store and found a half-empty bottle. I opened it and thought my father had come back in from the storeroom, the smell was so much his.

By the time I was ten, I'd wait for about four thirty in the afternoon, when I knew he'd be smashed, and bring groups of my friends into the store. We'd fill our pockets with candy while my dad was serving customers. My favourite was those long, thin red liquorice shoestrings. My friends were nervous about stealing, but I'd make it more and more obvious what I was doing.

I was challenging him to catch me. I *wanted* him to catch me. I wanted him to get angry with me and to hear him say something when he was drunk that I knew he meant.

Then maybe I could believe the other things he said to me when he was drunk. When he called me his princess and his angel.

He never said a thing, even when I was practically stuffing the shoestrings into my pockets in front of him. Even when I deliberately let them dangle out of my coat, in plain sight as I walked around the store.

'Too damn shitfaced to see,' I'd mutter, and dump the candy in the nearest trash can on my way home.

On my eleventh birthday he came home late, as usual, and brought me a big brown paper bag. 'Happy birthday, angel,' he said to me. 'I know they're your favourite.'

The bag smelled of cigarette smoke and beer; he'd taken it with him to Malone's.

Inside I found long, thin red liquorice shoestrings.

I stopped stealing after that. If my father thought that I'd only been after the candy, there was no point.

20

I had plenty of time to prepare for the Hallowe'en seance. Gina had invited a lot of minor celebrities to make up the audience, so all I needed was a hotel phone and internet access to find out everything I needed to know about them. It's amazing the things you can discover from a phone book and a map. And if you're willing to bend the truth a little and do a half-decent imitation of somebody's wife or PA, there's no end to what you can learn. For a live-broadcast TV show, preparation was going to make me feel a lot more secure.

With Harry's prying eyes safely in Northern Ireland trying to tell the difference between a satellite, an atmospheric disturbance, and ET's mother ship, I had free rein. It was two weeks when I didn't have to argue with Gina about whether he was staying. Though I didn't see much of Gina; she seemed always to be busy at something, and disappeared on our days off.

Two weeks was also enough time to prepare a special surprise for Harry.

I made several trips into London and used

up quite a bit of money and several good aliases making phone calls to the United States. By the time I was done, my knowledge of Harry Houdini was substantially extended. I knew that Houdini had been obsessed with spiritualism because he'd wanted to get in touch with his dead mother. And he was bitter against mediums because they'd never convinced him, even though he'd wanted them to be real.

I learned about the final test he'd devised for spiritualism: Houdini and his wife, Bess, agreed that when one of them died, they would try to contact the other from beyond the grave, using a secret code from their old mind-reading act.

I learned the code. I also learned several obscure facts about Houdini's life and the method of some of his tricks. I studied his letters and his interviews to learn his way of speaking. And I found out one interesting thing: Houdini bought a Spiritualist church in Worcester, Massachusetts, my home town, and hired a certain Miss R. Mackenburg to act as the Reverend Frances Raud. (F. Raud, for short. Houdini was such a card.)

Some well-chosen phone calls led me to Miss Mackenburg's closest living relatives. And from there to information about some books which the family had donated to the

Houdini Collection in the Library of Congress. By the time I finished my research, I had the details about one particular book, its physical description and a knowledge of its inscription written by F. Raud to H. Houdini ... and I hadn't directly contacted the Library of Congress once.

Here was a fact so obscure that only Houdini's ghost could provide it. With a little dressing up, delivered in code, phrased correctly, it could be an absolute killer.

It was going to lead Harry Blake on a merry chase for information. It was exactly the sort of fakery he suspected me of doing all the time, and he wasn't going to be able to prove it. It was going to show him, once and for all, who was the cleverer of the two of us. Maybe, after all his disbelief and his sneaky seduction and his random bits of information about me, it could even convince him that I was a genuine psychic. I couldn't wait.

★ ★ ★

'Wow,' I said.

The studio was amazing. All midnight-blue walls, with stars projected on to screens around the stage, scarves draped everywhere, and tall, elegant candelabra. Sort of a cross between a boudoir and a gypsy caravan.

'I told them 'mystical and sexy', to reflect your image,' Gina said. She stood beside me, looking over the room. 'I think they did a good job.' She bounced up and down and giggled.

Gina giggling? I'd never heard that before.

I looked at her closely. She was wearing a slim black dress, cut into a low V at the front and up into slits on the sides of her legs, to expose a flash of thigh above her shiny black leather knee-length high-heeled boots.

'I love your boots, Gina. Those are sex in a shoe.'

'Thank you.' She checked her classy gold watch, and then glanced at the door.

'In fact you're looking like a sex goddess all around. Expecting someone special?'

'Oh,' she said in a way that was supposed to be nonchalant, 'I invited Max DeMilo.'

'The rock star? Does this mean you're definitely doing his comeback tour?'

'I am.' Never mind the giggling, there was something in her voice I hadn't heard before.

'Is he still gorgeous? Still wear lots of leather?'

'He still wears leather,' she said, and her nonchalance was even more fake.

'And what's it like to hang out with a famous rock star? Is it as wild as it's made out to be?'

'It's . . . good.' She smoothed her glossy auburn hair. 'He's very grounded. Very comfortable with his fame. I think it will be productive to work with him.'

From the giggling and the boots, I sensed that this was somewhat more than just a working relationship.

'So is it a full house tonight?' I asked.

'Absolutely. Tickets were gold dust.'

'And did Harry reserve a seat? You got him one, right? At the front?'

'Yes.' Gina didn't look as annoyed as she usually did at the mention of Harry's name. My opinion of Max DeMilo immediately rose a few notches; any man who could mellow Gina Parker out a little bit was a man to be reckoned with.

'You should get in to Makeup,' she said, and then she looked over my shoulder and suddenly, Gina *glowed*.

Max DeMilo was nearly fifteen years older than the last time I'd seen him on MTV, but the years had been good to him. His longish brown hair had a little silver running through it, but otherwise he still looked the part of a pop star: high cheekbones, wide mouth, white silk shirt unbuttoned to show a smooth chest, black leather trousers that fitted him as well as they had in the eighties. The only major change was a very long brown woollen scarf around his neck.

'All right, Gina love,' he greeted her, looping his arm around her shoulders and kissing her swiftly but warmly on the lips. 'You must be Rosie,' he said to me, and held out his hand. He wore several silver and turquoise rings.

'Nice to meet you, Max.' I shook his hand. 'Glad you could make it. I hear you've got a new album coming out.'

'That's right, mate. Should be a laugh. Think Gina's gonna make a brilliant tour manager.' He squeezed Gina's shoulders and beamed down at her. I'd never seen her looking so thrilled.

'We're going to make a huge success of it,' Gina said.

'Yeah, babe, we're gonna have a lot of fun.'

'I'd better get to Makeup,' I said, and left them together.

Forty-five minutes later I looked into the mirror and wondered at the magic of cosmetics. The makeup artist had made me into something exotic, lush, with a few brushes and pots of glitter.

'They'll love you,' I whispered to myself. There was a knock at my dressing-room door. 'Come in.'

It was Harry. He paused in the doorway. 'Wow.'

'I've been saying that a lot myself,' I said. 'You look beautiful.'

'Thank you.' I spun my chair around so he could see my outfit: a chiffon dress the colour of the centre of a deep red rose, shot through with silver that would pick up the lights.

'I've brought you something.' He bent down out of sight in the hallway and came back in holding an enormous pumpkin carved with two slanted eyes and a toothy grin.

'A jack-o-lantern?' I cried. 'How cool is that?'

'It's to wish you luck.' He put it on the dressing table in front of me. 'Tonight is an important night.'

I narrowed my eyes. 'Since when are you rooting for me, Houdini?'

'I'm not rooting for you. I'm wishing you luck. You deserve to do well. You work harder than any medium I've ever met.'

He had no idea how hard I worked and how well I deserved to do. I thought of my message from Harry Houdini, and smiled.

Houdini had died on 31 October 1926. Harry Blake would be leaving this studio tonight a believer.

'I thought it was traditional to give a lady flowers,' I said.

'I considered it. But I thought the pumpkin

was more appropriate for you.'

I trailed my fingers over its plump orange surface. 'I'll put it on stage. Are you going to write about tonight?'

'It depends whether you give me anything to write about.'

I looked up into Harry's face, and dared to ask the question I'd been wondering. 'You've been travelling with me for a long time now, Harry. Haven't you found out enough about me yet?'

His keen blue eyes searched mine. 'Not quite enough. Not yet.'

He held my gaze for a moment more, then bent forward and brushed his lips against my cheek. 'You're on in ten minutes. Break a leg.' And he was gone.

'Oh, Harry Blake, you don't know half enough about what I can do yet,' I said to my reflection. 'But you will.'

21

'Here goes nothing,' I said, and downed the shot of whisky, as always.

I had the seating plan memorised and dozens of little facts stored away in my brain, to say nothing of the Great Magician's message from beyond the grave. It was All Hallow's Eve, the night when they say spirits walk the earth, and I was on the top of my Win/Win game as I walked on to the stage.

The lights dazzled and flashed and the cameras moved around to catch me from every angle. And yet I felt something missing as I talked with a radio DJ about his deceased sister, and a stand-up comedian about his vaudeville mentor. It was working, I had the audience in the palm of my hand — not to mention however many thousands watching at home — but it wasn't there. I didn't feel the buzz.

I knew too much. There were no risks, no dancing on the edge of falling down.

Except for what I was planning for Harry.

During the commercial breaks I sat on a high stool on stage and drank water. I was saving Houdini's coded message until near the end. It wouldn't have very much impact on this audience, I knew. But for the right person, it would be by far the most important thing that happened tonight.

'Five seconds, Rosie,' the floor director said as the third or fourth commercial break ended, and I slid off my stool and stood on the stage and wondered who to try next. The cuddly cookery writer to the right of the stage, who was wondering whether to try a new career as a novelist? The nightclub owner to the left, who'd been watching my tits and ass all night and who I thought I'd probably remind about his mother?

There was a scuffle from the back row. 'Rosie Fox!' a loud voice called.

I squinted my eyes against the light. 'Hello?'

A short, balding man was trundling up to the stage. His suit was creased and . . . was that the lights or was his suit purple?

It *was* purple. He stepped on to the stage and stood facing me, his legs akimbo, his hands defiantly fisted on his hips. 'I am the Fantastic Frederick,' he declaimed in a booming voice way too big for his body, 'and I am here to prove to the world on live television that I am a better medium than you, Rosie Fox!'

I stared.

Was this some live TV setup thing like *Candid Camera*? I looked at Gina, and her face was unmistakably shocked.

'Okay,' I said. 'Hi.'

'You.' He aimed an impressively trembling finger at my chest. 'You are a fraud, no more than a mere charlatan. The Fantastic Frederick has spoken with the spirits of kings!'

This time I looked at Harry. He was laughing and shaking his head. He hadn't set this up, then. This guy was a genuine kook. That meant that he didn't have any proof that I was a fraud.

Probably.

I smiled as widely as I could. From the corner of my eye, I could see two large men standing beside one of the cameras, awaiting my signal.

'That's great, Mr — can I call you Fantastic? As you said, we're here live on TV. Is there anything you'd like to tell the audience? Any messages you'd like to pass on from the world beyond?'

Fantastic Frederick's face crumpled. He looked down at the floor. I thought for a moment that he was going to burst into tears. Total loony, I thought, and put a hand on his purple shoulder to escort him off the stage.

He jumped under my hand, as if an electric

shock had hit him. I heard the audience laugh. 'I have a message for you,' he said. 'From your father.'

I took my hand from his shoulder. He smelled strongly of sweat and coffee. Probably why he was so jumpy. 'Is that right, Fantastic?'

'Yes. It's about shoes.' His stare was fixed on my high-heeled suede boots, and his booming voice had sunk to a mutter. Poor man, he was obviously mentally disturbed and he'd somehow gotten in off the streets.

'Do you like them?' I asked gently.

'Not those shoes. Something else. Shoes with laces. Red.' He raised his head and looked into my face, and as I watched, his eyes focused themselves. 'Red shoelaces. Your father says.'

It took a minute, his eyes locked to mine, before I realised what he was saying and what it meant.

Fantastic grabbed my hand and held it tight in his sweaty palm. I stood transfixed, my mouth full of the taste of red liquorice.

Then he was being pulled away from me, and I saw the two big guys from the stage crew and beside them Harry and Gina. The big guys gripped Fantastic's upper arms and steered him offstage. Harry held my elbow in his hand and drew me towards him. I breathed in his scent and felt my heartbeat start to return to normal.

'Are you okay?' he asked.

'Yeah. Yeah, I'm totally fine. He was a weirdo. Harry, we're on live TV.'

'They went to another advert break as soon as that man came on stage,' Gina said. 'You've still got forty seconds. Are you all right?'

My God, what was wrong with me? I'd been taken in, however momentarily, by the oldest trick in the business. A lucky guess. Lots of people have had red shoelaces at some point. Or red shoes with laces. Or they'd eaten red shoelace liquorice. It wasn't that unusual a candy, after all.

Fantastic Freddy was faking a fact from my father. Say that five times fast.

I swallowed hard and my smile returned to my face without my even thinking about it.

'I'm great.'

'Brilliant,' said Gina. 'You're doing really well. You've only got ten minutes and then it's over and we've got champagne on ice backstage.'

'You're a natural on television,' Harry said, warm and lazy and precise. 'It's easy tonight, isn't it?'

You wait five minutes and I'll show you easy, I thought. 'The spirits are definitely

willing,' I said, and Harry and Gina went back to their seats and left me alone on stage.

The floor director gave me the five-second warning again, and then the red light on the camera came on. The audience, who'd been whispering among themselves, quietened. I laid my hand on the head of Harry's jack-o-lantern.

They love me, I thought, and I made eye contact with my audience and the camera and said, 'Welcome back. Did you know that people carved pumpkins to scare spirits away?' I bent down and addressed the jack-o-lantern's grinning face. 'Not really working tonight, are you, buddy?' The audience, just having witnessed Fantastic as well as all my supposed spirits, laughed.

Ten minutes left in the show. It was time.

'I have one last spirit here, someone who's been waiting to talk with us for a long time. Someone who waited especially for tonight.'

Taking my time, I let my eyes travel over the audience, over every expectant face. It was silent. The right moment.

I let my gaze settle on Harry. I'd resisted looking directly at him during so many shows, it was almost a relief.

'It's a man,' I said. The words I needed to say were all ready in my head, in my mouth, on the tip of my tongue.

And they didn't come out.

I'd worked my butt off to hoodwink Harry, to play with his mind for once like he'd played with mine, and I could not do it.

I stared at Harry and I saw his blue eyes narrow. I saw *his body become alert, as it always did when he was searching out the truth in me.*

I raised my fingers to my temples. My carefully crafted lie waited. A thing of perfect beauty.

Instead, I tasted red liquorice.

I was trying too hard to steal something right under someone's nose. I already had Harry's attention.

'I'm sorry,' I said. 'He's gone.' From somewhere I raised a smile. 'I guess your pumpkin scared him off.'

A turn of my head, a swivel of my hips, and I was myself again. 'Not like this lady here,' I continued, focusing my eyes on the blank air towards the middle of the stage, 'who looks like she'd never be frightened by any old vegetable. She's waving her hands and shaking her head and she's saying something about' — I laughed — 'about a dirty mind, and she's saying it to *you*, sir.'

I pointed. The tits-and-ass guy did a double-take. The audience laughed.

I kept up my patter about the guy's mother

and stole a glance at Harry. For the first time I could remember during my shows, he wasn't looking at me. His eyes were lowered and his mouth was closed and straight.

Did he know how close I'd been to spinning him a story?

I remembered the cameras and turned back to the nightclub owner. The rest of the show was on exuberant autopilot, and the cheers had never been so loud.

Afterwards, I held a glass of champagne in my hand without drinking it and watched all the minor celebrities give each other air-kisses. I'd been air-kissed too, and had my hand shaken, and I'd been called 'amazing' and 'incredible' and 'gorgeous'.

And yet, right now, I was standing alone in a corner while my party went on without me. Even the tits-and-ass guy wasn't trying to pick me up after ogling me all night.

I knew why. I'd been too good. I was fun to watch on stage, but people were wary of getting close to me, in case I read their minds or started summoning more of their dead loved ones. I was the star of the evening, but when it came down to it, I wasn't a whole lot less freakish than Fantastic Frederick.

And for some reason, I hadn't been able to lie to Harry Blake.

'What a weird evening,' I muttered to

myself. I put down my drink, and found a high stool to sit on and watch the party.

I sensed rather than saw Harry come up to my side, from a warming of the air. He pulled up a stool beside me. It was high, but his feet touched the ground anyway. 'So about tonight. Was it trick, or treat?'

His voice, so familiar by now, was different, though I couldn't pinpoint how. The teasing banter still had a serious edge underneath, but there was something else, something darker.

'Treat. Of course.' I swung round to face him and crossed my legs, letting my dress drape over them.

'Something strange happened near the end when you were talking to me. What was that?'

I shrugged. 'I thought I had a message for you, but it turned out I didn't.'

'Are you sure the 'dirty mind' message wasn't for me?'

'I don't need the spirits to tell me that about you, Harry.'

Gina and Max approached us. 'Rosie,' Gina said, 'do you mind if I leave the party to you? Max and I still have some talking to do.'

Max winked at me.

'I don't think I've ever heard of a rock star leaving a party early,' I said.

'If there's one thing better than a load of

people in a room with free champagne,' said Max, 'it's two people in a room with free champagne. What d'you say, Gina? Ready to scarper?'

'Enjoy the party,' she said to me. 'Great show. We'll be all over the papers tomorrow, just watch.'

On their way out, Max swiped an unopened bottle of champagne and stashed it underneath his leather coat.

'Max DeMilo,' Harry said contemplatively. 'Now there's a man whose career is even deader than mine.'

'Gina thinks she's going to revive it. I bet she will, too.'

'She's a determined woman.'

I gestured to the room of quasi-celebrities drinking bubbly and talking crap. 'She put a small-time medium on prime-time TV.'

'No. You did that yourself.' He leaned a little closer to me; his knees brushed mine. 'You liked the fish and chip shop better, though, didn't you?'

I nodded. I wondered if the reason why I couldn't lie to Harry was because even after so short a time, even though I'd been trying to hide from him, he still understood me better than anyone else I knew.

'The people in Newcastle needed me,' I said. 'They wanted answers. These people want a laugh and their face on television.'

'Why are we here?' he asked. Trust him to always ask the right question.

'It's my party. Though I don't know anybody, and my manager has left to have wild, torrid sex.'

'So it's only you and me.' Harry was looking at me. Aside from that one moment in my show tonight, his gaze had been a constant in my life for weeks.

He didn't just see my body. He saw me.

I lifted my legs and rested them in his lap. His hands encircled my ankles, stroked up the suede.

'You and me and all these people,' I agreed. 'And nobody's talking to us. We're both too weird for this crowd, even at a seance.'

'I never thought I'd say it, but I'm starting to like being weird,' Harry said. 'Either *Amazing News* is getting to me, or it's you.'

I watched him. His hands were warm through my boots. I thought about all the trouble I'd gone to to impress him, and he'd never know.

'You're different tonight,' he said.

'How?' I asked, although I knew exactly how. I'd had one of the best cons of my life, and I hadn't used it.

And I was glad I hadn't.

'I can't quite say,' he said.

'Do you like it?'

His hands had reached the top of my boots, and his fingers touched the skin of my legs. 'I like it very much.'

'So do I.' I closed my eyes, savouring the feeling of his hands and how we were in a room full of people and none of them existed.

When I opened my eyes he was looking straight into them. He was relaxed, yet alert, every bit of his body and his attention focused on me. On the two of us.

'We're going to sleep together, aren't we?' I said.

22

'Yes,' he answered.

I swung my legs out of his lap and stood up. 'Let's leave now. I hate this party.'

He stood too. 'And I hate hotels. Let's take a taxi to my flat.'

'Yes.'

We didn't touch as we left the party without saying goodbye to anyone. We got into a taxi and sat side by side, silent. I looked out the window and watched the lights of London going by, and I was so aware of Harry that I knew we were breathing in tandem.

His flat was in an area I could tell wasn't fashionable. It was the basement of a Victorian house. I stood beside him as he unlocked the door. Everything in my body and in my mind was certain about what was going to happen next.

The hallway was uncluttered and smelled musty, as if he hadn't been there in some time. I stepped over a pile of letters on the doormat and stood against the wall, waiting for him to lock the door after us. Then he took my hand and led me down the corridor.

His bedroom had a bed, and dozens of books surrounding it. That's all I saw. Harry dropped my hand. He touched my cheek. I heard his breath, and the rustle of his shirt, and the parting of his lips as he opened his mouth.

'Rosie,' he said. I stepped forward into his arms and we kissed.

No time had passed since the first time. My mouth parted underneath his right away, and oh God, the taste of him, as right as his smell. I grabbed the front of his shirt and pulled him as close as I could. His hands on my hips, on my backside, crushed me to him. He was tall and strong but not so strong that I couldn't make him moan, deep in his throat, helpless with desire.

I pushed off his jacket. He pushed my dress down my shoulders and his mouth was on my breast. I nearly cried out with pleasure.

We fell backwards on to the bed, Harry on top of me and between my legs. I felt his breath on my neck, kisses on my chest. I tore at his belt and his fly; his stomach was under my hand, the thickening hair, my palm and fingers wrapped around the iron-hot, iron-hard length of him. Harry pushed my dress up my thighs, up around my waist, and I lifted my hips so he could slide my underwear down.

'Wait,' he muttered against my mouth, and rolled off me halfway to reach the bedside table. I stretched out my own arm and followed him, dipping into a drawer, pulling out a packet. We laughed, a quick breath, together. My fingers were beside his, tearing the condom open, rolling it on, guiding him to me. His tongue plunged into my mouth at the same time as he plunged himself deep, so deep that this time I did cry out, the noise muffled by his lips.

And then movement, no thought, no nothing, only Harry, better than I'd ever foretold he would be. A burning knowledge in the centre of my body.

It was endless. It was only a few seconds. I dug my fingers into his neck and his back and clenched my legs around his hips and panted my pleasure into his mouth, and I yelled, and I felt him pulse inside me, thrust hard as he came too. Still kissing.

Our kisses got slower as our breathing calmed. I felt his mouth widen against mine in a smile. I smiled too.

'That was fast,' he said. His voice vibrated in his chest and I could feel it in my nipples where they were pressed against his shirt.

'That was good,' I replied.

'That was more than good.' He pushed himself up on his arms and we looked at each other. My dress was pushed down over my breasts at the top, and up to my waist at the bottom. Harry's trousers and his boxers were around his ankles. We both still had our shoes on.

'Let's do it again,' he said. 'Only slower.'

'Only much slower. And naked.' I reached for the buttons of his shirt. He slipped his hand around my back to the zipper of my dress, undid it, and pulled it up over my head. We managed to get rid of my bra and his shirt at the same time.

Harry was still inside me. I felt him throb and grow. 'God, Rosie, you're beautiful,' he said, and ran his hands up my sides, over my breasts, up my neck to bury in my hair and pull me towards him for another deep kiss.

My whole body flushed with desire again. 'Harry,' I gasped when our lips parted for a second, 'I think we'll need a new condom before we start this again.'

He smiled. 'So we will. You'll have to forgive me, I haven't done this for a long time.'

He brushed a kiss on my lips and the tip of each of my nipples before pulling away and out of me. I missed him right away. But I had the wonderful compensation of watching him stand up, pull off the condom, and kick off his shoes and his clothes.

Harry Blake naked. I'd thought he looked good in clothes, but without them he was the most spectacular sight I had seen in my life. His body was sculpted in long lines, muscular and hard.

Especially hard.

He stood by the bed and looked at me, and let me look at him.

'Harry, you are totally hot,' I said.

'Thank you.' His eyes trailed up and down my body. My legs, still in my suede boots, were dangling off the side of the bed. I felt rumpled, abandoned and very sexy. 'I've wanted to see you like this from the moment I met you,' he said.

'I've been imagining you naked since the first time I saw you on TV,' I admitted.

Harry raised one eyebrow and grinned. 'Finally. I've found another perk of that job.' He leaned forward far enough to run one finger down the side of my hip, down my naked thigh to the top of my boot. I shivered.

'Did you really just say that you hadn't done this in a long time?' I asked.

He nodded, but his attention was on his hand as he found the zipper of my boot and drew it, slowly, down. 'Three years. Not since I lost my job at *The Times*.'

'You haven't had sex for *three years*?' Someone as gorgeous as Harry Blake? Surely that was against the laws of nature?

He waited until he'd pulled off my boot before he answered. He met my eyes. 'I had a girlfriend, but when the trouble started she left me. I haven't — it hasn't really been an issue since then. Until I met you.' He stroked the arch of my foot with his thumb. 'Since then it's been an issue.'

'Three years, though? Weren't you afraid you'd forget how?'

Deliberately, he stripped off my other boot. 'Does it appear to you as if I've forgotten how?'

'I'm not sure,' I said, and sighed as his hands and lips tickled up my ankle, the side of my calf. 'You'll have to show me a little more.'

'It's like riding a bicycle, so I'm told.' He nipped at the tendon at the back of my knee. He was half crouching between my legs, not yet on the bed with me. His soft hair brushed my thigh.

'Yes, but remember you broke your nose riding your bicycle.'

I was rewarded for my smart remark with a sharp bite on my inner thigh, making me squirm and giggle.

'I didn't hear you complaining I was out of practice a few minutes ago,' Harry said. He took hold of my hips and pushed me backwards on the bed so I was fully on it, and then he knelt on it with me. His glorious erection was pointing straight at me. I remembered the bliss of him pounding into me and I took a shuddery breath.

'Harry, I was so turned on at the thought of having sex with you that you could've read me the cricket scores and I would've come.'

He lay on top of me, propping himself up on his arms, pressing his chest to mine and letting his penis nestle between my legs. I loved the weight of him, his smell, how I felt when he kissed me and put all of his concentration into the kiss.

'Thank you,' he whispered when our lips parted.

I wrapped my arms and my legs languorously around him and whispered back, 'What for?'

'For wanting me so much.'

His voice sounded different. That darker tone. I pulled my head back from his so I could look into his face.

'Why haven't you had sex for three years, Houdini?'

'You didn't know me before I lost my job. I was different. It changed me. I'm' — I saw his eyes flicker upwards as he searched for the right words — 'damaged goods.'

His voice had the unmistakable huskiness

that happens when someone is telling a truth they don't want to tell.

And it stunned me. Harry Blake, the man who carried his broken nose and his ruined reputation with grace.

Now naked with me, more than physically, it seemed.

I shifted underneath him. When I pushed his shoulder, he rolled easily on to his back and I straddled his hips. I held his face in my hands and looked right into his eyes.

'Harry, you're not damaged at all.' I kissed his crooked, broken nose. 'Or if you were, you've healed into something different.'

I stroked my hands over his chest, savouring every inch of skin, the crisp hair, his heart beating underneath.

'Let me prove it to you,' I said, and reached into his bedside table for another condom.

23

'Yeah. It was bizarre, mate. I've never heard of anybody else being killed by a drum set.'

Max DeMilo settled back in his plastic chair and contemplated the fringe of his woollen scarf, secure in the knowledge that the entire audience was watching him agog. Except for Gina, who was watching him adoringly.

'But Nick loved his drums,' Max continued. 'That would've been the way he'd have wanted to go.'

I stood on the stage, nodding slowly and wondering where this was going.

Max had turned up in Scunthorpe a couple of hours before my show, bearing advance copies of his CD. Gina had gotten the theatre management to add an extra seat for him, and for fun, halfway through the show, I'd looked at him, pretended to listen to a spirit voice, and mentioned that there was a friend of his who wanted to say hello. I hadn't done any research on Max; I had no idea whether he had any dead friends or not, though in his profession it was a distinct possibility. I guess if he'd denied having any dead friends I could have faked a message from Elvis or Michael Hutchence or somebody.

But instead he'd shouted out, 'Nick?' and launched into a rather graphic story about how Nick, one of his drummers, had met his demise at the wrong end of a cymbal stand.

'Then again,' he added now, 'Nick was off his tits most of the time, so it's not surprising he came to a messy end. Though I thought the coke'd get him before the drums did. Well. That's a blast from the past. Tell him hi for me.'

'I . . . ' I paused, and glanced at Harry. I could see he was biting the inside of his cheek, trying desperately not to laugh. I was glad he was resisting, because I was dying to laugh too, and if he succumbed I wasn't sure I could keep a straight face.

'Nick can hear you, Max. He says hi. He wishes you good luck for the new album and the tour, and he's saying something about animals?'

Party animals, I was thinking, but Max nodded and said, 'Yeah, he liked my animals. You know that after I stopped recording I started up a llama farm. If there was one thing Nick loved almost as much as his drums, it was a good llama. He used to get pissed up and chase them all around the field; it drove me batshit. But it wasn't the llamas

232

that did for him in the end.'

I couldn't look at Harry. I couldn't. I'd pee my pants.

'Anyway, cheers for the message, mate,' Max said. 'I'm looking forward to this tour, you know? It's the journey, the journey that's important, you have to have a good time. Nick knew that.'

Max sat up and performed a salute to the empty air I'd been pretending to listen to. 'You did a good job, you touched a lot of people, Nick, I hope the journey's still good for you, mate.'

'It is,' I said. 'Better than you can ever imagine, he says. Thanks, Max.'

'My pleasure.'

There was light applause from the audience. I risked a glance at Harry. His mouth was clamped tight shut and his nostrils were flared. I transferred my gaze to Gina. She had that slightly dewy-eyed, slightly shell-shocked, hugely self-confident look that comes from having great sex, repeatedly. I knew I had it too.

I'd had a week of making love with Harry Blake in secret, stolen hours. We hadn't let on to Gina or anyone else what we were up to. No thoughts of the future, no worries about the past, just me and Harry and pure bliss. Underneath my shirt, I sported red marks on my chest from the rasping of Harry's beard stubble. My skin still tingled all over from what we'd done that afternoon. And before I'd raised my glass of whisky, Harry had slipped backstage to whisper in my ear some suggestions for what we could do that evening.

But first I had a job to do. I turned my private smile into a public one for my audience.

And then, looking at my audience, my smile melted away.

I'd missed the couple before. They sat to the left of the aisle, more or less exactly in the middle of the block of seats. They were in their twenties, and they held hands. Although the people around them were smiling, they weren't. The woman's face was drawn and pale; the man's eyes looked baffled, helpless. It was as if they sat in a private bubble of pain and fear.

Guilt pinched me. I'd been too distracted by my own happiness and Max DeMilo's bizarre anecdote to notice them.

The way the seats were set out, I couldn't get close to the couple, but I sat down on the edge of the stage, so at least my face was closer to their eye level.

'Hi,' I said, meeting their eyes, the woman first, then the man, then the woman again.

They both started slightly, the normal reaction at being picked out of a crowd. 'The lady with the brown hair and the green shirt, and her husband with the blue tie? Do you mind if I talk with you for a little while?'

They exchanged glances and tightened their hands together.

I felt my heart sink. I knew what it was. I'd seen it before, though not on this tour, and I hated it.

'I'm so sorry,' I said quietly. I wished I could get closer to them. 'Death is a difficult thing for everybody, but no one should have to lose a child.'

I heard the woman's small whimper of pain, as if I'd twisted a knife in a wound. I heard a little gasp of surprise from the audience, though I hadn't done anything amazing; this couple were so young, so united in their grief, so battered-looking, that there was only one thing bad enough.

The man half nodded, half shook his head.

No fancy guesses with this one. No risks or trying to impress. If I made a mistake, it could hurt even more; it could take away belief when belief was the only thing they had left.

The Win/Win game couldn't work when the loss was overwhelming.

They were young. Odds were, their child

had been very small when it died; odds were, it was their only one so far. I wasn't going to take chances on odds.

'What was your baby's name?' I asked gently, knowing that 'baby' could sound right for any age of child under ten, in this emotional context.

'James,' the man answered. His voice was hoarse. 'Jamie.'

'You know Jamie is with us, don't you?' I said. 'You must know he always will be. He loves you so, so much. You made his life happy.'

I couldn't give them any specifics without knowing the age of their child; words coming from a newborn, or a stillborn infant, would be grotesque. And yet I wanted to offer them something, some comfort, some feeling that their son really did still exist somewhere.

I closed my eyes, and I breathed in deep.

'Jamie is giving me impressions rather than words. I can smell something sweet, something almost like perfume, but not quite. I can feel a lot of warmth, I can feel something soft surrounding me, I can hear the steady beat of my mother's heart and her breathing. It's safe. I can see . . . '

I opened my eyes. 'I can see light. Lots of light, all around. And while I felt that the other things I could feel and hear and smell were things Jamie remembered from his life, this light is now. It's what he sees and feels right now, while he's here with us. Do you understand that?'

The woman was nodding, tears slipping down her cheeks.

Give them something to make them feel a little better, if only for right now.

'You made every minute of his life worthwhile,' I told them, gripping the edge of the stage with my hands, leaning towards them, giving them all of me that I could.

I heard a scuffle as somebody got up from a chair; I heard quick footsteps, and although I was trying to focus everything on the grieving couple, I followed the sound.

It was Gina. She was scrambling out of the front row, heading for the aisle. I saw her face; it was dead white, as if she'd had a horrible shock, or was about to be sick. She reached the aisle, staggered a little on her high heels, and headed for the exit.

I opened my mouth, trying to decide whether to call after her, but I heard somebody else shout, 'Gina!' and then saw Max following her. The theatre door slammed shut behind them.

Well. That was weird.

I shook my head to clear it, and turned my attention back to the couple. He had his arm around her and she was crying into a tattered tissue.

Screw the seats between them and me. I jumped off the stage and ran down the aisle, and saying 'Excuse me' all the way I climbed over people's laps and squeezed past the people who stood up, and I stood beside this couple and hugged them both, but it didn't really help. It was all too raw, too real.

In the end, I couldn't give them anything.

24

'Let's get out of here,' I said to Harry backstage.

'Are you all right?'

I stepped forward into his arms and let my head rest on his chest. 'Rough show,' I said to his clean cotton shirt. 'I hate dead babies.'

He tightened his arms around me and smoothed my hair. I relaxed into the feeling of Harry.

'And Gina freaked out.' I raised my head from his chest and looked at him. 'Do you know *why* she freaked out?'

'You're the mind-reader,' he said, still stroking my hair.

'That's right.' I stared hard at him, and then opened my eyes wide in false shock. 'Harry Blake! That's filthy!'

His smile helped me smile too. 'Let's walk back to the hotel.'

Being outside and having Harry's arm around my shoulders did make me feel better. I hugged his waist and felt my hip bumping against his thigh as we walked. The streets were quiet under the glow of orange lamps and silver moonlight. I took breaths of the damp air and watched it puff out in little clouds.

'How far to the hotel?' I asked after we'd walked for several minutes in silence.

'I haven't got the slightest. I've never been to Scunthorpe before.'

'No call for *Amazing News* here? Doesn't have a large werewolf population?'

'Let's hope not. It's a full moon tonight.'

' "Stick to the road. Beware of the moors",' quavered in my cheesiest *American Werewolf in London* impression.

'Bugger that,' Harry said, and steered me off the sidewalk, through the gates of a park. 'I want to find an isolated park bench and snog you on it. Or,' he leaned closer to me as we walked and murmured in my ear, 'an even more isolated park bench and make love to you on it.'

My insides jumped and dissolved at the same time.

Sex, I thought. The opposite of death.

Yeah, I could do with some of that.

I slipped out from under Harry's arm and ran down the path, howling like a wolf at the top of my lungs. I heard his footsteps and laughter behind me. When I found a bench sheltered underneath a tree, a little bit back from the path, I sprawled on it.

Harry landed beside me and grabbed me

240

and hauled me on to his lap. 'You're not getting away from me that easily, Rosalyn Jones,' he said, and kissed me.

Long, and deep, and soft. Harry Blake could kiss for England. I dug my fingers into his hair and melted into him.

'Markovitz Jones,' I gasped when we parted for air.

'Mmm?' His eyes were unfocused and his lips wet.

'My real name is Rosalyn Markovitz Jones. My grandparents didn't want me to have a goy name. They never approved of my father.' Hell, it wasn't as if he didn't know all about my family already, I might as well relax and tell him the truth about it.

His features stood out orange-coloured in the lamplight; I kissed a crooked path down his nose, then pressed my lips to the hollow underneath his jaw. I loved the textures of his body: smooth, rough, hard, silky.

'Like how your posh parents would be shocked at you taking up with a disreputable fortune-teller,' I said against his neck.

Harry's hands crept underneath my jacket and my shirt, encircled my waist, caressed upwards, slowly, on my bare skin. 'My family don't mind who I take up with as long as they don't start a nuclear war.'

'I think I can pass that test.' The November

241

air was chilly, but that made his hands and his mouth feel hotter.

Harry chuckled. 'I think they'd like you,' he said between kisses. 'Though they might take exception to your being American. They don't approve of US foreign policy.' The tips of his fingers brushed the bottom of my breast.

'Good thing we're only using each other for the sex, then,' I gasped.

He made a noise deep in his throat and bent his head to nibble and lick the skin of my neck.

I closed my eyes in bliss. With every caress the sad young couple, my helpless feelings, dissolved away bit by bit, being put away for later.

I opened my eyes again when I heard a sound. 'Harry, there's a guy walking a dog this way.'

'It's all right, werewolves never walk dogs,' Harry said, but he gave me one last lingering kiss and raised his head.

And then his hands tightened on my waist, tense and so unlike how he'd been touching me that I looked at him in surprise. He was staring at the man with the dog, and his face and body had gone still.

I looked at the guy with the dog. He was normal-looking, in his forties maybe, balding, leading a Jack Russell on a leash. He'd nearly passed us.

'Harry, what is it?' I asked.

'Spencer?' Harry said. His voice was low and full of an emotion I couldn't understand.

The man stopped and looked over his shoulder.

'Spencer!' Harry lifted me off his lap on to the park bench. The wooden seat was freezing after his legs, and I had to grab the armrest to stop from tipping over in surprise. He stood up.

The man dropped his dog's leash and ran.

Harry swore and took off after him.

The Jack Russell barked and ran after them both, his leash trailing.

'What the — ' I jumped off the park bench and sprinted after all three of them.

Harry caught up with the guy after about fifty yards, grabbed him by the shoulders, and the two of them tumbled to the ground. For a breath-stealing moment they wrestled, and then Harry was on top, pinning the other man down.

The Jack Russell reached them before I did and jumped on to Harry's leg. He dug his stumpy legs into Harry's jeans and tried to sink his teeth into his thigh and bark at the same time.

I snatched the dog off of Harry. 'Who is

this guy?' I demanded, holding the squirming, barking, snapping animal as tightly as I could.

'I don't believe you had the balls to stay in the country,' Harry growled into the man's face. 'You knew what I'd do to you if I ever saw you again.'

'I — I'm visiting my mother,' the man gasped. 'She just moved to Scunthorpe.'

'Why'd you do it? Why'd you set me up?' Harry's voice was wilder than I'd ever heard it. His hands were white-knuckled on the man's shoulders.

Harry Blake, the eternally cool, the always comfortable, was on the verge of losing it.

'Holy shit, is this the guy who gave you that fake memo and made you lose your job?' I asked.

'And everything else,' Harry gritted. 'Why did you do it, Spencer?'

'I got paid lots of money, of course,' Spencer said, and then yelped as one of Harry's hands closed on his throat.

'Harry!' I cried. I wanted to touch him, to calm him somehow, but my hands were full of dog. 'Please don't kill this guy, it's not worth it. Please, Harry.'

Harry didn't appear to hear me, but after a moment he hauled the guy to his feet.

'Walk,' he said, twisting Spencer's arm

244

behind his back and holding it tight.

'Do you think you might let me go?' Spencer asked as they walked towards the park bench we'd vacated, with me following.

'After I've got some answers.'

Both Harry and Spencer were breathing hard; clouds puffed from their mouths as they walked. I looked around the park. There wasn't anybody else in sight.

Harry pushed Spencer down on to the bench and sat beside him, still holding his arm. 'All right. Tell me who paid you to give me that forged memo.'

'Why should I?'

The Jack Russell writhed its compact body, scratching me with its blunt claws and snarling and snapping at my face.

Jesus. The thing was a miniature canine Jaws. I wrestled with it until I found a position that worked: my arm around its back legs, pinning them, and my other hand gripping the scruff of its neck.

'You're not going to hurt my mother's dog, are you?' Spencer asked.

'Don't be stupid, I wouldn't hurt an innocent dog,' I said. 'You, though, you're an asshole. I'd be happy if Harry broke both of your legs.'

'Who was it?' Harry said. 'Was it Greene?'

Spencer's laugh was cut off by a gasp of

pain as Harry wrenched his arm. 'Why would an MP pay me to publish something that put his own reputation at risk?' he said when he got his breath back.

'I trusted you,' said Harry, and he sounded so sad and angry that I wanted to drop the dog. 'We risked a lot for each other. And you did it for money?'

'It was a hell of a lot of money. And you were easy to trick. Like a knight in fucking armour, too busy looking for the next crusade of truth to see what was under your nose.' Spencer let out a laugh, half a giggle, strange coming from a middle-aged man.

I looked around the park again. 'The coast is clear, Harry. You can hurt him if you want.'

'I don't need to hurt him. He's going to tell me who paid him.'

Spencer snorted. 'Why, do you have a lot of money to pay me too?'

'I'll tell you what I've got. Desperation.' Harry spoke quietly into Spencer's ear. 'Greene's had everything out of me. My job, my money, my life. But he's bored and he's looking for someone else to sue. And I can track you down now, Spencer. Your mother didn't know where you'd gone three years ago. But she does now. And I can find out her address within ten minutes.'

The dog barked. I tightened my grip on it

and strained my ears to hear every word Harry was saying.

'I was too distracted by my world collapsing around me to find you before. It won't happen again. And when I find you, I'll make sure you get indicted for fraud. And then I'll open you up for Warren Greene MP and his dozens of lawyers.'

It was very quiet. Even Jaws Junior shut up.

'You know I can do it,' Harry said. 'I've got nothing to lose.'

I felt the dog's rapid heartbeat against my chest. I think mine was going as fast.

'Marcus Wilson,' Spencer said. 'I don't owe the fucker anything; he stopped paying me two years ago. Can I have my mother's dog back now, please?'

Harry didn't say anything. He let go of Spencer. Spencer stood up and shook his arm from the shoulder.

'Marcus Wilson,' Harry repeated. 'Saint Wilson. What does he have to do with Warren Greene?'

'Nothing. Greene was bait. Everybody knew you were dying to bust him. Wilson knew if you were offered a story about Greene, you'd take it. And you did.'

Spencer held his hands out for the dog. I looked at Harry. The moonlight and street-light only lit up half of his face, but I could see him thinking, making connections, searching for the truth.

I handed over Jaws Junior. 'You're scum, and you should get this thing a muzzle.'

'Nice to meet you too,' said Spencer. 'I hope the two of you are very happy together.' He walked away as fast as he could, holding the dog, trailing the leash behind them.

'Harry.' I sat beside him. 'Are you okay? Who's Marcus Wilson?'

He didn't appear to see me. He was breathing rapidly, and his eyes were focused on a point far away.

I touched his hand where it lay on the bench. 'I think we did pretty well with that.'

I could feel him tense and trembling. He looked down at his hand, with mine on top of it.

He pulled his hand away.

'Harry?'

He stood up.

'Houdini? You all right?' I stood too.

He looked at me. In the orange light, his blue eyes were an uncertain colour.

'Let's find a cab,' he said.

'Sure.' I walked beside him to the park entrance. He made no move to touch me, so I made no move to touch him.

He hadn't been able to keep his hands off me for the past week. Even before that, whenever the opportunity arose. But he was upset; I could understand why sex was the last thing on his mind.

I thought about how I'd rested my head on his chest after my sad show, and I shoved my hands into the pockets of my jacket.

Harry flagged down a passing cab, and when it stopped, he opened the door for me. He was always doing that — opening doors, stepping aside to let me enter rooms first — so I didn't think twice about it until I sat down on the back seat and noticed he hadn't climbed in after me. He shut the taxi door.

I heard him telling the driver the name of our hotel through the open front window, and giving him money. I scooted over to the side where he was and rolled my window down.

'Aren't you coming?' I asked.

'I need to be alone,' he said.

'Hold on.' I opened the cab door and got out. 'Houdini. Not so fast.'

He'd begun to walk away already. 'Rosie, I said — ' he began.

'No. Wait a second.' I stood with my hands on my hips. My breath puffed out. I felt mad enough to be breathing steam.

'You don't get to brush me off,' I said. 'The whole thing with this Spencer guy and this Wilson guy might be none of my business, but I'm here. I'm involved. I kept that damn dog from chewing off your ass.'

'Rosie, you don't — '

'Shut up. You've pried into every area of my life that you possibly can. And you're sleeping with me, Harry. We're friends. You owe me some honesty.'

I felt that he owed me more than honesty, though I couldn't have said exactly what.

Harry looked at me for a long time, his forehead creased, his eyebrows drawn together in a frown. As if he were concentrating fiercely on every part of my face.

Finally he nodded, though it looked more like he had come to a decision than like he was agreeing with me. He took a long, deep breath, and then let it out in a plume of mist.

'Okay,' he said. 'You're right. I should be honest with you.' He raised his hand to his forehead and rubbed it, as if to get rid of his frown. 'But not tonight, Rosie. I need to think. Tomorrow, all right? We'll talk tomorrow morning.'

I didn't know what to do with my hands, with my words, with myself. I couldn't argue with his desire to leave me.

'Take the cab,' he said. And then he walked away.

25

My hair was frizzing from the damp evening air. I smelled of dog. I had smears of mud and grass on my clothes. A hot bath was probably the best thing.

Instead, when I got back to the hotel, I went to Gina's room. The morning was a long way away. I didn't want to be alone. And I wanted to know why Gina had run out of my show.

When I got there, Max was sitting on the carpet in the corridor, his back against the wall beside the door. 'Hey,' he greeted me.

'Is Gina all right?' I asked.

'No. She wanted to be alone. I told her I was going to the bar, but I ended up staying here. Thought maybe I could do some good.' He wrapped his woolly scarf tighter around his neck. 'I'm mostly getting a sore arse.'

'Can you hear anything?'

He shrugged. 'She took a shower.' He held out a key-card to me. 'Here, you try. You're a bird, you might have better luck.'

Gina was sitting on the bed applying makeup with the help of a compact mirror. When I stepped inside, she looked up,

251

mascara wand in hand. 'Rosie? What are you doing here?'

'I wanted to see if you were all right. I got a little worried when you ran out of my show.' I sat beside her on the bed, and she stiffened even more.

'It was nothing,' she said.

'You looked awful. I've never seen you run out of a room full of people before.'

'I'm fine now.'

I watched her apply mascara to her left eye, as precisely and coldly as she did everything when she was around me. With every small stroke of the wand on her lashes she built up the silence between us.

'You're hurting about something,' I said. 'Let me help you. I can help people heal. It's what I do.' I reached out to touch her, and she flinched away.

'Don't,' she said.

'You don't want me to touch you because you think I might see something about you,' I said, and then I knew: her secret, her distance from me, why she'd run out, everything.

'You think I might contact your dead baby.'

Gina dropped her mirror and her mascara as she stood up. The wand made a dark blotch on the carpet. 'Stop.'

But I was right.

'Losing your child was your one failure, wasn't it, Gina? And every single thing you do — the perfect clothes, the perfect makeup, your travel iron, your mobile phone with you all the time — it's to prove you're not a failure any more. Because if you can succeed at everything else, maybe it wasn't your fault your baby died.'

It came out of me in a triumphant rush. I stood too, facing Gina, the puzzle pieces fitting together in my head, not even having to guess or play the chances. I felt light, exultant, as if I were full of helium, as if the world were in the palm of my hand.

'What has he said to you?'

Her voice was a broken whisper.

I blinked and saw the woman whose mind I'd been reading. Her face had lost all its colour under its makeup; her eyes were wide, her mouth, not yet lipsticked, slack. She looked like a very scared young girl.

Oh, shit.

This wasn't a Win/Win game. This was a violation.

I sank back down on to the bed. 'I am so, so sorry.'

'You talked to that baby tonight, so they can talk. What did he say? What did he tell you about me?'

She stood completely still. A tear ran down

one of her cheeks, taking a black smear of mascara with it.

'Gina, I — '

She knelt on the bed beside me and took my hands in hers. Her fingers were like ice. 'Tell me. What does he say? I was only eighteen. I wanted a different life. But I didn't want him to die. Does he know that?'

'Gina, I'm sorry. It wasn't your fault.'

'Talk to him,' she said, and gripped my hands harder.

Gently I took my hands away. 'You can talk to him yourself, Gina. If you want him to, he'll hear you.'

I stood and left her there. I'd manipulated her and prodded her and seen her as a challenge. I wasn't the one who could offer her comfort.

Max was still sitting on the floor in the hallway, wrapped in his soft woollen scarf. He rose when I came out the door. 'I think she needs you,' I said to him.

On my way back to my room, I paused at Harry's door. I raised my hand to knock, to see if he'd come back yet, and then forced myself to shake my head and go to bed alone.

26

For a whole week I'd had Harry sleeping with me every night. He was the type who curled around you, breathed into your hair, and protected you with his sleeping body. I felt unanchored. I had uneasy dreams.

When I opened my eyes, the clock beside my bed said 9.27. I pushed myself out from underneath the covers and into the bathroom. A hot shower helped. Then I stood in front of my suitcase and wondered why I was worrying about what to wear to talk with somebody who'd seen me with no makeup and morning breath and hadn't seemed to care.

I threw on jeans and a V-neck shirt that I knew flattered my figure, put on makeup and brushed my teeth. Then I went down the corridor to Harry's room.

'Come in,' he replied to my knock. When I walked in, he was at the hotel-room desk, tapping at his laptop. He was wearing the same clothes as last night. His chin and cheeks had a blur of blond stubble. His bags were packed and waiting on his untouched bed. He stood as I entered.

'Rosie,' he said, running his hand through his hair. It looked like he'd been doing that all night. 'I was going to find you in a minute. I'm leaving.'

I nodded. Yeah, of course. He had his whole life to sort out. Other than great sex and a couple of articles, why would he bother to stay with me?

'Going to find the guy who paid Spencer to give you the memo?' I asked nonchalantly.

'Marcus Wilson. Yes.' He felt his unshaven face. 'Please excuse the way I look. I haven't slept.'

'I can tell.' He looked gorgeous. And, after all the tenseness of last night, he seemed to be his normal relaxed self again. Unlike me. I felt empty-stomached, wanting.

'Who's Marcus Wilson, and why did he want you to lose your job?' I asked.

'I suppose he's not so famous in America.' He gestured to the bed for me to sit down. I did. He stayed standing.

'Marcus Wilson is a philanthropist,' he said. 'He's the heir to the Wilson pharmaceutical empire, which he sold for an enormous amount of money when he was in his thirties so he could set up a charitable organisation to help sick children. Heaven's Hope Foundation. Heard of it?'

'That, I've heard of.' I crossed my legs and

hugged them to my chest, to stop myself from getting up and doing something uncool. Like taking Harry's beard-stubbled face in my hands and making him look at me again like he'd been looking at me for the past week.

'The press calls him 'Saint Wilson',' Harry said. 'His foundation raises millions of pounds a year to help research treatments for childhood disease. He's Princess Diana and Bob Geldof rolled into one. He's good-looking and adored by the public.'

'And this is the guy who paid a lot of money to get you discredited? What does he have against you?'

Harry leaned back against the desk and crossed his arms. 'I think the real question is what I might have had against him. He never struck me true for some reason. I don't know why. Instinct. I was poking around, feeling out some investigative lines about him, and for months I kept on coming up against blank walls. Receiving polite advice to back away, from some quite powerful people.'

'What had you found out about him?'

'Nothing. At least, not yet. I knew there was something, though. I'd got hold of a lead, a former employee, and I was about to follow it up. And then Spencer passed me that memo.'

'You're thinking that maybe you were on the brink of discovering something.'

'And he wanted to stop me. That's right.'

'So you're leaving to pick up your investigation where you left off. To clear your reputation.'

'Yes. Though that's not the only reason.' He tugged on his hair as if he wanted to put it in order. 'I want to know the truth. I want to know what really happened.'

'Of course you do. Plus, if you can get a really big story on him, something spectacular, maybe *The Times* will give you your job back.'

For the first time since I'd come into the room, Harry looked straight into my face and smiled. It was the smile he'd given me on the first morning we woke up together. Warm. Real. A little bit surprised. He came and sat down beside me on the bed.

'I said I'd be honest with you,' he said. 'When I first heard about your train crash prediction, I thought you might be a story like that. Something big enough to get my career back. I suspected that you might have caused the crash in some way, for publicity.'

'You what?' I gaped at him, but he was still smiling.

'My opinion of psychics was not high.' He reached over and stroked a lock of my hair behind my ear. 'When I met you, I knew you hadn't done it.'

'Well, that's a relief,' I said, but the thought that Harry had suspected me, even for a second, was disturbing.

'You cared too much. You feel other people's pain as much as you feel your own. I knew that as soon as I saw you backstage in Birmingham, the night after the crash.'

I laughed uneasily. 'I thought I'd hidden how upset I was.'

'You're not very good at hiding things, Rosie. Not from somebody who knows how to look.' Harry took my hand in his. 'But you're very good at hiding things from yourself, I think. You don't know why you're here in England, do you?'

I narrowed my eyes at him. 'I've got a tour here. What do you mean?'

He held my hand up toward the ceiling, and then brought it to his lips. ''Here goes nothing',' he said.

'Harry. Do you mind telling me what on earth you are talking about?'

'I'm talking about the toast you do to your dead father before every single show.'

I pulled away from him. 'That's not a toast to my father. It's a ritual, to — '

'To connect with your dead father before you go on stage. Why do you drink whisky?

259

You don't like it. It makes you gag. Why not vodka, or gin, or grape juice?'

'It was the only thing they had backstage before my first show. Years ago. It got to be a habit. It helps me get more receptive to the spirits.'

'Your father drank whisky, didn't he?'

My throat burned as if I'd downed a whole bottle. 'Yeah, but that's not — '

'And he was English, and here you are in England trying to find him. Even though he's dead. Every night you hope he'll talk to you. And he doesn't.'

I stood up. 'I'm here in England because Gina arranged a tour.'

Harry shook his head. 'It's about more than the job, Rosie. I saw you in that chip shop reciting the 'Our Father' and holding back tears. I saw you when Fantastic Frederick said he had a message from your dad. He left you, and you want to know why.'

An ache, a punch to the gut, stealing my breath.

'How do you know this stuff?' I whispered.

He stood and moved close enough so I could feel him imprinted on my body. The touch-memory of all we had done. He smoothed my hair with his fingers.

'It's what I do,' he said. 'It's my job to know these things.'

He ran his thumb against my mouth, slow and tender. He held my chin in his hand and kissed my skin with his breath.

'Just like I know you're a fake,' he said.

27

I was up against the desk anyway. I couldn't back up any more.

'No you don't,' I said.

'I do.'

He was way, way, way too close. I slipped out of his gentle embrace, ducked under his arm, and retreated to the other side of the room.

'You can't prove it,' I said.

'I can.'

'I am not a fake.'

I was rattled from the stuff he'd said about my father. That was the reason why I sounded like an idiot. Obviously.

Harry held up his hands. 'You asked me to be honest, Rosie. I am. I think it's time you stopped lying to me.'

'Houdini, I know you're very clever. And you're trying to rattle me. But I thought we'd gone beyond this, you and me.'

'We have. And that's why I'm telling you I know you're a fake.'

My laugh was the fakest thing ever. 'What are you trying to do, Harry? Write a killer article? I thought Marcus Wilson was the ticket for getting your career back. Not me.'

'My career has nothing to do with it. Not any more.' He sat on the desk in that completely comfortable way he had. 'This is about your career. The one based on the assumption that you have supernatural powers. And you don't.'

I perched on the side of the bed and willed my muscles to look relaxed.

'How do you figure I do everything I do?' I asked. 'Hidden transmitters? Stooges in the audience? Someone dressed up in a sheet? Go ahead, I'd love to hear your theories.'

'I don't have theories, I have facts. You don't need stooges or transmitters, although you may have used them in the past, before I started following you. You use a combination of inspired guesswork, audience feedback, and statements that are vague enough to apply to many different people. You manipulate your audiences into the best frame of mind for believing in you, and you give them exactly what they want to hear so that they have an investment in trusting you. It's the same trick every psychic uses, only you're charming and beautiful and a born actress. And you care. It's a brilliant combination.'

I rolled my eyes and shook my head. 'Houdini, you're going to have to do better than that. You can't prove any of this stuff.

And it doesn't explain my train crash prediction.'

'I've already worked out your train crash prediction,' he said. He came and sat beside me on the bed. I turned sideways so I could look him full in the face, show him I wasn't scared of him.

Though I was.

'I'm sorry, Rosie,' he said, his voice soft. 'I like your act. I like how you use it to try to cover up how you really feel. It's one of the reasons I'm so attracted to you. But your feelings about your father don't mean that you should be lying to other people about their dead relatives.'

'Harry, I honestly do not know what you're talking about. I didn't fake that prediction about the nine twenty-seven to Swansea. I'm not lying.'

'Rosie,' Harry said. He put his hand on the bed and leaned toward me. 'Rosalyn. I know about your father's shop. At nine-two-seven Swansea Road.'

If I hadn't been sitting down, I would have fallen over.

Nine-two-seven Swansea Road, Worcester, Massachusetts, USA. Markovitz's General Store and Deli, between a drugstore and a dry cleaner's. Corned beef, chopped liver, Hebrew National hot dogs in a glass counter at the back. Rows of kosher dills in jars, matzoh ball mix, gefilte fish and toilet paper. At the front, red liquorice shoestrings in a plastic-lined box, and my Anglican father with his hand on a bottle of Wild Turkey, touching it like a friend.

It was the fact in the back of my mind, forgotten until the moment Harry said it, like the big Muppet's name on the train from Milton Keynes. And now it was a huge, blinding certainty, something that was as much a part of me as the deaths of those six people had become.

I didn't say anything. I was seeing the 927 in black numbers on gold stickers on the glass door, and smelling whisky and red candy and dust. Harry must have thought I was trying to think up a denial.

'You guessed,' he said. 'You were thinking of your father, as you often do, and you saw a woman with her bag packed and you knew the theatre was close to the train station. You pulled a number and a place out of your memory and did something dramatic. If you'd stopped that train, or even delayed it by a minute, you could have claimed you'd averted a disaster, and had a room and a platform full of witnesses. As it was . . . you guessed right.'

I shook my head. It hadn't been a guess.

Harry was right about my father's shop, but that was a coincidence, or a cosmic joke. The prediction was true. It just happened to be connected to my father.

It seemed like a lot of things were.

I blinked and swallowed. 'I didn't think I thought about my father that much,' I said. 'He was a drunk. He was never there even when he was alive.'

Harry looked as if he was about to say something else, but he paused, his eyes intent on my face as if he were reading me. He sat back. 'You didn't know where you'd got the number and place, did you? You thought you'd taken a random guess.'

'No,' I said. 'I knew that train was going to crash. I was absolutely certain of it. I was terrified. It was one of the most real feelings I've ever had.'

I stared at the bedspread. Before, I'd been afraid of Harry finding out my secret, of losing my job. But now I felt as though I was losing a lot more.

'You don't believe me, though,' I said.

Harry stood up and put his hands in the pockets of his jeans. 'The facts speak for themselves.' He walked around the desk and closed his laptop.

'I wrote an article for *Amazing News* last night explaining what I've discovered about you,' he said, his voice detached. 'I emailed it to my editor this morning.' He opened up his case and slid the laptop into it.

'It'll be printed in Thursday's edition, and of course the nationals will pick it up after that. You've got a week left of your career. It's up to you whether you cancel your shows up till then. I wouldn't blame you for carrying on for as long as you can, and you're not doing anybody any actual harm. But I can't let you go on telling lies indefinitely. I'm sorry.'

He was *sorry*? For ruining my career and dumping me on my ass?

Forget sad. I was angry. I was furious. I wasn't going to let Harry do this to me without a fight. I jumped to my feet.

'That's bullshit, Harry, and you know it. You can't prove anything. Just because I could have done it with guesswork doesn't mean I did. You don't have anything more on me than you ever have.' I swiped my hair out of my eyes, and added, 'If you wanted to end things between us, you could've picked a hell of a more honest way.'

My voice was loud and harsh, but Harry continued winding up cables, packing them, and buckling up his laptop case.

'I have proof,' he said.

'And what might that be?'

'It was on national television. During the

Hallowe'en seance there was a nightclub owner ogling you all night. I knew you wouldn't be able to resist somebody like that. Remember you told him his dead mother sent her best wishes and a message that he should keep his hands to himself? His mother ran the London Marathon this year. She's the healthiest eighty-year-old I know.'

I clenched my fists.

'You set me up,' I said.

'I put information where you were likely to find it, if you were cheating. You chose to use it.' Harry shrugged. 'You set yourself up.'

He was being so casual, so self-assured.

'Uh-uh. You set me up. And on that same night you saw me fall for your lies, you slept with me. You . . . ' I stepped back, baffled at his betrayal. 'I trusted you.'

'Come on, Rosie. Don't play righteous.' His voice sounded reasonable, but he raked one hand through his hair. 'You were lying to me too. You've been lying to me all along. That didn't stop you from sleeping with me. The only difference is that I already knew you were lying.'

'No. I was doing my job. I wasn't lying to you. I couldn't. I tried — '

I stopped myself. I couldn't tell him about the Houdini lie. It would be more evidence for his smug *Amazing News* article.

'You fed me information and knew I'd take it,' I said. 'You did to me exactly what Spencer did to you. God!' I threw my hands up in the air. 'And I was feeling bad for you, Harry, I was on your side when you found Spencer. But you're the same. Except you did it to a woman and then took her to bed. You're . . . '

I dropped my hands. 'I thought you were one of the good guys.'

'I'm sorry you feel that way.' I had never heard Harry's voice so clipped, so proper. 'It isn't the same thing, of course. I've never been a conscious fraud, and I haven't been lying to people more or less constantly for the past eight years, as you have. But you should feel free to think anything that makes you feel better.'

He slung his laptop case on to his shoulder and picked up his jacket from the chair. 'If you don't mind, I've got to catch a train to London.'

He was every inch the cold British gentleman as he walked to the bed and picked up his packed bags. Every wrinkle of his clothes was exactly where it was meant to be, his posture was elegant, and his face was perfectly impassive.

He'd lied to me about a lot more than the nightclub owner's mother. He'd lied with every touch, every smile, the banter between us, every time he'd met my eyes and made me feel like laughing out loud. Every kiss in the night, every whispered desire, the way he protected me with his body as he slept.

God, he had lied to me in his sleep.

I hurled myself between him and the door. 'Not so fast. We're not finished talking about this.'

'You're too upset to talk.'

'Harry, I am never too upset to talk. If you haven't learned that yet, you're a lousy reporter.'

The smallest of smiles softened his mouth. 'I have noticed that.' He put his bags down. 'Rosie, I'm sorry about what this article will do to you. But I don't have a choice in the matter. The truth is the truth, and it's got to come out. It isn't personal.'

His clipped tone was gone, but my anger wasn't.

'You bet it's personal, Houdini,' I said. 'You've known about this for a week. How come you've only written the article now? You delayed the all-important truth for a week so you could spend a little time fucking me?'

He winced a little at the verb. I'd meant him to.

'I wasn't planning on writing the article at all,' he said. 'Once I knew the truth, I was going to keep it to myself. I like you, and you weren't doing any harm, and I genuinely believe that you do most of what you do for unselfish motives. Maybe I shouldn't have got involved with you.'

'Don't use euphemisms. You had sex with me.'

'All right. I shouldn't have had sex with you, knowing what I knew. But I wanted to, Rosie. I really wanted to.' He scrubbed his face with his hand; I could hear his palm rasping against the shadow of beard stubble. 'I still want to.'

And just like that, my body yearned for him so intensely that I felt as if we were already touching, as if he were moving inside of me. I wanted him as much as the first time we'd had sex.

No. No euphemisms. Made love.

I had to blink, hard, to hold back the tears.

He hadn't made a single move towards me, but I stepped away anyway. 'I can't,' I said. 'Not any more.'

'No. I can't either. Seeing Spencer last night made me realise what lies can do, what they've done to me. You're making money out of deceiving people, and that's wrong, no matter how I feel about you.'

He took a deep breath and sighed it out, and for the first time since I'd walked in the room, he looked tired.

'You know what I lost, Rosie,' he said. 'My principles are all that I've got left.'

You had me, I thought.

I wasn't going to cry in front of Harry. It was far, far too easy for him to read my emotions, and I didn't want him to read this one.

'I'm sorry,' he said.

'Get out.' I stepped aside, holding my head high, my body straight and proud. He picked up his bags again.

As he passed me and went out the door, I breathed his smell.

Effortlessly right. And totally wrong.

28

I hated my father. He was a drunk. He was a coward. He couldn't keep down a job unless his in-laws gave it to him. He never made it to any of my school plays, or heard my teachers talking about what a good student I was. For as long as I could remember he had promised me we would move out of Worcester, go to England, make a new start, just the three of us; we'd be happy. We never even got out of the state.

While he was alive, he reduced my mother to a woman who nagged and pretended, who had fights with her parents behind closed doors, who found fault with me whenever she could, who cried in the evening, hiding her face behind the *TV Guide*. When he was dead, he made sure that I couldn't talk with her, so strong was my resentment of her love for that photograph and the fictional memory.

I loved him more than anything in the world.

One Thanksgiving vacation, when I was still at U Mass, I went out for a walk after my mother's dry turkey and my grandparents'

273

questions about what kind of a job I was going to get with a degree in ancient history, for God's sake, and why I couldn't've studied something in business. I'd started charging money for tarot readings the week before. I had eighty-four dollars cash in my pocket and I was wondering where I could get a bus to on a holiday.

I walked into Malone's bar before I even knew I meant to do it.

'You twenty-one?' grunted the big-bellied bald man behind the bar. Malone, I guessed, though there was no Irish brogue, only wide Massachusetts vowels.

'Twenty-three,' I lied, and sat on a stool, leaning on the sticky bar top. The place was a smoke-hazy cave of red vinyl and fake wood panelling. A Guinness sign lit up the taps and the rows of whisky on the back shelves. I wondered which one my father had drunk.

'A Guinness, please,' I said, and watched Malone pour the black liquid into a glass. He stopped the flow when the glass was two thirds full and came back to my end of the bar. There were six or seven people in the room, all male, mostly sitting at the bar. Malone stood, his arms crossed over his fat belly, and studied me. I kept my chin up and my eyes steady and rather bored, as if I'd walked into scruffy Irish joints every

Thanksgiving of my life.

'Do I know you?' he asked. 'You look awful familiar.' It didn't sound quite like a come-on line, but it could be one.

'Don't think so,' I answered, my voice friendly but neutral. 'I've never been in here before.'

He shrugged and grunted, and went back to pour the rest of my drink. When he put it in front of me it had a shamrock drawn in the creamy foam on top. I was surprised at the nicety, in this place.

I took a sip. I'd never had Guinness before. The foam was velvet on my lips, the liquid cold silk on my tongue. It tasted richer than my mother's turkey gravy.

When I looked up, Malone was still staring at me. 'No offence,' he said when our eyes met. 'It's that you look so familiar.' He gestured towards his face with his stubby hand. 'Your hair, and your face. Your eyes, I guess.'

I took another sip of Guinness. 'You might remember my father, he used to come in here a lot. Ed Jones.'

The smile broke over Malone's face like a sunrise. 'Ed? You Ed's daughter? Rosalyn? Hell, no wonder I recognise you. He had his picture of you out of his wallet every night.' He held his hand out to me and I shook it. It

275

was softer than I'd expected.

He was nodding enthusiastically. 'You were a kid in that picture. You still have that same hair, though. Dark, curly. Nice. Ed talked about you all the time, what a pretty daughter he had.'

'He did?'

'Charlie! Glen! Come over here and meet Ed's daughter, Rosalyn Jones.' Malone beckoned to two of the drinkers and they came over and shook my hand, bathing me in their beery breath and their sympathy for my father's death seven years before. They told me what a good guy he was, what a good listener. They talked about his accent, and his great stories about London, and his inability to understand American football.

These two men, drinking in the afternoon on Thanksgiving Day, knew more about my father than I did.

Malone laughed. 'You're full of crap, Rosalyn. You're not legal age yet, you must be, what, twenty?' He tapped the side of my glass. 'It's okay, though, I don't mind. I remember when you were born. Ed was buying all night. He must've dropped three or four hundred bucks. He was so proud of you.'

The Guinness had started to taste bitter. I finished it, and I listened to stories, and I thought about all the hours my father had spent with these people while I was born and grew up and waited for him.

'He really loved you, Roz,' Charlie said, gripping my shoulder, wiping at his blurry eye. 'Said you were his princess. Malone, let me buy Roz another drink.'

'No thanks,' I said, and I made my excuses and left these men, who only wanted to please me, to their bar and their memories.

I started the tarot readings in earnest after that, and then seances, and after I finished college I didn't get the job my grandparents thought was so important but instead travelled from psychic fair to carnival and learned to tell people exactly what they wanted to hear.

But I didn't listen for what *I* needed to hear in what they told me.

★ ★ ★

After Harry left me, I walked for hours around Scunthorpe. I didn't see where I was going, I just looked up enough to avoid being hit by cars.

Harry was right about one thing. I'd chosen my career because of my dad. I hadn't known it; I hadn't believed in life after death. I thought I'd done it for the attention, for the risk, because I was good at it, because it helped other people. And all of those reasons were true.

But I still did it for him.

The couple who were walking in front of me went into a pub, and I followed them. The pub was clean and bright, with shiny brass things on the walls.

'Half a pint of Guinness,' I said to the bartender, 'and a whisky, no ice.'

'Any particular whisky?' he asked. I looked at the rows of bottles on bright mirrored shelves.

'Whatever the best one is,' I said.

I took my drinks to a table in the corner. I held the glass of amber liquid up to the ceiling in a toast to heaven.

'Thanks for trying to save those six people,' I said. I wasn't sure whether I was talking to my father or to myself — whether my one glimpse into the future had come from beyond the grave, or from the depths of my own subconscious.

I wasn't sure whether it really mattered.

I took a deep breath and downed the whisky, and I felt its fire in my belly and throat.

And then slowly, sip by sip, I drank my Guinness and thought about all the messages my father had left me, while he was living and after he was dead.

29

When I got back to the hotel, I went straight to Gina's room and knocked, bracing myself for her anger.

When she opened the door she was dressed, but she didn't have her makeup on. Behind her I could see what looked like Max's bare leg sticking out of the end of the bed.

'What's wrong?' she said immediately.

'Jeez. Anybody would think you're the psychic.' The old line fell flat.

She frowned. At least she didn't look angry. 'You look like hell and you smell like a pub. Are you all right?'

'No, not really,' I said. 'Listen, Gina, I have to tell you something very important and I need to take you out to lunch to do it.'

'Why do you have to take me out to lunch?'

'Because if we're in a public restaurant it's less likely you'll hit me.'

Max appeared behind Gina. He was wearing a white bathrobe and his brown hair looked tangled. 'Hey, can I come too? I'm always intrigued by a good catfight.' He put his arm around Gina's shoulder and she leaned against him.

'Gina looked looser, clear-eyed. Obviously Max had been able to give her some comfort. She checked her watch. 'We've got to get to Hull this afternoon for your show tonight. It's not far, but — '

'Don't worry about getting to Hull. Honestly. That's going to be the last thing on your mind. I'll meet you in the lobby in fifteen minutes, all right?'

I spent the next fifteen minutes getting a restaurant recommendation from the front desk and then prowling the lobby.

What was I going to say?

Hey, I didn't really talk to your dead baby, I just manipulated you into telling me your deepest, darkest secret, and by the way, you now look like a fraud too. No hard feelings?

I threw myself into one of the chintz armchairs scattered through the lobby. 'Maybe I should catch a plane home,' I muttered. 'Clear out of here and let the shit hit the fan without me. Nobody in America's going to care about a fourth-rate English newspaper like *Amazing News*.'

But it was bravado. Even before I said it I knew I couldn't do it. I owed Gina the truth.

'Where's Harry?' Gina asked when she and Max came down. 'I though you two were attached at the hip these days.'

'He's gone,' I said, and Max, with the rock-star sixth sense he seemed to have when a distraction was needed, leapt in with a long-winded story about this weekend he'd once spent in Spain, filling up the silence as we drove to the restaurant so that Gina couldn't ask me what was wrong before I was ready to say it. And I wasn't ready to say it, not until we were seated around a table in an Italian restaurant, and we'd ordered, and I'd toyed with the breadsticks and my glass of mineral water and the bottle of olive oil on the table and there wasn't anything else to do.

'Okay,' I said. 'Here it is. I can't really talk with dead people.'

What finesse. What tact and delicacy. I fixed my eyes on the checked tablecloth and ploughed on.

'I've been faking it for years. I guess at things. You know, play the odds, say obvious things that fit most people, get all vague about when things actually happen, manipulate people's answers. I'm not really psychic. Just a good con woman.'

Total silence from the rest of the table.

'So Harry found this out. And he's sent an article to his editor about it. He says it'll be published a week from today. So we're going to have to cancel the rest of the tour.'

The silence stretched out. And out. I stared

and stared at the tablecloth and I felt very small. Not small enough to disappear, though. Unfortunately.

'I'm sorry I let you down. It wasn't on purpose, although really I guess it was, because I've been lying to you. And I should've taken your advice, Gina, and got rid of Harry a long time ago, but I — '

The tears I'd swallowed in Harry's room filled my eyes and clogged my throat. I wiped my face with my hand and kept on talking, my eyes low and wet.

'I liked him. And anyway it's not Harry's fault that I lied to you, it's mine. I'm sorry.'

I stood. The wooden chair scraped against the wooden floor. I couldn't look at the others; I couldn't make myself see how they felt about me.

When it came down to it, my father and I had a lot in common. We were both liars, and we were both cowards.

I turned to leave, but before I could get to the door my eyes filled with tears and I couldn't see anything, so I stopped.

I heard another chair scrape back and then I felt Gina's arms around me.

It was a messy cry, a sobbing, sniffing, racking wet cry. I could feel myself leaving a damp patch on Gina's perfect jacket. She stood there and held me and stroked my back and let me use her clothes for Kleenex. Eventually, I subsided into hiccups and sniffles.

'Excuse me,' a voice said beside us. Gina and I looked over to see the Italian waiter.

'I was wondering if you have stopped crying now, madam? Because the kitchen is holding your food.' He shrugged apologetically.

I glanced around the restaurant. All the other customers were looking at us. Hopefully there were no reporters among them.

'I'm done crying.'

'Okay. Good. I will tell the kitchen, thank you.'

For the first time, I dared to meet Gina's eyes.

'I'm sorry for what I did last night,' I said. 'I didn't mean to hurt you.'

She looked at me for a long time. Then she nodded, and took my hand, and led me back to the table.

I sat down beside her, still holding her hand. If Max joined the circle, we could have a good old-fashioned table-tipping seance. Though I'd never really liked table-tipping; I was too fond of delicate shoes. Table legs tended to put irreparable dents in your mules.

I guessed that was one thing I wasn't going

to have to worry about any more, at least.

The waiter brought our plates of pasta. Nobody made a move to touch them.

'I never said how I felt until I thought he was listening,' Gina said finally.

Now Max did reach over and take Gina's hand. 'He was listening, babe. Like Nick was listening to me last night. You can talk to the dead all you want. They don't mind. The trick is getting them to talk back to you.' He looked at me and winked. 'Without taking drugs,' he added.

The waiter moved around the table with a giant pepper mill, twisting it over our plates. He looked concerned that we weren't eating yet. When it was clear that none of us was going to pick up a fork in the immediate future, he retreated a short distance away, hovering and frowning.

'It's not bad going when you think about it,' Gina said. 'You're the most famous medium in Britain and you don't even have any psychic powers. That's quite impressive.'

I laughed wryly. 'I think I might be even more famous when Harry's article is published. People love it when somebody's career is ruined.'

I thought about how the news of Harry's career implosion had travelled all the way to North America.

I turned to Gina. 'You trusted me with your career and I blew it.'

'I'd still be advising people on mortgages and ISAs if you hadn't hit it big. You don't need to apologise for that.'

'At least you've still got Max's tour.'

'Yes. I've still got Max.' They exchanged a warm look. 'And I'd be very surprised if your career were over, Rosie.'

I shook my head vehemently. 'No. I'm not doing any more shows. I've had enough of lying to people. I've been found out; I'm stopping.'

'A woman of principles.' Max nodded. 'I like that.'

I let his words sink in. Principles. Looked like I had some, maybe, after all.

And as Harry had said, they were just about all that I had left.

'Is everything all right?' The waiter had clearly found it too difficult to stay away and was now hovering over our table. His frown had deepened to epic proportions.

'It's fine; we're being intense,' I told him. 'I think we need to appreciate this man's food,' I said to Gina and Max. Our hands loosed each other, and we picked up our forks.

I took a bite of my linguini alla marinara and smiled up at the waiter. 'Delicious.'

He waited until he'd received a similar reassurance from each of us before he went away, looking a lot happier.

'I'll cancel your shows, if that's what you want,' Gina said.

'Yes, that's what I want. It's going to cause trouble, isn't it?'

Max spoke up. 'I know what the tabloids are like. Harry's story isn't out till Thursday, but if you cancel the rest of your tour they're going to say something about it.'

'I suppose you could say you were sick,' Gina said.

'No. I want to stop lying. It doesn't make sense to tell a lie to stop lying.'

Gina considered. 'So what do you want me to tell the venues and the press?'

'Nothing. They'll find out on Thursday. Just cancel the shows, refund everyone's money.'

I could see the managerial part of Gina's mind ticking away. 'We could scoop Harry's story and sell an exclusive to a paper. Rosie Fox admits she's a fake. It could pre-empt the bad publicity and give you control and a lot more celebrity status.'

God, that would annoy him, I thought, and then I realised that it wouldn't. Harry had bigger fish to fry than Rosie Fox. He had Saint Wilson and his own crusade for the

286

truth. He'd look at any headlines about me and raise one eyebrow and smile an indulgent smile, thinking, *That was something I used to think I cared about . . .*

Anyway, what was the point of preserving celebrity, if all I wanted to do was tell the truth for a change?

'No,' I said again. 'I don't feel like getting into a media tug-of-war. The best thing is probably to lie low for a while and let the press speculate why I've cancelled my shows, and wait for Harry's news to come out.'

'You don't want to fight it?' Gina said.

'I don't want to fight Harry,' I replied, before I thought about it. But that was the way it was. It was like stealing candy from my father's shop: it had hurt when I thought he didn't notice or care. I didn't need to feel that all over again.

'I don't want to leave the country yet either,' I said. 'But I do need to get away somewhere. Out of Scunthorpe.'

'If you want to lie low, you can go to my llama farm in the Dales,' Max said. 'It's miles from anywhere.'

'A llama farm?'

'Yeah, babe. Fresh air, no pressures, big woolly animals. You'll love it.'

'That sounds like it would work,' I said. 'It

will keep me out of trouble anyway. Thanks, Max.'

He gave me a cheeky grin. 'Hey, doll, that's what friends are for.'

30

Fresh air. No pressures. Big woolly animals.

God, I was bored.

I shifted my backside on the window seat and looked outside at the acres of rolling fields, green even in November. Max was in one of the pastures with Gina. I could see him talking and gesturing as they approached a group of brown and cream llamas. She held out her hand and stroked one of them with the very tips of her fingers.

I had to admit it, Gina was doing well with the llamas. I'd tried to pet one of them the day before and it had spat at me. Max had assured me that it wasn't spitting at me, it was spitting at another llama and I'd just happened to be standing in its path, but I'd decided to keep away from them anyway.

That left watching television, or reading, or trying to learn how to knit llama wool. I'd only been here a day and a half and I was bored to tears with all of those options. The only place to walk to was the village miles down the road, and I couldn't even do that because there was a big photo of me on the front page of one of the tabloids and I didn't want to get spotted. Hopefully tomorrow there would be some real news to chase me out of the papers. I'd never wished so hard for a political scandal in my life.

I picked up one of the tabloids from the floor next to the window seat, and read the article about me again. It said I had MYSTERIOUSLY CANCELLED my sold-out UK tour, TOTALLY BAFFLING fans and raising speculation that I had INEXPLICABLY LOST my AMAZING PSYCHIC POWERS. It was accompanied by a photograph of me in my red dress, the night of the Hallowe'en seance.

They had the answer to my baffling behaviour right there, if they only knew it. That was the night that Harry Blake had set me up.

I sighed and shook my head. Having all this time on my hands meant I had leisure to think about two things: Harry Blake, and the loss of my career. The two things that I wanted least to think about.

For the first time in a long time, I had no role to play. I had nobody to be except myself. I couldn't be Rosie Fox, psychic, any more. And if I wasn't her, who was I? Rosalyn Markovitz Jones? I'd never known how to be her in the first place.

Had it been like this for Harry, I wondered, when he lost his job and his money and his car and his reputation and his life, and had to start all over again?

At least Harry could still *write*. Mentally I went through my CV. I could read tarot cards, pretend to talk with spirits, fake a variety of supernatural phenomena, and (once) predict a rail disaster. Only the last one was even remotely a marketable skill in today's fast-paced business life, and I never wanted to do it again as long as I lived.

I supposed I could type.

And what then? A nine-to-five job?

The prospect seemed so . . . boring. No shows, no risk, no audience. No Harry.

Really no Harry.

I sighed and opened the tabloid again. I needed distraction, mindless gossip, a horoscope to snigger at. I flipped through the pages, and stopped short.

SAINT WILSON'S HEAVENLY PARTY, said the headline, next to a picture of a man in a tuxedo. He was in his fifties, fit, tall, and handsome. Silver streaked his brown hair; his teeth were perfectly white. In his arms he held a child, about three years old, who wore a tinsel halo and a T-shirt with the Heaven's Hope logo.

'So you're the guy who screwed up Harry's

life,' I said to the photo, and began to read the article.

Ten minutes later I was striding across the pasture towards Max and Gina.

'I'm going to a party,' I announced when I was in earshot.

'Cool,' said Max, looking up from examining a llama's foot.

'A party?' Gina asked. 'I thought we were lying low.'

'I'm sick of lying low. It's better to go out with a bang than to fade away. I want to go to the Heaven's Hope charity ball tomorrow night in London.'

Gina frowned at me. She had a clump of llama dung on her shoe. I decided not to say anything.

'That ball will be crawling with reporters,' she said.

'I'll practise beforehand. Look.' I smiled dazzlingly at the imaginary cameras. 'No comment,' I said, waving away phantom journalists.

'I'm not sure this is the best move for your career.'

'What career? Come on, Gina, my career is deader than a dodo. I can at least have some fun. You're my manager, it's your job to get me a ticket.' I held up the article. 'The newspaper says it's not sold out yet.'

She looked worried. 'Tickets are going to be very expensive.'

'Do I have lots of money?'

'Well, a fair bit. But you've cancelled all those shows, and the column for *Cosmo*, and with nothing booked for the foreseeable future you should be caref — '

'I'm not a careful person. Come on, Gina, get me a ticket. I can afford it. It's for a good cause, right? Sick children?'

'Yes, but — '

'Gina.' I put my hands on my hips. 'I am going stir-crazy on this farm. There's nothing to do and the llamas all hate me.'

'Hey, they don't hate you,' said Max.

'Oh yeah? Why is that one humming at me?'

I wasn't joking. A big dark brown animal was staring at me through its long lashes and making a humming noise.

'She's just humming,' Max said. 'She's not humming at you. Relax, babe. The llamas can feel your fear.'

'Rosie.' Gina stepped between me and the humming llama and put her hands on her hips too. 'Why do you want to go to Marcus Wilson's charity ball?'

I regarded Gina. She didn't have a hair out of place. Her clothes were perfectly pressed and coordinated. Somehow, even the llama dung seemed to match. But I'd had practice now, and I could see the real concern for me in her perfectly made-up face.

'I need to find something out.'

'That's quite a vague answer.'

'Yeah, I know. But I can't tell you any more right now, it's not my secret to tell.'

She wasn't going to let me get away with that. 'Let me guess. Are you planning to do your psychic act one more time?'

'If I have to.'

'I thought you said you were through with lies.'

I bit my lip. 'I know. It's just . . . I want to help one more person. Then I'm done.'

Gina held my eyes with hers. 'Does this have anything to do with Harry Blake?'

I opened my mouth to say no, and then remembered I wasn't a fake any more. I shut my mouth, but Gina got all the confirmation she needed from the sheepish expression that was probably all over my face.

She frowned at me. 'I don't want to see you getting hurt, Rosie.'

'I won't.' I already was.

'He won't pull the exposé even if you do manage to help him. He's a reporter. The story comes first.'

'That's not why. I want to show him that I'm not just a con woman. I want to prove that even though my act's a lie, there's some value to it. I've helped lots of people. If I can help Harry, he won't be able to look down at me any more.'

And if he still looked down on me . . . well then screw Harry Blake. I'd have proved it to myself.

'You want him back.' Her voice was accusing, but sad.

I bit my lip again. God, lies would be a lot easier to deal with. 'No. I mean yes, I do, but I'm not stupid.'

'Are you sure?'

I sighed. 'I've spent my whole life loving a man I couldn't trust. I'm not going to do that again. Believe me. I want to even things out between us, and then I'm going to let him go.'

I saw the exact moment when Gina's face turned from stern to soft, when she decided to trust me.

'All right,' she said. 'I'll get you a ticket. But if you say anything to any of those reporters, I will feed you to these llamas.'

31

As soon as I walked through the door I was looking for Harry.

It was a stupid thing to do, I know — why on earth would Harry Blake come to a charity ball put on by the person who, if Spencer had told the truth, was his greatest enemy?

But intelligence had nothing to do with it. It was pure, dumb, helpless hope that made me stand at the side of the ornate ballroom and search the crowd of well-dressed people for a beacon of blond hair.

I craved the sight of him like my father had craved the whisky that killed him.

I took another look around, this time actually noticing my surroundings. The walls crawled with plaster ornamentation, the ceilings soared, the chandeliers hung like ice daggers. Vast flower arrangements filled the room with the scent of lilies. The whole place vibrated with beautiful, glamorous people laughing and sipping champagne.

I stood up straighter and took a quick look down at myself to make sure that my dress, or what there was of it, was covering the parts it was supposed to cover. I didn't have a shot of whisky, but I didn't need one any more.

I took a deep breath. *I am beautiful*, I told myself. *I am clever and perceptive, exotic and amazing. They will all love me.*

Marcus Wilson wasn't going to know what had hit him.

I wasn't the most beautiful woman in that room, not by a long shot. I recognised models and actresses, some of the most talented and gorgeous people on the planet.

But my hair tumbled around my shoulders like a gypsy princess's. My dress was of midnight silk, and I wore jewellery of moonstone and silver, cloudy and glimmering like a crystal ball. My three-inch-heeled shoes carried me as easily and as smoothly as enchanted slippers. My bracelets jingled soft music as I walked across the room.

And heads turned in my wake.

I was witchy, I was bewitching. I was different from everybody else. I had a bright red mouth and silver hoops dangled from my ears and *I could talk with the dead.*

I heard groups of people go quiet as I approached, and erupt into whispers after me. A few of the braver ones returned my smile.

'It's all a bunch of nonsense,' I heard one

woman say loudly. 'They say she's lost it anyway.'

I paused and made eye contact. Then I smiled enigmatically and moved on, leaving her silent and wondering what guarded secret I had lifted from her brain.

For a moment I felt sad. I was going to give up all of this power.

But not tonight. Tonight I had it in the palm of my hand.

I spotted Marcus Wilson holding court beside the champagne bar. I stood a little distance away from him, accepted a glass of champagne from the barman, and watched.

He was a very handsome man, in a classic style, like the hero of a black-and-white movie. He had a strong jaw and chiselled features and the silver hair at his temples made him look dignified and urbane. His formal clothes were tailored to his tall, muscular body. While he held a glass of champagne, he didn't drink it.

He had an aura around him. I don't mean that in any mystical sense; it was the way he affected the people in his vicinity. Everyone around him was smiling, and they brightened still more when he spoke with them. Their smiles were genuine, not toadying or seeking to impress. These people liked him.

And he liked them liking him. I couldn't

hear what he was saying, but I could see the compliments, the congratulations. He shook hands, and patted men on the back, and touched women's arms, subtly flirting.

Marcus Wilson was a man in his element, and every single movement he made showed it.

I leaned my arm on the polished bar and watched him openly. Why would a happy man pay to ruin somebody's career?

Marcus glanced up from speaking with one of the people in his group, and caught my eye.

I held it.

From this distance, his eyes looked grey, but I couldn't be sure. I saw that he wasn't listening to the person standing next to him.

I smiled an intimate, lowered-eyelids smile. Sipped my champagne without shifting my gaze.

He lifted his own glass to his lips. He was mirroring my action — consciously or subconsciously, I couldn't tell, but it was the first time I had seen him drink in fifteen minutes.

'Rosie? Do you mind if I have a word?'

The question came at the same time that one of Marcus's companions touched his arm and he looked away. I turned my attention to the man who'd addressed me. He had very short red hair and his dinner jacket fitted him badly.

Reporter.

'Sure. What's your name?'

'Don. Are you enjoying the ball?'

'Immensely. What paper do you work for, Don?'

'*Now* magazine. I was hoping you could tell me, why have you cancelled all the dates on your sold-out tour?'

'I'm sorry, Don, I don't have any comment on that.'

A bulb flashed. I held my glass up in a toast and said 'Cheese' for the second shot.

'Is it true that you've lost your psychic powers?'

'Strangely enough, I don't have any comment on that either.'

'What about your train crash prediction? Does it bother you that — '

'Forgive me for interrupting, but may I have this dance?'

Marcus Wilson interposed himself between Don and me. And he was a presence: a tall, broad expanse of impeccable man. I could smell his spicy cologne.

'Yes, you may,' I answered.

He held out the crook of his arm. I slipped my hand through it and he escorted me toward the dance floor.

'I apologise for stepping in,' he said. His voice was deep, a little bit rough around the edges. 'I thought perhaps that reporter was bothering you.'

'Nothing I couldn't handle. But thank you for rescuing me, anyway.'

'I noticed you were watching me.'

'You're right. I was.'

He glanced down at me with grey eyes that were amused and intrigued. 'Have we met?'

'Not before tonight. We shared newspaper space a couple days ago, though.'

'Did we? Which newspaper?'

'Friday's *Sun*.'

'Ah!' He snapped the fingers of his free hand. 'You're the spirit medium, aren't you?'

'That's me. Rosie Fox.' We had reached the dance floor; Marcus steered me through gyrating couples towards the centre of it.

'Lovely to meet you, Rosie,' he said. 'I'm Marcus Wilson.' I knew the introduction was only for form's sake; I'd made it clear I recognised him already. He enjoyed saying the words, though; there was a slight deepening of his voice, a little lingering on the consonants.

And he didn't look like a habitual *Sun* reader. He must keep up with his own publicity.

'Lovely to meet you too, Marcus.'

He paused in the middle of the dance floor and turned to me. 'Before we start dancing I think it's only fair to lay my cards on the table. I don't believe in you.'

I laughed lightly. 'What, do you think I'm too good to be true?'

'No, you seem real enough.' His gaze flickered down over my body as he said it. My dress revealed a good amount of cleavage and leg, and clung like skin everywhere it covered.

'What I mean,' he said, after he'd had an eyeful and had returned his attention to my face again, 'is that I don't believe in ghosts. No offence intended.'

I pretended to consider. 'I don't usually dance with sceptics, but for you, Marcus, I'll make an exception.'

'It must be my lucky night,' he said, and put one hand on my waist and took my other hand in his, ready to dance.

His hand was warm, dry, large, and enfolded mine completely. Our skin touched and I looked into his grey eyes.

And it hit me like a slam of recognition, sharp and certain.

There was something very wrong with Marcus Wilson.

32

Deep down, underneath his urbane handsomeness, below the awards and the charity and the tailoring, there was something cold, something dark and desperate, and it made my skin crawl and go clammy.

He started to move and automatically my body followed his.

I didn't want him to see in my eyes what I could feel. I moved closer to him, nearly leaning the side of my face on his chest. The skin of my cheek touched the lapel of his jacket.

Wilson made an amused, satisfied sound in his throat at how eager I apparently was to plaster myself all over him. His hand slid from my waist to the small of my back, holding me against him.

My breasts touched his chest; my thigh brushed his with every step we took. Each cologne-spiced breath brought me closer to him. There were goosebumps on my arms. A small trickle of sweat wound its cold way down my cleavage.

I closed my eyes and gritted my teeth and tried to reason this through.

This man had ruined Harry. That could be why I saw something wrong in Marcus Wilson's eyes and felt it through his skin. To pay a man to betray another man, to calculate an enemy's downfall in secret — those weren't the acts of a moral human being.

And then there was my professional experience, my talent at observation. I knew already that I could reach conclusions with the speed of intuition, process facts in my subconscious. It was how I'd known Gina had a secret before she'd told me, how I'd picked up Geordie slang from a radio show.

Or maybe there was that third option. The option of the nine twenty-seven to Swansea. The knowledge beyond myself. The warning.

Which one was it? I asked myself. Fact? Observation? Or warning?

Because if it was the third option, I should pull myself out of Marcus Wilson's arms and head for the door as quickly as my three-inch heels could carry me.

'You're a wonderful dancer,' he murmured. I felt his breath stirring my hair.

Right, Rosie. He's a man, not a train crash, and you can handle him.

'I think the person doing the leading should get the credit,' I said, tipping my head back and looking up into his face again.

The corners of his eyes crinkled when he

smiled. 'Tell me something. What's it like to read somebody's mind? Is it playing the odds? Or do you have a set technique that you use?'

'I listen and feel for vibrations,' I answered, 'and then try to make sense of them. At times the information I get is vague, and at other times it's quite specific.'

'What vibrations do you pick up from me?'

I'd wanted to do a reading of Wilson and find out what I could discover, and now he'd straight out asked me for one. I narrowed my eyes and pretended to concentrate.

'You're a complex person, Marcus. For example, you're very social and outgoing, but when you have something you want done, you're extremely efficient at arranging it.'

Yeah, like paying to ruin somebody's life. If I'd hoped to get any reaction to that, I was disappointed. Marcus only smiled at me and kept dancing.

'You're famous, but you have things you'd like to keep to yourself,' I continued. 'There are two sides to you, the public and the private, and if you're honest, you'd prefer the two of them didn't mix.'

'Hmm.' Marcus guided me in a graceful turn on the dance floor. 'Isn't everyone like that to some extent? Aren't you?'

'Yes. But then again, it's my job to be mysterious.' I tossed my hair back from my face, and his gaze lingered on my neck, and downwards to where I pressed against him.

'What else?' he asked.

'How am I doing so far?'

'Not bad. Not bad at all.' I didn't think he was talking about my reading. Or my dancing.

'You're obviously kind; you've built your life around other people. But you're not a stereotypical do-gooder. You like to take risks. You enjoy the thrill.'

I was getting closer here; I could tell from the minute tightening around his eyes. My description fitted the profile of a person who'd built a successful charity by himself, but it also fitted Marcus's language. *Playing the odds. Lay my cards on the table.* He used metaphors of chance.

'Am I right?' I asked.

The song ended, but Marcus didn't let me go. 'You'll have to find out, won't you?'

'I guess I will.' I winked at him.

His smile was broad and very self-assured. 'I have to speak on stage in a moment. May I get you another glass of champagne?'

I'd hardly sipped my first one; as far as I knew, it was still sitting on the bar where I'd left it. 'Sure,' I said.

He escorted me back to the bar and supplied me with a glass, then checked his watch. 'It's time for me to announce how much we've raised this evening. I'll be back.' He touched my bare elbow lightly. 'If you like.'

'Of course. I have to finish my reading, don't I?'

I watched Marcus walk across the ballroom and step up on to the stage. He was introduced by a short man spouting a series of superlatives and then he took the microphone.

I made my way closer to the stage to observe him more closely. I was beginning to think I might have started to understand something about Marcus Wilson. As he spoke I watched his actions rather than listening to his words.

Yes, this was an act. He couldn't fake a faker: every gesture was slightly too perfect. His voice was a little bit too sincere, dropping to a hush as he spoke about the children he'd visited in hospital, rising to nearly a shout when he announced how much money the ball had raised.

The Saint Wilson we saw on stage was a carefully rehearsed image that he wanted the world to see.

Two or three times his eyes met mine in the crowd. I didn't make any pretence of not watching him. From weeks of having Harry in my audience, I knew exactly how seductive it was to have somebody with eyes only for you.

The room burst into applause. It echoed from the high ceilings and practically swayed the chandeliers. Marcus came down from the stage and worked the crowd, shaking hands, patting backs, accepting congratulations and praise. By the time he made it to me, he was flushed, grinning widely, exultant. He took my hand and pulled me towards him. His body felt very hot.

'Come away with me for an hour,' he murmured in my ear. 'Nobody will miss us; we can return before the end. Go through the door near that flower arrangement.' He gestured discreetly with one hand to what looked like a mountain of lilies against one wall. 'I'll meet you in ten minutes.'

He didn't wait for me to agree before he was gone, back to his fans.

I rubbed my hand against the side of my dress as I walked towards the mountain of lilies. Their scent grew stronger as I got closer. I hated lilies. They smelled like death.

I reached the door, breathing in the air of a thousand funerals. I stepped through the door into a grey-painted corridor and waited for Marcus.

He was less than ten minutes. 'Quickly, let's go,' he said, and took my hand and led me down the corridor through a maze of passageways and doors. He'd done this before, the quick secretive escape. Or at least planned it. I'd been right about the risk-taking.

We went out into an alleyway, round the back of the building to his car. He opened the door for me and I sank into the leather upholstery.

Marcus's cheeks were still flushed and his eyes were glittery with excitement; his breath was coming quickly, and he drove his car fast. And yet his conversation, as he took me away from the ball, was polite, charming, and detached: asking how long I'd been in the country, describing his own trips to America, recommending places I must see in Britain and in Europe during my stay.

He hit a button on a device mounted on his dashboard to open a gate, and we pulled up into the driveway of a large house. He came round to open the door for me and gave me his arm to escort me in.

'Wow,' I said as we walked into his house. 'This is gorgeous.' The entrance hall was enormous, all gleaming wood and under-stated lighting, with a curving marble staircase leading up from the middle. 'I thought you gave all your money to charity, but obviously not.'

'I do pay myself a salary. But this is the house I grew up in. I inherited it from my parents.'

'Oh, are your parents in spirit?' I asked. 'Is that why you invited me back here, to get in touch with them for you?'

'No.' He chuckled. 'I told you, I don't believe in ghosts. I invited you back here because you are an incredibly attractive woman.'

Marcus pulled me close, as close as we'd been when we were dancing, closer, and then he kissed me.

He was a good kisser. Technically. He was sensual, and slow, and yet passionate, but while his lips and his body were warm on mine, I was instantly cold again.

Wrong, this man was wrong. It was like being pressed up against something reptilian and insistent.

I forced myself to raise my arms and wrap them around his neck. A kiss, and then I'd try to get some more information. A kiss was nothing.

And what did he need to hide, my chilled brain wondered as he kissed me; what did he need to keep hidden away from everyone so much that he would destroy Harry, destroy his career and everything he loved most? Was Wilson a liar? A thief? A murderer? A rapist?

310

He tangled his hands in my hair and brought me closer to him. His tongue briefly touched against my lips.

I couldn't fake this.

I stepped back and pulled my mouth from his. 'Marcus, do you think I could have a drink?' I asked.

'Oh. Of course. What kind of a gentleman am I?' He laughed, and looped his arm around my waist. 'Come into my study, I've got a bar in there.'

We walked down a hallway, our steps muffled by the thick carpet underfoot. I'd only known this guy for less than an hour and I knew already that he'd have a couch in his study big enough for two people to lie down on.

He opened a door and switched on a light. It was a big room, lined with bookcases, dominated by — I'd guessed right — a huge leather couch and a big mahogany desk, and —

'Harry?' I said, struck, strangely, by pleasure as much as surprise.

33

Harry's eyes were wide and startled. He stood behind the desk, one hand on the computer. His black clothes made his hair look bright. I saw him pull something from the side of the computer with one gloved hand and put it in his jacket pocket.

Marcus strode past me into the room. 'Who the hell are you and what are you doing in my house?' he thundered.

Within a split second Harry had recovered from the shock of being discovered. Somehow, with his hand in his pocket and his body relaxed yet alert, he looked completely at home in his enemy's house. Which, presumably, he'd snuck into while his enemy was out.

'You know who I am, Wilson,' he said.

'How'd you get in here?'

Harry glanced at him contemptuously, and then turned his attention to me. 'What I'd like to know is why *you're* here, Rosie. Did you see a chance for some publicity that would revive your career?'

His eyes travelled over my skimpy dress, my high heels, and my rumpled hair. They lingered on my mouth, kissed free of lipstick.

'Or are you still turned on by danger?' he asked.

His words were like a slap. I rubbed the back of my hand against my mouth.

'I was trying to help you,' I said.

'If you two are quite finished, I'm calling the police,' said Marcus. He pulled a mobile phone out of his pocket and pressed a button.

'Go ahead,' Harry said easily to him. 'I think they might be interested in what I've found on your computer. Not even hidden with a password. Were you so certain you wouldn't be found out, Wilson?'

Marcus paused.

Harry walked around the big desk and then leaned against the front of it. 'For one, the numbers of several offshore bank accounts in your name. For another, a record of the deposits you've made into them over the past few years. More than ten million pounds, all of it siphoned out of Heaven's Hope. You could cure a lot of sick kids with that money.'

'What's on my computer is none of your busine —'

'You made it my business when you paid Spencer to destroy my career. I was following up Heaven's Hope accounts when you fed him that memo. This time I'm making sure of my facts before I publish anything. I've already got my evidence.'

'You've stolen files from my computer. Give me the disk,' Marcus said, with all the command of a person used to having his orders obeyed.

'I'm wondering what you've done with the money you've embezzled. It seems to go out of your accounts as quickly as you put it in. You've got expensive habits, but they're not out of reach of your salary. I'm thinking possibly — '

'Gambling,' I said.

Harry's head snapped in my direction. 'How did you know that?'

'He's addicted to risk,' I told him. 'That's probably why he had the files right there on his computer, it probably gave him a charge. I recognise the symptoms. I've got a few of them myself.'

'Give me what you've stolen.'

Marcus's voice was rough, low, and dangerous. Both of us looked at him. He was standing next to an opened drawer of his desk, pointing a gun at Harry.

'Holy shit,' I said.

'Give it to me,' Marcus repeated.

'No,' said Harry. 'You won't shoot me.'

Marcus's laugh was humourless. 'Blake, there's only one thing that matters to me, and that's my reputation as head of Heaven's

Hope. I need it, and I'll do whatever it takes to keep it. Give me the disk, and if you're lucky I'll only ruin your career again. There isn't much to ruin these days, though, is there?'

I didn't even see how it happened. One moment Harry was casual-looking, leaning confidently against the desk even with a handgun pointed at him; the next he was on Marcus, his gloved hands clamped around his wrists, wrestling with him. The gun was between their bodies.

'Harry, what are you doing?' I yelled.

What happened next had the heart-freezing clarity of a dream when you know something's going to go horribly wrong and you're powerless to stop it. Every movement was magnified, every colour sharpened, every smell unbearable.

It was exactly as I'd felt on the platform of Reading station, trying to stop the train.

I stepped forward, reaching for the two of them. Marcus was taller and broader than Harry, but Harry was younger. I heard Marcus grunt, I saw Harry twist his arm, I heard a deafening explosion, and then the world paused.

When it started again I was screaming Harry's name, and I'd reached him and grabbed the cloth of the back of his jacket.

He was still standing. They were both still standing. 'Oh my God, are you all right?' I gasped.

Marcus half fell, half staggered backwards. His grey eyes were wide with shock; his mouth was slack and open. Blood was flowing — no, spraying and gushing from the top inside of his leg. He fell on to the thick carpet. I could hear his breathing, harsh and raspy and wet. The air was full of a metallic, burnt smell.

'Wilson! Jesus, Wilson, I didn't mean to — ' Harry stripped off his jacket. He knelt beside Marcus, pressing his jacket to the wound, tying it around his leg. Marcus's trousers were already soaked with blood all the way to his knees. 'The bullet must have hit an artery. Hold on, we'll call an ambulance and — '

The room exploded again.

Harry flew backwards.

For a moment I stared at the gun, falling from Marcus's pale bloodstained hand.

And then I was at Harry's side where he lay on the floor. Harry who was wearing black, and I couldn't see how red his blood was as it pumped from his chest, but I could see it on the cream carpet, and on the skin of his neck, and droplets in his bright hair.

Harry, oh God, my Harry, who was staring

up at me with his blue eyes full of pain, who was trying to breathe, who *I could not lose.*

In that split second I knew it. Not a vision of the future, but a feeling of the future. A knowledge of years ahead stretching out, echoing, empty. The future with Harry dead, Harry lost beyond all returning.

For that split second, the fear paralysed me.

It was the worst fear I had ever had. It was worse than being on platform four of Reading station, worse than the day my father had died.

I watched Harry's blood soaking the carpet, and pulled in my breath with a sharp hook of anguish. Then I launched myself to my feet and grabbed a throw from the big couch and pressed it to Harry's chest.

'Don't die, Harry,' I whispered.

He raised his hand and applied pressure on the cloth himself. 'Get the gun away from Marcus,' he said. 'Call 999.'

'Don't die,' I said.

'I'm trying not to,' he said. 'Go.'

When I got to my feet I was light-headed, a roaring filling my ears. Marcus lay very still by the desk. He was still breathing, but unconscious. From the puddle around him, he must have lost a great deal of blood in a very short time. I kicked the gun away from his limp fingers, underneath the desk, before tightening Harry's jacket around his leg.

I'd dialled 911 on the phone on the desk before I remembered I was in England and had to dial 999 like Harry had told me. I didn't know the address, just had to repeat 'Marcus Wilson' over and over again. It was a replay of a nightmare, impotent and never-ending, trying to communicate information I didn't know over the phone to strangers. Finally they understood me.

'Four minutes,' I said to Harry, hanging up the phone and kneeling at his side again. I put both my hands on the throw. It was already soaked through. Harry's face had gone very, very pale. I kissed his forehead. His skin was cold.

The fear hit me again, twice as bad.

'Don't die, Houdini,' I said. My teeth were chattering. 'I need you to hold on here. No escape acts.'

The corner of his mouth twitched. As if he were trying to smile.

'I forgot to say I like your dress,' he said, his voice barely a whisper. And then his blue eyes unfocused, fluttered shut, and his head lolled to one side.

I put my hand to his neck. His pulse was steady, though fast and weak. He was still breathing. He wasn't dead.

And yet there was so much blood.

I pressed. And pressed. And waited for the ambulance to come.

'Don't die, Harry,' I said over and over again. 'Don't leave me. Don't go.'

Hoping that this time, I could change the future.

34

I was still pressing and pleading when the emergency services came through the front door and managed to find us in the big house.

Paramedics surrounded Harry and pushed me out of the way. I stood, clutching the throw trying to understand what they were doing, and failing, and asking 'Is he going to be okay?'

One of them took me by the shoulders and made me sit down on the huge couch. 'Have you been shot?' she asked me, wrapping a blanket around my shoulders.

'No. Is Harry going to be all right? It looked like he was shot in the chest but that doesn't have to be bad, right? He can still live?'

'Is all this blood on you from him? Or have you been hurt?'

Why was she asking if I was hurt, when Harry was unconscious, maybe dying? I glanced down at myself and saw that my dress was clotted with blood. My bare arms were smeared with it, and my hands were pure red. My fingers felt slippery.

I heard a tearing sound from Harry's direction and jumped up to watch them cut off his shirt. Oh Lord, even more blood than I'd thought. I staggered backwards and the paramedic caught me.

'You're in shock,' she said. 'Lie down.' She wasn't a big woman, but she forced me on to the couch and put a pillow underneath my feet. 'So you're not hurt?'

'No, I'm fine. Is Harry going to survive? Please check.'

'He'll be all right.'

I had no idea whether that was the truth or something she was saying to calm me down. But the reassurance was enough to allow my mind to free itself for a moment from fear, and it was then that I noticed that the room was also full of police. Four uniformed officers and two men who looked like detectives clustered around the desk, pointing at the gun.

And then I started thinking. I jolted upright and ran across the room to where the paramedics were lifting Marcus on to a stretcher. He was still unconscious and looked worse than Harry, if possible.

Harry's jacket lay in a pile on the floor. I picked it up. It was warm and sticky.

'Has he lost a lot of blood?' I asked, although any idiot could see the answer to my question in the crimson stain on the carpet. I wanted to show some concern for Marcus in case the police were watching while I dug into the pockets of Harry's ruined jacket and curled my fingers around the bit of plastic I found.

The paramedic draped the blanket round me again. 'Putting pressure on the wound was probably what saved him. They'll both be fine once we get them to the hospital. Come on, sit down. The police want to speak to you.'

I watched Harry and Marcus being wheeled out of the room. Then I sat on the couch with the bit of plastic hidden in my fist and answered the policemen's questions about what had happened.

I'd come home with Marcus from the charity ball, I said. We'd gone to the study, where we met Harry. We had a discussion and Marcus pulled a gun. Harry tried to take it from him and Marcus got shot in the struggle. No, Marcus had been holding the gun the whole time. While Harry was trying to help him, Marcus shot Harry. No, I didn't know how Harry got into the house. He probably walked through the front door, I hadn't noticed it being locked. For all I knew, Marcus had invited him.

Okay. So that wasn't quite the truth. And

I'd decided to be a truthful person.

But there are lies, and there are lies. Harry had been in the house finding out information about the man who'd ruined his life. He'd been wearing gloves and there wouldn't be any proof he'd touched the gun or the computer. Marcus was the real criminal. I was telling the moral truth, if not the literal truth.

And sometimes the moral truth is more important.

'What was the discussion about before the shooting?' asked one of the policemen. He wasn't wearing a uniform, but he talked and held himself just like a cop on TV. I wondered how much of TV was based on what real cops were like, and how much real cops based what they were like on what they saw on TV.

Telling the truth for this one was a no-brainer. 'Harry had discovered that Marcus had embezzled something like ten million pounds from Heaven's Hope Foundation. They were talking about that. Then Marcus took the gun out of his desk and threatened Harry.'

I saw the policemen exchange a look. I also saw that I might be here for a long time, once they started asking questions. And every minute was another minute the ambulance was driving Harry further from me, and if his

323

injuries were fatal I might never see him again because I was stuck here talking with these cops.

'Excuse me, I'm not feeling very well,' I said, and then I let my eyelids flutter shut and collapsed back on the couch in my best impersonation of a faint.

That's how I got to ride in the back of a second ambulance to the hospital. There, a kind nurse noticed that I was shaking and my skin was freezing and she gave me a set of scrubs to put on instead of my bloodstained dress. The part of my mind that was still holding on to some normality noticed that the scrubs looked really silly when paired with my three-inch heels. She checked me over and said I was fine and gave me a plastic cup of sweet tea and showed me where to wash Harry's blood from my skin. As I watched it swirl down the drain of the restroom sink, I thought about how he'd felt under my hands, breathing shallowly.

I waited. Sometimes I sat on a plastic chair; mostly I paced the shiny tiled floor. The cops came into the waiting room twice to ask me more questions. The piece of plastic from Harry's coat was a flash drive. I still held it hidden tight in my fist, as if it were the key to keeping Harry alive.

Eventually a doctor approached me. 'You

were at the shooting tonight?' she asked.

Instantly I was on my feet. 'How's Harry? Is he all right?'

'Are you his partner?'

No, I was the woman he'd dumped and then assumed was seducing his greatest enemy. But that fact wasn't going to get me any information.

'Yes,' I said.

'He's had surgery to have the bullet removed. It missed his vital organs and lodged in his shoulder. He's going to be all right.'

I sagged into the plastic chair with relief.

'Have you contacted his family?' the doctor asked.

Guilt rushed in to replace the relief. Harry Blake knew every single detail about my family and my origins, and I didn't even know his parents' names.

'No, I don't know them. They live in Surrey. He has a sister called Clarissa but I don't know where she lives.'

The doctor nodded. 'All right. He can contact them himself when he wakes up.'

'He's still unconscious?'

She saw the lines of worry on my forehead and smiled reassuringly. 'We've given him a big dose of painkillers and they knocked him out. He'll be sore, but he'll be fine. Honestly.'

'Can I see him?'

'I have no objection, but we'll have to ask the policeman they've got stationed outside his room.' We started walking down the corridor. She shook her head. 'It's been quite an exciting night here. Police and reporters everywhere.'

'Is Marcus Wilson going to be okay?' The bastard deserved to suffer lots of pain for what he'd done to Harry and for stealing all that money from those kids, but I wouldn't wish death on anybody.

'The bullet punctured his femoral artery — that's the big artery in your thigh. He's had surgery and he's received some blood. He should be all right too. Both of the victims were very lucky. Mr Blake is in this room.'

A uniformed cop stood outside. The doctor had a few words with him and he nodded.

I paused at the door. 'Are you sure he's asleep?'

'He should be for some time. Go in,' she said, her face kind. 'He won't know you're there.'

This time when I saw Harry, the feeling went beyond pleasure.

He was bare-chested, and his shoulder and half his chest were covered in bandages. His eyes were closed and there were dark blue smudges underneath them. A clear tube ran

326

into the nostrils of his crooked nose. His lips were colourless, his skin pale. His hair still had streaks of brown blood in it.

And when I saw him, I felt a bubble of joy growing in my stomach, exploding into my chest, filling my entire body from my toes to the ends of my hair. It was more than relief. It was pure happiness.

Harry was alive. He was breathing, his heart was beating. He'd wake up and talk and walk and look around him with that keen, intelligent curiosity.

After the way he had talked to me in Wilson's study I knew there was no way in the world that we were getting back together. There had been contempt in his voice, and even though I didn't deserve it, it showed me that he wasn't willing to think of me as somebody who could be trusted.

But even though he was lost to me, he wasn't lost. Even if I never saw him again, he would still *be*.

I practically skipped to his bedside. I touched his forehead and pushed back a lock of silky hair. He was breathing softly; I put my hand in front of his face and felt the air coming from him. I laid my finger on the side of his neck, and felt his pulse beating strong and the warmth of his skin. I laughed aloud.

Next to Harry almost dying, his setting me

up seemed like nothing in comparison.

And somewhere along the line I'd forgiven him for that. He'd done it to discover the truth, and to Harry, there was nothing more important. By his own lights, he'd done the right thing. Since I had spent my entire life living according to my own personal moral code, who was I to be angry with him?

I'd been lying since I was thirteen. Harry had showed me the reason why I'd been doing it. He'd helped me make my peace with my father.

I bent down and kissed the side of his mouth. He stirred slightly, looking for a moment as though he'd started a sleepy smile, the kind he'd given me when he was lying beside me late at night.

'I love you, Harry,' I said, and my voice shook with joy.

I didn't even know I was crying until a tear landed on Harry's cheek. I wiped it off, and kissed him again, longer this time, feeling his breath like a caress on my face. His lips were warm and dry. He smelled of antiseptic and hospital sheets and the clean chemical smell of bandages, but he still smelled like Harry.

His left arm, with its IV line, was on top of the sheets. I opened his hand and curled his fingers around the flash drive. It would be the first thing he noticed when he woke up.

I left him sleeping and went down the corridor. I couldn't stop smiling. I glimpsed my reflection in a window. I looked like a total freak — I had panda eyes, a bloodstain on my forehead, hair that looked like a mop, and the widest grin I'd ever seen.

I love Harry, and he's going to live. It felt like the most miraculous thing in the world. I danced down the corridor, the tapping of my heels echoing in the bare, clean silence.

The reporters weren't hard to find; they were camped outside the entrance to the hospital, smoking and drinking tea and chatting to each other. One of them recognised me as soon as I walked out the door, and within seconds I was surrounded.

'Rosie, can you tell us what's happened to Marcus Wilson?'

'Rosie, did you witness the shooting? Who shot who?'

'Rosie, you were seen leaving the Heaven's Hope ball tonight with Marcus Wilson; will you please comment on your relationship?'

'Which one of you is from *The Times*?' I asked. A woman stepped forward. 'Great. I need you to call your paper and find an editor who worked with Harry Blake and tell him to get his butt down here. Harry's got a story for him.'

35

The ecstatic happiness lasted for a day, more or less.

In theory, and when you're addled from having witnessed a double shooting, it's fine being happy about falling in love for the first time in your life and deriving great joy from the mere fact that your loved one is alive.

In real life, and when the adrenalin has worn off and you've had time to think about it, being in love with somebody you can't have makes you really, really miserable.

I went back to Max's llama farm. Max and Gina weren't there; rehearsals had begun for Max's tour. I had nothing to do again, except for walking the six miles to the nearest shop every morning to buy a newspaper. In wellies and one of Max's old llama-wool sweaters nobody was going to recognise me anyway. I liked the Yorkshire landscape; it felt older than Massachusetts, with the layered marks of all the generations who had lived here. The mud and the cold and the rain felt cleansing, somehow. I was even beginning to make friends with the llamas, who seemed friendlier. I guessed I didn't have any more fear for them to feel.

Tuesday morning I picked up *The Times* in the little village shop and the headline shouted at me right away. CHARITY BOSS EMBEZZLED MILLIONS.

Harry Blake was listed in the byline as one of the investigating journalists. Seeing his name made my stomach twist.

I took the newspaper outside and read the article sitting on a stone wall. Wilson had been funding a gambling habit, as I'd suspected. He'd kept it secret for years, and once he'd worked through his personal fortune he'd started stealing from Heaven's Hope. From what I'd seen of him, I thought he'd enjoy the deception. The article said he'd regained consciousness and was in a stable condition in hospital but had refused to comment on the allegations, either about the embezzlement or about shooting Harry.

The sidebar on the second page was written entirely by Harry, most likely from his hospital bed. HOW WILSON COST ME MY CAREER, the headline said. There was a thumbnail photo of Harry, serious and beautiful and wild-haired. As I read his words, I could hear his voice speaking them, somehow lazy despite his precise diction.

He put the blame on Wilson and on Spencer, but acknowledged his own fault in believing the scam. He sounded fair and honest.

I folded up the newspaper, put it in the nearest bin, and walked the six miles back to Max's farmhouse.

Odd to think that from now on, the closest I would get to Harry was reading his words.

Including the words he'd written about me, exposing my lies, which would be published in two days' time.

★ ★ ★

The next morning I didn't walk to the village. It felt as if everything was over, and I was just waiting for the curtains to close before I gave up and went home. I spent the day lying on the couch with a llama-wool blanket pulled up to my chin, staring at the brown roses on the couch cushions. For a rock star, Max had the ugliest furniture.

I would be okay. Eventually I'd find another job, I'd discover who I was, and I'd enjoy the present again. I had found out how to tell the truth. I could hold on to that.

But Harry Blake was everything I'd never known I'd always wanted, and I would never see him again. If he got his job back at *The Times*, I couldn't even watch him on *Amazing TV*.

I used to think this was a Win/Win game, I thought, and buried my face in the cushions.

There was a knock on the door.

I didn't know anybody around here. I didn't move. Couldn't if I'd wanted to. Maybe it was a damn reporter.

'Go away,' I whispered.

I heard the letter box squeak open. 'Rosie,' a voice called through it. 'It's me.'

Harry.

I could move.

I bolted off the couch and to the door. I had on my Ramones T-shirt and mud-spattered jeans and my hair was a rat's nest. Who gave a shit. I opened the door.

He was wearing jeans and sneakers and his leather jacket with his left arm inside, draped in a sling. He looked tired. He was pale; the skin under his eyes still looked bruised.

God, he was beautiful. So much more than words or a photograph or an image on TV. A big, complex, mortal man.

'Rosie,' he said.

I itched to touch him. Not to seduce him, not even to kiss him. Just to smooth his hair, run my fingertips over his face, coax colour and life back into it.

I didn't.

'Hi,' I said. 'Good to see you're alive.'

'I need to thank you,' Harry said. 'Thank

you for saving my life. Thank you for getting me my job back.' He sought out my eyes with his, and held my gaze. 'Thank you for everything.'

I ran my hands through my hair to give them something to do, got them caught in a snarl. 'You should still be in the hospital.'

'I discharged myself this morning.'

'How'd you know I was here?'

'I called Gina.'

Gina had told Harry where I was. She was obviously not holding a grudge against him for ruining my career and therefore hurting hers, unless she thought I'd finish off Wilson's job and kill Harry myself.

'You were shot a couple of days ago,' I said. 'You'd better come in and sit down and have a cup of tea.'

He followed me inside and sat down on the couch. The brown roses did nothing for his complexion. I left him there and went to the kitchen to put the kettle on.

Thank you for everything? What did that mean? Why was he here? What did he want? Why were my stupid hands shaking?

'I didn't only come here to thank you.' His voice behind me in the kitchen doorway made me jump. 'I need your advice, too.'

'I thought you had all the answers already, Harry.'

The bitterness in my voice surprised me.

'I don't.' He leaned against the kitchen counter, but something was different. His hand grasped the edge of the counter too tightly. His long body radiated tension and uncertainty.

Somewhere along the line, Harry Blake had lost his ease.

'I need your advice about Marcus Wilson,' he said.

I took two flowered mugs down from Max's mug tree and dropped a teabag in each of them. 'What do you need my advice for?' I asked. 'Thanks to you, the truth has come out. He deserves everything that's coming to him.'

Harry didn't reply. He didn't reply for so long that I stopped watching the kettle and looked at him again. Max's kitchen was painted olive green, and that didn't do anything for his complexion either. His face was drawn. Haunted.

'You don't know, do you?' he asked.

'Know what?'

'Marcus Wilson is dead.'

The teaspoon I'd been holding clattered on to the floor.

He reached into the inside pocket of his jacket and pulled out a newspaper. I took it from him.

The headline and the first paragraph told me immediately. Marcus Wilson had hanged himself the night before in his hospital room, using his bed sheets, while policemen guarded the door from the outside. Seventeen hours after the news of his crime was published, he was dead.

'I remember having breakfast with you when you saw the photographs of the people who'd died in the train crash,' Harry said. 'You felt as if you were at fault, didn't you? You felt that since you'd foretold their deaths, you should have prevented them?'

I could only nod.

'I hadn't thought about that properly. I knew you hadn't caused the crash, but I didn't think about what your guilt meant. Coincidences don't make people feel guilty. You only feel guilty if you could have prevented it.'

Exactly.

'You really saw that train crash coming, didn't you?' he asked.

'Yes,' I said. 'I did.'

'I believe you,' said Harry.

The kettle boiled. I poured the water. Steam kissed my face. I thought, *Harry believes me*.

'I caused Marcus Wilson's death.' Every one of Harry's words was deliberate, clearly pronounced. 'I didn't know he was going to kill himself. But it's my fault he died.'

There were a lot more important things than making tea. I faced Harry with my hands on my hips. 'You didn't kill Marcus Wilson, Harry.'

'Is that how you dealt with the deaths of those six people on the train? By denying you had anything to do with them?'

I dropped my hands. 'No.'

'What *did* you do?' He leaned towards me, as if only I could give him the answer he wanted.

'I tried to accept that I'd done all I could.'

'And has that worked?'

'Not really,' I said.

Harry slumped back against the counter. He drew in a deep breath and let it out.

'I've been obsessed with finding out the truth,' he said. 'When I lost my reputation the truth seemed to be all that I had left. It was the only part of me that I still recognised. But Spencer was right. I was too busy with my crusade to see what was right under my nose.'

He hit the counter with his fist. 'If I hadn't investigated Wilson he would still be alive. *The Times* has offered me a job again, and my reputation is going to be cleared, and it's all I ever wanted, and God, Rosie, I feel wrong.'

His voice was full of pain. Rational reassurances didn't work in this situation, I knew, but they had to be given anyway. 'Okay, Harry, feel as guilty as you want. But I'm going to tell you a few facts. You didn't commit Wilson's crimes. He did. You didn't hang him with his sheets. That was his choice. The man was addicted to risk. He was going to be found out sooner or later. And when he *was* found out, it was inevitable that he'd crash. I watched him; he loved being Saint Wilson. He wasn't strong enough to see his reputation and his image being destroyed.'

I took one step closer to Harry. 'He wasn't as strong as you were, Harry, when the same thing happened to you.'

'Or as strong as you'll be,' he added quietly, 'when the same thing happens to you.'

I retreated and braced myself against the sink, holding the edge of it to keep myself in place. 'We'll find out tomorrow when *Amazing News* hits the stands, I guess.'

Harry stood up straight and took the step towards me I'd taken back. 'My way of dealing with losing my reputation was to cling on to my integrity at any cost. I was wrong. Integrity isn't about facts. I shouldn't have written that article. I shouldn't have set you up. I didn't see that Wilson was going to die, and I didn't see that I wasn't only attacking your career. I was attacking you. I hurt you.'

A lump rose in my throat. I spoke around it. 'You said once that neither of us could separate the professional from the personal.'

'I thought it was all professional. And I was wrong about that too. It was all personal. Wilson was personal. And everything absolutely everything between you and me.'

You and me. I held on tighter to the sink behind me, feeling the stainless steel warming under my fingers.

'It was always personal with us, Rosie. Since the minute I met you. And I didn't let myself see it. You chose your career so you could talk to your father. I chose to investigate you because I wanted to be near you.' He closed his eyes and shook his head. 'I was an idiot.'

I swallowed. 'You were an idiot for wanting to be near me?' I asked, although I knew that wasn't what he meant, because I wanted to hear more about him wanting to be near me.

'I was an idiot for thinking that my lies were any different from yours, and thinking I could use my article to sidestep our relationship. For being self-righteous and setting you up.'

'Just an all-round idiot I guess is the term you're looking for.' The kitchen was warm, but I was trembling.

He laughed and for a moment his face was full of life. 'I can think of worse terms that apply, and I'm glad you're not using them.' He sobered. 'I might be able to make some of this up to you, Rosie. I've talked with my editor at *Amazing News* and I've got him in touch with Gina.'

'In touch with Gina? Why?'

'They want you to replace me on *Amazing TV*. And part of the deal is that they'll drop my article. You're worth more to them as a psychic.'

I took a moment to let that sink in.

'You negotiated this, didn't you, Houdini? From your hospital bed or something?'

He shrugged. 'I'm beginning to learn that the pure unvarnished truth isn't always the only option. Sometimes you have to do what feels right.'

'And it feels right to you that I should keep on pretending to talk to spirits?'

Harry inclined his head. 'It's up to you, Rosie. It was never my decision to make.'

I stared at the cracked green linoleum on the kitchen floor and I thought about it.

I could keep my career. I could keep the power, the mystique, the attention. I thought about being on stage, seeing belief in the audience's eyes. How good it felt.

I could keep on helping people. I could keep on pretending I had all the answers people needed.

I could keep all these things I'd thought I was going to lose.

Maybe, even, I could keep Harry.

At the age of thirteen I'd seen the way the world works. *Given the choice between a beautiful lie and an ugly truth, most people will go for the beauty wherever they find it.*

And my lie was a beautiful one. So beautiful that I'd believed in it for a long time without knowing it.

But it wasn't real.

I'd been holding my breath the entire time I'd been thinking. Now I let it out and shook my head.

'No,' I said. 'I'm done with the spirit trade. I don't want to manipulate people any more.'

Harry smiled. I felt as if I'd passed a test, although he hadn't been the one who'd set it.

'I don't want you to publish the article, though,' I blurted out, and then I had to figure out why I'd said that. But the answer was obvious.

'I'm quitting being a medium. But I helped a lot of people, Harry. And I helped them because they believed I could talk with their dead loved ones. If they find out that I lied to them, they're going to feel horrible. They could lose something they really want to believe in. Give it some time before you publish it.'

Harry shook his head and looked at me, warmth and wonder in his blue eyes.

'See, Rosie,' he said, 'this is why I love you.'

He froze. Standing stock-still in Max's kitchen, tall and strong and wounded and hurting and precious.

'Did I say that out loud?' he asked.

I wasn't sure whether to believe my ears either.

'You said it,' I confirmed. 'Did you mean it?'

Slowly, Harry nodded. 'I mean it. I didn't think I'd say it that way. Or' — he looked around him — 'in a kitchen. But I do. I love you.'

'It just came out, without you expecting it,' I said. 'Things like that do, when they're real.'

Like my prediction. Like the moment I'd known that I could not bear to see him die.

'When I was in hospital I couldn't stop thinking about when you read my tarot cards,' he said. 'You said I was going to get justice and that I was going to be hurt. And you said I wouldn't know the woman I loved until the truth about her hit me between the eyes.'

He took another step towards me. He

reached out with his good right hand and stroked my hair, a slow caress I felt all the way down to my toes.

'You're my Queen of Swords,' he said softly. 'The person who cuts through the bullshit. The person who sees who I really am.'

That ecstatic happiness started to seep back in again, filtering through the cracks in me, filling up the emptiness.

'Harry,' I said, 'I love you too.'

I let go of the sink and let myself go to him. I wrapped my arms around his waist and held on as tight as I could. He held me with his good arm and I breathed in his smell. Heard his heart beat. I felt his body against mine, effortlessly right. And then I kissed Harry Blake and felt only pure, burning certainty.

At last, a beautiful truth.

Other titles published by
The House of Ulverscroft:

HE LOVES LUCY

Susan Donovan

Most women would *kill* to have access to personal trainer Theo Redmond. But Lucy Cunningham's starting to wish she'd never met him! Marketing exec Lucy's original idea for a reality TV show, in which Theo transformed someone from flabby to fabulous, hadn't featured *her* being the star . . . Balancing the need to lose weight against being watched by the whole of Miami, Lucy sweats her way into a new life. And as things also heat up between them, could chocoholic Lucy and Gym Bunny Theo be about to discover that true love lies somewhere between pizza and Pilates?

THE EX-WIFE'S SURVIVAL GUIDE

Debby Holt

Sarah Stagg thought she had it all: a lovely husband, twin teenage sons, a cottage in the country. Then her husband, an amateur thespian, leaves her for his leading lady, her sons go off to India, and Sarah is left alone and single. The path of a discarded wife is strewn with hazards and humiliations, and Sarah needs to acquire survival skills. Help (and hindrance) is at hand in the form of well-meaning neighbours, a psychopathic mongrel, an unassuming plumber — and an unwelcome role as Mrs de Winter in the forthcoming Ambercross Players' production of *Rebecca*.

SKIN DEEP

Catherine Barry

Finn has felt unhappy with her chest size since she was a girl and decides that her dysfunctional childhood, failed relationships and poor job prospects all come down to the fact that her image is lacking. Indeed, post-operative Finn's life changes dramatically, but is it all she imagined it would be?

LUCY BLUE, WHERE ARE YOU?

Louise Harwood

Lucy Blue is not the sort of girl to pick up a stranger in a snow-bound airport and she's certainly not the sort to then leap into bed with him in a motorway motel . . . Yet this is a strange, once-in-a-lifetime day, and in any case nobody will know and they'll never meet again . . . But actions can catch up with you and secrets have a way of being told, and a spectacular gesture means that this time Lucy just can't walk away.

FOR MATRIMONIAL PURPOSES

Kavita Daswani

'Who needs you to be happy? I want to see you married this year.' This is the view of Anju's mother, in the time-honoured tradition of all mothers, but particularly that of the fond Indian parent. Anju now works in New York, living the sophisticated American lifestyle — almost. But when she returns home to her parents in Bombay — usually for another family wedding — she finds herself reverting to the traditional daughter role. At each visit another prospective suitor is brought forward. But what sort of man does the very modern Anju want? How important are her family, her country, her traditions?

EAT, DRINK AND BE MARRIED

Eve Makis

Anna's head reels with plans to escape life behind the counter of the family chip shop on a run-down Nottingham council estate. Her mother, Tina, wants nothing but the best for Anna. She thinks that Anna should forget going to college, learn to cook and find herself a suitable husband. Mother and daughter are at loggerheads and neither will give way. Anna's grandmother, Yiayia Annoulla, is her ally, telling her stories about the family's turbulent past in Cyprus. Anna longs for the freedom enjoyed by her brother, Andy, but it is only when family fortunes begin to sour that she starts to take control of her own destiny . . .